OBSESSION

Other books and audio books

by Traci Hunter Abramson:

Undercurrents

Ripple Effect

The Deep End

Royal Target

Freefall

Lockdown

Crossfire

Backlash

Smoke Screen

OBSESSION

A NOVEL BY

TRACI HUNTER ABRAMSON

Covenant Communications, Inc.

Cover image: *Mic in Blue* by Podgorsek © iStockphotography.com

Published by Covenant Communications, Inc.
American Fork, Utah

This is a work of fiction. The characters, names, incidents, places, and dialogue are either products of the author's imagination, and are not to be construed as real, or are used fictitiously.

Printed in the United States of America
First Printing: September 2011

17 16 15 14 13 12 11 10 9 8 7 6 5 4 3 2 1

ISBN: 978-1-60861-392-2

To Jana Lynn, Connie, and Paula,
for constantly showing me the value of friendship

Acknowledgments

Thank you to the wonderful people at Covenant for helping me bring this book to light, especially Kathy Jenkins, who always offers me so much support and encouragement; Kirk Shaw, who challenged me to try something new; and Samantha Van Walraven for her constant willingness to help me work through my ideas and for all her efforts in ushering this book through the editing process.

As always, thank you to Rebecca Cummings for her continued willingness to read everything I write and for all her invaluable insight.

I also want to thank my friends at the FBI who continue to share all of those little details that help me write what I enjoy. Thank you to my sister, Tiffany Hunter, for relating so many of her experiences with working backstage at the Grammys. Her insight was truly invaluable.

And finally, thank you to all of the readers who continue to support my journey in discovering which story comes next.

Prologue

Water shimmered behind her, nearly the same color as her dress. Only a sliver of light cut through the darkness, but it was enough for him to see her delicate features and the way her blonde hair flowed past her shoulders. A slow smile crossed his face, one of appreciation and anticipation.

He took a step forward.

She took a step back.

His voice was low and eerily calm. "Don't be afraid."

"What do you want from me?" She asked, her breaths coming in rapid, short gasps. "You said—"

"Here." He lifted the single rose he held until it was in her line of vision. The stem was slightly crooked and still held its thorns, jagged in comparison to the delicately curled blood-red petals. The breeze caught its fragrance, mixing it with the subtle scent of the swimming pool behind her. His eyes gleamed with expectation as he held the flower out to her. "This is for you."

Only briefly did her eyes focus on the rose before they slid to the gloved hand that held it. When she looked up once more, her eyes darted around the expansive backyard as though she were looking for a way out, a way to free herself. She took another gasping breath and another step back, and his excitement shifted to dread.

He shook his head. She had to know how perfect things would be once they were together. He edged closer. "What's wrong? Don't you want it?"

"It's late." Her voice quivered. "I need to go back inside."

He felt the stab then, swift and clean as the hurt and betrayal clawed inside him. It was all going wrong again. Pain exploded in his chest as though bursting to get out. The shadows began closing in, settling onto his shoulders, into his heart and mind.

Even as he stared at the light and beauty in front of him, he welcomed the familiar weight, the comfort of the darkness he could lose himself in. His voice was raw when he asked the question, the same question that echoed from a previous night, a previous pain. "Why won't you love me? I only want you to love me."

"I don't understand . . ." Her voice faded, and her eyes widened as she saw him lift his other hand. She opened her mouth, maybe to question, maybe to scream, but no sound came out. Only the muffled gunshot overshadowed the rhythm of the water gently lapping behind her.

He stared down for a long moment.

It could have been so perfect. But, no, she couldn't have been what he'd always wanted. With a shake of his head, he assured himself that next time would be different. Next time she would understand that they belonged together. He dropped the rose beside the lifeless figure on the ground and then silently disappeared into the night.

Chapter 1

Three quick raps sounded at the door, followed by a deep male voice. "Ten minutes, Miss Blake."

"Thank you," Kendra called out. Her stomach pitched and rolled with nerves, and her breath shuddered out as she anticipated her upcoming performance. At moments like this, she wondered why she had chosen to pursue a career that kept her so firmly in the spotlight. Then she reminded herself that the spotlight would follow her regardless of what she did. She'd been born famous.

Her first baby pictures had netted a cool three million dollars and had appeared on the covers of countless magazines, the result of some enterprising hospital employee who realized "Baby Girl Blake" was none other than the daughter of renowned actor Sterling Blake.

Now, twenty-five years later, Kendra was all grown up, but the spotlight still hadn't faded.

As the music from the opening act continued to pulse through the air, she closed her eyes, willing her body to relax. She had worked hard to get to this point in her career, to make a name for herself beyond just "Sterling Blake's daughter." The Grammy she had taken home a few nights earlier had certainly helped distance her public image from that of her father's. Now, if she could just gain a bit more freedom in her private life.

Only three years had passed since she had demanded the right to control her own career, her own finances, even her own independence. All her life, her father's overprotective nature had restricted every aspect of her life, from where she went to the friends she kept. Finally, she was stepping out on her own and beginning to discover who she was and what she wanted.

As terrifying as facing a crowd of twenty thousand could be, at least she knew this was her choice. She also knew that once she let herself get lost in her fans' emotions, the nerves would disappear, and she would remember why this agony was worth it.

She turned to face the lighted mirror on the wall of her dressing room and straightened her shoulders with determination. Dozens of red roses reflected behind her, tokens from various fans and friends. They also served as a reminder that a single comment to the press could take on a life of its own.

Leaning forward, she touched up her makeup and then muttered to her reflection, "Okay, you can do this."

Just then, her cell phone rang, and Kendra scooped it up from among the clutter of makeup on the counter in front of her. When she read the caller ID, her lips curved into a smile.

"Hi, Grandpa."

"How's my little girl?" William Blake's voice carried over the phone at full volume.

Kendra's nerves settled into a dull ache. "Nervous."

"What are you nervous about? All those fans of yours love you, and I know you'll put on a good show."

"You always say that." Her smile widened.

"And I'm always right," he insisted. "When are you coming to visit?"

Kendra considered for a minute. "My last concert is tomorrow night in San Francisco. Maybe I'll head over to Phoenix this weekend."

"Good, good. I was just telling your grandmother this morning that it's been too long since we've seen you," he said. "And who knows when that sister of yours will stop gallivanting around Europe."

"Sienna will be home as soon as she finishes shooting her new movie. Besides, we just saw you at Dad's house in Malibu for Christmas," Kendra reminded him. "That was only a few weeks ago."

"At my age, a few weeks can seem like forever," he said in a serious tone, even though Kendra knew he was fighting a grin. "And with that army of bodyguards your father keeps around, we could hardly have a decent conversation without an audience."

Kendra laughed now, her nerves forgotten. "You're the one who made him so paranoid. He says growing up with a dad in the FBI showed him how many crazy people there are in the world."

"Excuses, excuses." William chuckled.

Another knock sounded on her door. "I've got to get going, Grandpa. I'll call you tomorrow or the next day and let you know when I'm coming."

"Good luck tonight."

"Thanks."

Kendra hung up and crossed her dressing room. She pushed the door open, and Dustin Brady instantly appeared at her side. She glanced over at the forty-two-year-old former Marine who had been on her security detail since she was sixteen. His presence reminded her that she hadn't completely broken free of her father's influence.

At least she had finally managed to reduce her security team to a single bodyguard, but even that change had been hard won. Kendra reminded herself that it wasn't Dustin's fault that her father insisted she have a bodyguard. She tried to keep her resentment out of her voice. "Are we all set?"

Dustin nodded. When several members of Kendra's band approached, Dustin seemed to blend into the background like a silent sentry. The band members all moved toward the stage, waiting as the crew finished the set change. The buzz from her fans was both energizing and a little unnerving.

Kendra closed her eyes and took a deep breath. She could feel the energy around her, the impatience of the crowd. A wave of nausea threatened, and she took another deep breath to steady her nerves. She knew she should be used to this by now—the crowds and the adrenaline rush that always came before a concert—but even after four years, she always felt like she was walking out onto the stage for the first time.

"Are you okay?" Zack Prescott asked as he stepped up beside her.

Kendra nodded and looked over at him, the newest dancer in her entourage. A dimple flashed in his pretty-boy face—a hint of infatuation showing in his expression. She supposed she should be amused that he was still a bit starstruck, but at the moment, all she could think about was filling her lungs with air and hoping she didn't look as awful as she felt.

"I'm fine. It's just nerves."

"Really?" Zack's eyebrows went up. "You've already had three number-one albums, and you still get nervous?"

Kendra didn't answer. Instead, she focused on her cue and managed a weak smile. "Okay. Showtime."

Zack gave her an odd look before getting swept onto the stage to take his place with the other dancers. The stage lights were off, and Kendra could barely make out the movement as the crew made the final adjustments to the set.

Anticipation bubbled inside her as the stage lights came on and the crowd's buzz intensified with excitement. *I can do this*, she told herself, just like she'd done hundreds of times before.

She heard her name announced and heard the rumble of the crowd turn into a roar. With her heart pounding wildly, she forced herself to move into the spotlight.

One hand pumped into the air; the other grasped the microphone. "Hello, Los Angeles!"

The roar erupted, punctuated by high-pitched squeals, and Kendra was suddenly grateful her earplugs were in place. Through her earpiece, she could hear the transmission from her manager followed by the notes of the opening song.

The deafening noise from the crowd slowly faded, quieting as her voice began blending with the music. Then all she could hear were the words she had written and her smooth voice, joined by thousands of others.

Chapter 2

Lights glared through the windows of the elegant house nestled against the side of Camelback Mountain. The landscaping was subtle, blending into the surrounding desert. Music blasted through the air, the words of some rapper competing with the voices inside the house.

Moving forward quietly, Charlie Whitmore gripped his weapon and prayed no shots would be fired tonight. His hands went clammy as a memory flashed into his mind, the memory of the last time he had been forced to draw his weapon. Charlie gritted his teeth, refusing to let the images of that night in DC fully form.

He had moved to Phoenix to start fresh, to work where no one knew him. Here, he was just another FBI agent, someone who had sworn to protect rather than someone who needed to be protected. Tonight, he was on equal footing with the other members of the four-man team, and they had a job to do.

Agent Ray Underwood motioned to Charlie, and together they made their way to the front door while the other two agents positioned themselves near the rear entrance in case their suspect tried to rabbit out the back.

The man who reportedly lived inside was known to his neighbors as a pillar of the community, an example of the American dream. Charlie knew better. According to the FBI's latest information, thirty-four-year-old Terrence Colter had built his small fortune by exploiting teenage girls, luring them into the dark underworld of pornography.

The FBI's Phoenix office had been investigating Colter for months, but solid evidence had been hard to come by. They had the proof now, but it had come with a high price: the life of a fourteen-year-old runaway from Albuquerque.

Charlie's stomach curled at the thought of what this man had done—using the young girl to profit his business and then killing her when she crossed him. The girl had tried to call for help, her screams alerting a nearby pedestrian.

The witness had gotten only a glimpse of the man running away from the scene of the crime, but the general description had matched their suspect. A fingerprint lifted off of the victim's watch had confirmed their suspicions, and Charlie expected that DNA testing would prove that the skin under the girl's fingernails belonged to Colter. Finding the murder weapon would be the icing on the cake, but one way or another, Terrence was looking at a long sentence behind bars.

Charlie's heart pounded against his ribs as they reached the front door, and someone inside cranked the music up to deafening. Ray shifted to the side of the door and lifted a hand to knock. As he pounded his fist against the door, he heard a scream rise above the music.

Ray shouted, "FBI! Open up!"

Charlie couldn't make out the muffled sounds over the music, but he thought he heard glass shattering against a hard surface. With his weapon already drawn, Ray slammed a shoulder into the door and forced it open. Charlie followed behind him, his eyes already scanning inside for movement.

The dining room to the left of the front door was empty, and both men quickly focused on the activity down the hall. They moved toward the music and into a huge living room that stretched along the back wall. Flood lights were set up around the room, along with a camera on a tripod. One of the lights was on the ground, fragments of the light bulb scattered beside it.

Standing in front of the camera was a hollow-eyed girl wearing a flimsy robe. Her bloody lip suggested that the scream had come from her. The fact that the man standing next to her was holding a knife practically ensured it.

"FBI! Drop the knife, and keep your hands where I can see them," Charlie shouted, his gun trained on the man with the streaked blond hair.

Terrence turned, his eyes hot with anger and indignation as the girl quickly moved out of his reach. His words were lost in the music, but Charlie caught the general gist of the obscenities being shouted at him. Then Ray shut off the music, and the protests sputtered out.

"What do you think you're doing, bursting in here like this? I told Rinaldo that I'd have the prints to him by tomorrow."

Charlie's eyebrows lifted. The music had obviously masked his words when he had identified himself, and it appeared that Terrence had mistaken who they were and why they were here. "Maybe you didn't hear me the first time." With his weapon still trained on the suspect, he reached into his jacket pocket and retrieved his ID. "We're with the FBI."

"There must be some mistake. I haven't done anything wrong." Little beads of sweat formed on Colter's upper lip. "You need probable cause before you can come breaking into someone's home."

"We have a warrant." Ray pulled the folded court document from his pocket as the other two agents entered through the back door. "This gives us the right to search the premises. Now drop the knife, and place your hands on your head."

"This is absurd." Colter stared at the gun Charlie was still pointing at him and slowly opened his fingers and let the knife drop to the floor. "I haven't done anything wrong."

Charlie's jaw twitched, but he held his position as Ray stepped forward and cuffed him.

Ray squeezed the cuffs a little too tight and said the words Charlie had been waiting for. "Terrence Colter, you are under arrest for the murder of Megan Robertson."

"Megan?" The girl in front of them shrieked. "She's dead?"

Charlie nodded, but before he could offer any explanation or condolences, he caught a glimpse of movement out of the corner of his eye. Charlie swung around to face the stairway and saw a gun and the hand that held it.

"Drop it!" Charlie ordered as he took aim and let his eyes glance up at the man's face.

He saw the intent immediately. He had seen it before. In one seemingly effortless motion, Charlie shifted to the left as a shot rang out. Then Charlie pulled his trigger. The gunshot merged with the man's cry of pain as the man jerked back against the stair railing and then slid to the floor.

* * *

The floor vibrated as Kendra's captivating voice filled the STAPLES Center in Los Angeles. The chaos backstage calmed as everyone's attention shifted to the stage and the woman singing in the center of it.

Lingering in the shadows, he watched and waited as the crew settled in to enjoy the show. The first song drew tremendous applause, and Kendra bantered with the crowd before segueing into the next number. As the third song began, he stepped out of his hiding place, now certain that no one would notice him.

He moved down the hall and past the main-level dressing rooms, fully aware that he didn't have to worry about keeping his movements quiet. The tremendous noise from the music and the crowd would drown out any sound he might make.

His fingers gripped the cardboard box he held, and his eyes focused on his target. He passed the green room, glancing briefly at the cluster of chairs inside where the band could relax before and after the show. In front of him was the deep stage, only a small portion of which was currently being used for the concert. A thick black curtain sectioned off Kendra's band from the dark backstage area that was crowded with various equipment.

He was nearly to the edge of the center curtain when he noticed Kendra's bodyguard approaching. Unlike everyone else backstage, his attention wasn't on the performance, but rather, his eyes scanned the area looking for anything out of place.

Annoyance shot through him in a quick burst. Why was Dustin here right now? Why wasn't he on the other side of the stage where he was supposed to be?

Moving quickly, he stepped behind the curtain and let the deep folds of heavy fabric surround him. His heart raced for a moment. Then he remembered why he was here. He was supposed to be here to take that next step toward his future, the future he had been waiting for.

He peeked out into the wings of the stage where Dustin was still standing like a Doberman anxious to sniff out trouble. His jaw clenched as he considered his options. He couldn't let Dustin see him, but he certainly wasn't going to let him ruin his plans.

Shifting to the left, he felt something beneath his foot and heard the muffled clang of metal rolling on the floor. His heartbeat jumped into his throat, his eyes darting to Dustin to see if he'd heard the sound or sensed the movement. To his relief, Dustin hadn't moved from his spot; he was still standing stage left where he could monitor the backstage activity.

He let an expulsion of breath escape, and he looked down at the long, thin length of metal beneath his foot. Leaning down, he picked it up and discovered that it was a section of a microphone stand.

He set his package beside the curtain, and his gloved fingers curled tightly around the cold metal as he watched and waited. Several minutes passed before Dustin finally shifted his body to look down the hall, leaving his back exposed.

Seizing the opportunity he had been waiting for, he moved quickly, wielding the piece of metal like a weapon in the air. Then without any hesitation, he brought it down with force, and it connected with the back of Dustin's head.

Dustin's moan was silenced in the music as he collapsed on the floor.

With some effort, he leaned down, gripped the larger man's arms, and dragged him behind a riser. Once he was satisfied that Dustin was no longer visible, he moved back to where he had left his package and made his way deeper backstage.

The boards beneath his feet vibrated with the music as he surveyed his possibilities. Risers, floodlights, and various musical equipment were crammed together in no apparent order. He noticed the wide spotlight located near the edge of stage left, not far from where the opening band's drums were still set up on a riser. He considered the angles and the possibilities as one song ended and another began.

He stopped and listened, his heart squeezing in his chest as Kendra began singing his favorite song—a slow ballad about searching for love. Even though she couldn't see him, he knew her words were meant for him.

Soon she would find out what they could have together. He let himself dream of their future for a minute, of that moment when she would finally see him for what he really was—the only man who could ever truly love her. Ah, she was a fool—a beautiful fool—for not seeing it already.

Drawing a deep breath, he slowly opened the box he held to reveal the homemade explosive that he had designed himself. Slowly, methodically, he connected it to the underside of the spotlight and set the timer. He stared down at it, double checking every detail as the song ended and the noise from the crowd spiked again.

As Kendra Blake started into another song, he contemplated how her fans would react when they experienced the surprise he had in store for them. She deserved more than what her fans could give her, and soon they would understand that she wasn't performing for them.

She was performing for him alone.

A single press of a button started the countdown. He shifted back into the wings of the stage, where he could peer through the curtains. Kendra's blonde hair bounced with her movements as she crossed the stage, her voice captivating the audience. She was perfect, more perfect than any of the others. She was his now, even if she didn't know it yet.

In a few minutes, she would learn that she wasn't safe in front of all these people, and finally, he would have her to himself.

With a sense of anticipation rushing through him, he started down the hall and listened to the words Kendra sang for him.

* * *

Kendra stared out at the crowd, wondering if she would ever get used to this overwhelming feeling of seeing people singing along to a song she had written. Her legs felt like rubber as she moved with the music, but she didn't care. She was as captured by the fans as they were by her.

Only after she finished the last song did she begin to feel the exhaustion and the sweat dripping down her back. She exited stage left the moment the lights dimmed. The entire arena was encased in darkness for a brief moment before the houselights were brought up. Then the rumble of applause crescendoed as the crowd demanded yet another encore.

"Are we going back out again?" Zack asked as he joined her, looking out at the crowd.

Her shoulders lifted. "I try to draw the limit at three encores."

"Come on, Kendra," Ben Artina said, tapping his drumsticks together. "This is our hometown. Let's give them one more before we send them on their way."

Kendra considered briefly, and then she nodded and lifted her hands in surrender. "Why not."

She signaled the stage manager, and a moment later the houselights began to flicker and then dim. Instantly, the crowd erupted with deafening screams and applause.

A new wave of energy pulsed through Kendra, her previous nerves long forgotten. She grinned at her band and then glanced over at her manager, who was standing in the wings.

A flicker of surprise rushed through her when she noticed that Dustin wasn't in his usual position at the edge of the center curtain. A little red flag went up in the back of her mind, and her brow furrowed slightly. Not once could she remember a time when he hadn't been at her side the moment she'd stepped off the stage.

Then she heard her cue, and she let herself get swept up in the moment. She jogged onto the stage, all thoughts of Dustin quickly forgotten.

The drums started and set the beat. The keyboard joined in, followed by the guitar and bass. Then Kendra lifted the microphone, and her voice filled the arena once more, the music competing with the rumble of the crowd. She moved from one side of the stage to the other, reaching a hand out to connect with the fans in the front row.

When the guitar player started his solo, she moved back across the stage, her steps timed to the beat of the song. Out of the corner of her eye, she caught a glimpse of movement. Then she noticed Dustin stumbling near the edge of the stage.

Her first thought was that Dustin was back where he was supposed to be, but then she noticed the way he grabbed onto the curtain as though he couldn't quite support his own weight. One part of her brain was tuned into the music, listening for her next cue, but the other part let an underlying sense of concern flood through her as she saw Dustin take a staggering step forward.

One of the backstage security guards rushed to his side, and Kendra tried to focus once more on the music and her upcoming cue. Then she saw Dustin motion wildly toward the stage. She wondered what could have upset—

Before she could finish her thought, an explosion rocked the stage and everything seemed to happen in slow motion. Curtains and equipment crashed down behind them. Shards of glass and mangled metal spewed through the air. Intense screams erupted from the crowd.

Kendra's microphone flew out of her hand, and the blast sent her body hurtling through the air. She could see the stage floor rising too quickly, and she slammed down hard on it.

To her right, Ben's drums flew off of their riser, and Ben was thrown to the floor beside them. In front of them, the other band members and the fans dropped to the ground in an effort to avoid the flying debris.

From the depths of the stage, flames spiraled upward, and smoke filled the air.

Before Kendra could try to sit up, footsteps sounded, and she felt hands pulling her away from the heat and the flames. Dazed and confused, Kendra could only stare as her fans crowded toward the exits and chaos reigned.

Chapter 3

Charlie walked into his sparsely furnished apartment and locked the door behind him. He toed off his shoes and then immediately reached for the remote to turn on the television. A late night movie wasn't something he would normally watch, but at least the dialogue would help drown out the silence.

The events of the night replayed through his mind as he shrugged out of his suit jacket and tossed it over the back of the couch. He sat down, immediately dropping his head into his hands as he fought back his emotions. His stomach curled at the realization that someone had tried to kill him—that someone had nearly succeeded.

Charlie took a deep breath, a silent prayer of gratitude running through his mind that he had survived another shooting. On the heels of that silent prayer was a new resolve to hide this part of his job from his family. He reached for the framed photograph on the end table and stared down at it. His parents stood in the center, surrounded by their children and grandchildren.

His gaze lingered on the woman beside him in the photograph and on the diamond ring sparkling on her left hand. He never would have guessed the day that picture was taken that only two weeks later, one dream would come true while another would shatter. When the memory of that last day with Lisa flashed into his mind, he didn't even try to fight it.

Charlie hung up the phone, both thrilled and stunned at the news. They wanted him. The FBI wanted him. Everything he'd ever dared hope for was about to be his. In a few short months, he would be married to a beautiful woman whom he adored, and now the career that he had secretly dreamed about for the past four years was going to be his.

Barely able to contain his excitement, Charlie quickly finished getting ready for his engagement party that would begin in a matter of minutes.

Then he hurried down the stairs of his childhood home and headed straight for the guest room.

He rapped on the door, his smile widening when Lisa pulled it open. As always, her short chestnut-brown hair was perfectly styled, and her makeup was flawless. Her dark brown eyes met his expectantly. "Are the guests here?"

"I don't know," Charlie said, even as the doorbell rang. "I have some great news. I just got a job offer."

Her face lit with anticipation, and she reached for his hands. "Already? I thought Harrison & Bates wasn't making their decision until next month."

"The job isn't with Harrison & Bates." Charlie's eyes were alive with excitement. "I got accepted by the FBI."

She stared blankly at him before she echoed, "The FBI?"

"I can't believe I made it in. I'll find out next week when I'm scheduled to start at the FBI Academy."

"Wait a minute." Her voice was incredulous. "You already accepted the job?"

"Well, yeah," he said, puzzled by her expression. "Why wouldn't I?"

"You accepted the job without even discussing it with me?" She pulled her hands free of his and took a step back. "How could you do that?"

"Wait a second. Is it the fact that I didn't talk it over with you first or is it the job itself that's the problem?"

"I can't believe you would seriously consider taking a job like this."

Charlie felt his reality shift before his eyes. "I thought you would be happy for me. This is a job I've dreamed of getting for years."

Lisa shook her head and crossed her arms firmly across her chest. "You'll never make any real money, and it certainly won't be of any use to you when it comes time to run for office."

"I never said I was going to run for office. Where did you get that idea?"

"Your father, for one. He said that with your personality and your law degree from Georgetown, you could take his job someday if you wanted it."

"Just because I could *run for office doesn't mean I want to," Charlie said, his heart squeezing in his chest. "The idea that I would try for Dad's seat in the Senate when he retires has been a running joke in my family since I was a kid. I don't think anyone ever really expected that it would happen."*

Lisa held up one hand. "So let me get this straight. You're telling me that the man I plan to marry has no other ambition in life besides carrying around a gun and playing policeman every night. What am I supposed to do? Sit around and clip coupons?"

Charlie stared down at her, his mind trying to comprehend how this woman he thought he knew had turned into someone else right before his eyes. "You're in law school too. I thought you wanted to work until we started a family."

"Yes, because it looks good for a politician's wife to have a solid résumé."

"You can't be serious."

"Of course I'm serious." Lisa rolled her eyes before staring up at him. "I spend six months dating someone from a solid family, someone who is going places in life, then all of a sudden, he's going to walk away from all the opportunities sitting in front of him to go play cops and robbers. That's not what I thought I was signing up for. What else have you been planning for our future without telling me?"

Charlie took a deep breath and then took a deliberate step back, disgust and confusion warring with each other. "I'm starting to wonder if you really love me *or if you love the idea of marrying the senator's son."*

"Of course I love you, but that doesn't mean I'm willing to see you throw your future away." Lisa took a step forward and ran her hands up his chest to rest on his shoulders. Smiling seductively, she continued, "Sweetheart, you're destined for more than working a menial job with minimal pay. We should be thinking about celebrating our future together. I'm sure we can find a more suitable job for someone with your connections. Why don't you go call the FBI and tell them you changed your mind?"

Slowly, he shook his head and took a step back. All he could see were two paths before him. He could be the man Lisa wanted him to be and try to fill his father's shoes, or he could follow his dreams and forge his own path—alone.

"I have changed my mind," he said softly. "But not about the job."

Lisa's shock had quickly turned to fury. When she had stormed out of the house a short while later, she had left Charlie with a diamond ring, two nonrefundable tickets to the Bahamas, a houseful of family and friends, and the stunning realization that he had nearly married a complete stranger.

Looking back now, Charlie knew that Lisa had let him see what he had wanted to see. He had gotten distracted by the outer package without taking the time to know the woman within. He promised himself he wouldn't make that mistake a second time.

Charlie indulged in one last look at the photograph before setting it aside. Lisa wasn't part of his life anymore, and it was time for him to start looking forward instead of living in the past.

* * *

"Can you think of anyone who could have set off the explosive device at your concert?" Detective Dan Eadelton asked gently. "An old boyfriend or someone you might have fired recently?"

Kendra shook her head, her body still trembling even though she had arrived home more than an hour before. An ambulance attendant had checked her out and bandaged the minor cuts she had sustained when she was thrown to the floor. Then she had been allowed to go home. She still couldn't believe that someone had planted a bomb backstage. A small bomb, according to the detective—but a bomb nonetheless.

Dustin had been the closest person to it and was currently at the hospital in stable condition. Ben, her drummer, had suffered a broken arm, and several other people backstage had been taken to the hospital for various broken bones and burns. Kendra considered it a minor miracle that more people hadn't been injured.

She tried to concentrate on the detective's questions, despite the constant throbbing in her head. "I haven't dated anyone recently, and it's been more than three months since anyone left the band."

"Who was that? Why did he leave?"

"Adam Templeton," Kendra said. She saw the light go on in the detective's eyes, but she expounded on her answer anyway. "He signed a contract as a solo artist with my record label. It was time for him to branch out on his own."

"Have you received any threatening letters or phone calls? Any unusual fan mail?"

Kendra shook her head, but she turned to Greg Young, her manager, for confirmation.

"She always gets a few obsessive letters from fans, but nothing out of the ordinary," Greg told him. "Of course, we've had a few nasty e-mails about Kendra winning best female artist at the Grammys."

"What kind of e-mails?"

"Just fans of the competition complaining that someone else should have won," Greg told him. "From what I understand, this kind of thing is pretty common."

"The e-mails might be, but bombs sure aren't," Detective Eadelton said. "I suppose it's possible that some obsessed fan got backstage and set off a bomb to scare Miss Blake. For now, I would suggest you stay home for at least a couple of days while we pursue our investigation."

Greg looked from the detective to Kendra. "As much as I hate to do it, I think it's only logical to cancel your concert tomorrow night. Ben can't play, and I'd rather not bring in a last-minute replacement under the circumstances."

Kendra nodded, not sure if she should feel relieved or disappointed.

Detective Eadelton stood and took a step forward. "I assume you have a security system here in the house, but we'll have a cruiser parked outside just to be safe." He handed Kendra a business card. "Please give me a call if you think of anything else."

Kendra managed to nod as the detective turned and Greg escorted him out. Then she felt reality crash over her. She knew what it was like to have strangers watching her constantly, limiting her activities. She remembered all too well the lack of privacy, the overwhelming feelings of invasion and oppression. Her chest tightened, and she tried to fight back the anxiety that threatened.

A moment later, Greg returned and held out a cordless phone. "Kendra, I'm sorry, but your father is on the phone."

The mention of her father kicked her anxiety into high gear. She had to force herself to reach her hand out to take the phone. She could already imagine her father's reaction to the news that someone had bypassed security, overpowered her bodyguard, and then planted some kind of bomb backstage. The fact that her parents hadn't already shown up on her doorstep confirmed that they were still in New York, where her father was scheduled to appear as a guest on one of the late-night TV shows.

She stared down at the phone for a moment and took a steadying breath. "Hi, Dad."

"Baby! Oh, it's so good to hear your voice," Sterling said, his voice both relieved and concerned. "Are you okay? I can't believe someone got past your security."

Kendra glanced down at her arms, at the ugly scrapes and minor burns that had resulted from the explosion. "I'm fine."

"And I'm going to make sure you stay that way. I'm sending a car to pick you up and bring you home," he told her. "Your mother and I will catch the next flight out."

A fresh wave of panic rushed through her at the thought of moving back into her father's home, of living with a dozen guards and the carefully controlled schedule, of losing her right to make any decisions for herself without her father's permission. "No, Dad. I'm staying here. There's no reason for you to come home early."

Sterling hesitated briefly, and then his determined voice came over the line once more. "If you won't move home, then we'll enhance your security. I've already talked to Bruce Parsons. He and Alan can be over there within the hour. Alan can take over for Dustin until he gets out of the hospital."

"I don't want a house full of security people." A wave of nausea threatened as Kendra considered what it would mean to have her father's head of security take over her protection again. "I'm fine. Really."

"Kendra, you aren't fine. The bomb at your concert could have killed you."

She swallowed the lump that formed in her throat. "But it didn't."

"I'm not going to take chances with your safety," Sterling insisted. "Bruce and Alan will be at your house shortly. Let them help you."

Kendra swallowed her objections, already knowing her father would ignore them. Instead, she simply said, "Good-bye, Dad."

"Be safe, sweetie. I love you."

"I love you too," Kendra said softly and then hung up the phone. She stared at it for a long moment. An image of what her life would soon be like flashed into her mind and pressed on her. What little privacy she had gained would disappear the moment Bruce Parsons walked through her door.

His paranoia, his insistence on constant surveillance, would stifle her just as it had during her teenage years. Bruce's son, Alan, seemed to understand her almost desperate need for some space, but undoubtedly, he would follow his father's instructions and effectively smother whatever creativity she still had left.

As a teenager, Kendra had locked herself in her room with her guitar to find peace and solitude. Writing music gave her that sense of freedom she always craved but could never quite grasp. Bruce's men didn't know how to protect her without hovering, without invading her personal space.

How often had she discovered a wonderful melody or figured out the perfect lyrics only to have them skip right out of her head when a bodyguard came knocking on her door? How many times had she attempted to take a walk on the beach to gather her thoughts only to be told she couldn't go? Could they not understand that she needed time alone—time without a constant audience?

Kendra stood up, her urge to flee surpassing all logic. She grabbed her phone and pressed speed dial. Her knees were shaky, so she lowered herself onto the couch as she heard the sleepy hello. Tears threatened when she opened her mouth, her voice low. "Grandpa, I need your help."

Chapter 4

William Blake hung up the phone and looked up to see his wife standing in his office doorway. She shivered against the chill in the room and pulled her robe more tightly around her.

"Who was on the phone?"

"Kendra."

She took a step forward, concern evident on her face. "What's wrong? Is she okay?"

"Everyone's fine." He slipped his arms around her and gathered her close. "A bomb went off at her concert tonight."

Hannah pulled back enough that she could see his face. "What?"

"She's okay, but her bodyguard ended up in the hospital."

"Sterling isn't going to want her staying in that big house alone."

"I know. He's sending part of his security team over there right now, but she'll be gone by the time they get there."

"What do you mean? She isn't running away again, is she? I know Sterling can be overprotective, but this isn't the time to argue about security."

"I agree. That's why she's coming here, at least until I can find a better solution." He saw her processing his words and knew that she understood his concerns.

Her eyebrows furrowed. "You're worried you won't be able to protect her by yourself, aren't you?"

"Maybe . . . but I definitely think it's time for me to pull in a few favors." He leaned down and kissed her forehead. "Why don't you go back to bed? I need to make a phone call, and it's going to be at least six hours before Kendra gets here."

"She's driving?"

William nodded. "I don't like it either, but it's safer than flying."

Her eyes narrowed. "You think someone would try to follow her here?"

"I think I'm not going to take any chances with Kendra or with you." He nudged her toward the door. "Go get some sleep. I need to make that call."

With a reluctant nod, she gave him a kiss and then disappeared back down the hall.

William glanced at the clock and considered waiting for a couple hours so his old FBI buddy could get some more sleep. Then he shook his head. Kendra was family, and she had the same stubborn streak that William had passed along to her father. She was adamant that her grandfather could give her the privacy and safety she so desperately craved, but he knew better. As much as it pained him to agree with his son, Kendra needed a bodyguard, whether she wanted one or not.

* * *

Elias Washington hung up the phone and rubbed the sleep out of his eyes. He glanced over at his wife, who was lying peacefully beside him, and was grateful that she had learned years ago to sleep with earplugs.

He slipped out of bed and headed straight for his office. William's call had woken him up shortly after three o'clock, and he wanted some time to consider his friend's request before the morning briefing.

As the agent in charge at the FBI's Phoenix office, Elias knew no one under his command would question him if he assigned a protection detail to Kendra Blake, even though the explosion in Los Angeles was technically outside their jurisdiction. Assigning protection to someone who potentially didn't want it would be a lot trickier, especially considering William's other request. He wanted the agent assigned to his granddaughter to either be one of his female operatives or someone who was LDS, preferably both.

Since Kendra knew most of his agents, his options were limited. Elias knew it was going to take some time to look through his personnel files, to consider his options, and to identify the right person for the job.

He powered on his laptop and automatically opened his e-mail. An urgent message caught his attention. He opened it and read through the disturbing details of the woman found dead the night before along with a request from the LA office for some extra support in hunting a possible serial killer.

Elias shook his head and headed for the shower. Whether he liked it or not, this workday had already started, and it was going to last well into the night.

* * *

Kendra stared at her grandfather, still not quite sure what to think. She was exhausted after not sleeping at all last night, not to mention everything else that had happened. She must have misunderstood what he was telling her. "You want to assign me a security team?"

"It wouldn't be like the bodyguards your father keeps around. I just want some of my FBI friends to keep an eye on things for a while, at least until the police finish their investigation."

"You know I can't live like that anymore. That's why I came here." She shook her head, already feeling like the walls were closing in on her. "I can't do it anymore, Grandpa. I just can't. You used to be FBI. I'll be fine here with you."

William let out a sigh. "If whoever planted that bomb at your concert was trying to hurt you, he might be able to track you here, and I definitely don't want you staying at your condo here in town. I just don't know if I trust myself to keep both you and your grandmother safe."

Sickness and nerves sloshed inside her, and her face paled. "I never really thought about that."

He rubbed a finger along his snow-white mustache, the way he always did when he was thinking. "Did you tell anyone that you were coming here?"

"No." She shook her head. "I left a note for my manager, but I didn't tell him where I was going. I just said I'd be gone for a few weeks so he could handle the press. I also wanted him to know that I plan to be back in California in time for a couple of benefit concerts next month."

"In that case, I do have one other idea."

"What?"

"You could stay in one of our cabins in Pinewood for a few weeks. Not many people go up there this time of year, and you'd be able to have that peace and quiet you've been wanting."

A glimmer of hope speared through her as she considered what it would be like to truly be by herself for the first time ever. Part of her couldn't believe that her grandfather would send her somewhere alone, but hope overshadowed her doubts. "Could I really do that? You think it would be safe?"

William nodded. "A lawyer friend of mine is going to be staying in the little cabin. He picked up the keys yesterday, and I think he was heading up there today, but the cabin you normally stay in with your parents is empty."

Kendra threw her arms around her grandfather. "That sounds perfect. Thank you."

He motioned down at the sandals on her feet. "Did you pack any other shoes besides those?"

"My tennis shoes are in my gym bag in the trunk."

"In that case, why don't you let your grandmother get you some breakfast, and then you can try to take a nap. I'll load up some supplies and check out the car before you head up the mountain."

"Thanks, Grandpa." Kendra nodded and kissed his cheek. "I love you."

"I love you too."

Chapter 5

Charlie entered the briefing room, his stomach still a bit unsettled after the events of the night before. He'd slept restlessly all night, images of gunfire infiltrating his dreams with annoying regularity. Determined to appear unfazed by the fact that he had shot someone, he moved forward and exchanged greetings with a few of the men and women he worked with before taking a seat on the left side of the room. A minute later, Special Agent in Charge Elias Washington walked in and took his place at the front of the room.

The chatter ceased immediately.

Elias set a file on the podium beside him and spoke in a grave voice. "I'm sure you have all heard of the Malibu Stalker."

A wave of assents rippled through the room. Charlie looked around. Concern showed on everyone's faces, confirming to him that he was the only person in the room who didn't know who this Malibu Stalker was.

In that moment, he wasn't sure what was worse: being the new guy in the Phoenix field office and not knowing what they were talking about or being back at FBI headquarters where everyone knew him as Senator Whitmore's son.

Biting back a sigh, Charlie lifted a hand to get Elias's attention. "I know I'm the new kid on the block, but who exactly is the Malibu Stalker?"

As expected, everyone turned to stare at him. Thankfully, Elias answered without any animosity. "He's a serial killer the Los Angeles office has been tracking for the past three years. He's the prime suspect in six murders, including this most recent one. All of the victims fit the same general description. Tall, blonde, early to mid-twenties." He hesitated before lifting his eyes to look out at the room. "They found another victim last night. The medical examiner places the time of death to be about four days ago. The victim was supermodel Joslyn Korden."

Charlie's gut clenched as he considered the challenges of identifying the culprit. From his training, he knew that serial killers typically looked like normal people and could be exceptionally difficult to recognize.

"The LA office has asked for some extra support from us on this case. They specifically asked for agents who have prior experience with serial killings." Elias looked around the room, and then his gaze settled on Daryl Montgomery, one of the senior agents in the room.

A knowing look passed between the two men, and Daryl nodded. "I'll go."

Elias nodded his approval. "Assemble your team, and check in with Rick Michaels in LA. He's taking the lead on this."

Charlie listened quietly as the morning briefing continued and various new assignments were passed out. He was surprised that he wasn't given any new cases, especially after he and Ray had closed down the pornography ring the night before.

When the meeting concluded, Elias motioned in his direction. "Charlie, I need to see you in my office for a minute."

Charlie nodded, acutely aware of the surprise on the faces of several fellow agents—surprise that rippled through him along with a combination of curiosity and concern. During all of the weeks he had been in the Phoenix office, Elias had never asked to see one of the junior agents. Of course, this was also the first time since his transfer to Phoenix that anyone had been involved in a shootout with a suspect. Afraid to speculate as to the reason he had been the only agent singled out from last night's incident, Charlie stood and followed Elias out into the hall.

* * *

Elias settled behind his heavy oak desk and watched Charlie fold his six-foot-three frame into the chair across from him. He plucked Charlie's personnel file from a stack of folders on the left side of his desk and slapped it open in front of him. Elias didn't need to read the information in front of him. He had already memorized it.

Charlie Whitmore: twenty-nine years old, a Georgetown University Law School graduate, a recent transfer from the Washington DC office, and the son of Senator James Whitmore. A few casual inquiries had also revealed that, like his father, Charlie Whitmore was a practicing Mormon, and the incident report from the night before proved that he knew how to handle himself on the job.

He also appeared to be without any personal entanglements at the moment that might complicate his upcoming assignment. From what Elias had gathered from his file and the rumor mill, Charlie hadn't dated anyone seriously since breaking up with his former fiancée shortly before entering the FBI Academy.

Elias tapped his fingers on the arm of his chair. "I have an assignment I'm considering you for, but I have a few questions first."

Only a hint of curiosity sparked in Charlie's eyes as he leaned back slightly, as though getting more comfortable before the interrogation that was about to begin.

"I understand you're Mormon."

Charlie nodded, one corner of his mouth lifting slightly. "That's right."

"Have you ever met Kendra Blake?"

"The singer?" Charlie asked, his eyebrows drawing together. "I've heard of her, but I've never met her."

"Good." Elias leaned back more comfortably in his own chair. "Her grandfather retired from this office a few years ago, but he's asked for a favor, and I think you may be the person who can help."

"What kind of favor?"

"She needs protection," Elias said simply. "There was an incident at her concert in Los Angeles last night. A bomb went off backstage, injuring several people. Her bodyguard was knocked unconscious during the show, and we're moving forward with the assumption that Kendra may have been the target."

Charlie's voice was professional when he asked, "How many people will be on the protection detail?"

"Just you."

"Just me?" Charlie straightened, and confusion flickered over his face. "I don't understand."

"You're not a woman, which is a minor downfall, but you're one of only four agents in this office who hasn't met her," Elias admitted.

"Why would that matter?" Charlie asked. Then his eyebrows lifted, and understanding dawned. "Wait a minute. You want me to protect her without her knowing about it?"

"Exactly."

"I'm confused. How does everyone else in the office know her? And why don't you want one of the other new transfers to work this with me? And what does it matter that I'm not a woman?"

Elias chuckled at the last question. "It matters that you're not a woman because Kendra has a protective grandfather, but I'm going to trust that you won't give him reason to worry. And Kendra has been into this office dozens of times over the past few years with her grandfather. She even performed a benefit concert for us to help raise money when Ray Underwood's little girl was fighting cancer. She hasn't just seen the other agents. She's talked to them and knows most of them by name," Elias explained. He lifted one hand and gestured vaguely toward the door. "As for giving you backup, the other three agents are heavily involved in cases I can't pull them off of right now. With where you'll be staying, we won't have to worry about anyone tracking Kendra down."

Elias went on to explain that the assignment was actually in Pinewood, a sleepy summer town twenty miles south of Flagstaff, and then relayed William's plans for Charlie's living arrangements.

Charlie listened intently and then finally asked, "Do you really think Kendra will even let me talk to her? She has to be freaked out about what happened at her concert."

"William mentioned to her that a lawyer friend of his would be staying in one of his cabins. She's only a couple of years younger than you, and with your family background, I'm sure you can find some common ground."

The muscle in Charlie's jaw jumped. "Excuse me?"

Hit a sore spot, Elias thought to himself, even as he appreciated how quickly Charlie controlled his emotions. "You were raised in the fishbowl of Washington politics. Kendra grew up in the limelight of Hollywood. That should give you some common ground."

"Forgive me, sir, but how did you know about my family? I didn't think background checks were included in personnel files."

"Normally they aren't, but because of the sensitivity of this assignment, I asked headquarters to fax yours to me."

Charlie nodded, his lips drawing together in a thin line. "If it's all the same to you, I'd appreciate it if that information could stay between us."

"Don't worry, Charlie. You won't get any special treatment here." Elias stood up and glanced at his watch. "I'm going to have Ray Underwood coordinate with the LAPD about the bombing at Kendra's concert. I want you to hand off all your active cases to him so he can reassign them for now. Then go home and pack. I want you settled into that cabin by this afternoon."

Charlie stood as well and nodded.

"And, Charlie?"

"Yeah?"

"Remember, this is a sensitive situation. I expect you to keep the details to yourself and report directly to me."

"Yes, sir."

Chapter 6

Snowflakes danced in the wind as they drifted downward. Kendra switched her windshield wipers to high. The roads were becoming more treacherous by the minute. When her grandfather had checked the weather reports two hours ago, the forecaster had insisted that this winter storm would hit well north of Flagstaff and miss Pinewood completely. Obviously, someone had miscalculated.

Her fingers gripped the steering wheel tightly as she took her exit, slowly steering the car down the ramp that led into town. The roads were already covered with several inches of snow, and only a single set of tire tracks disturbed the pristine white.

She shook her head as she considered her current situation. She couldn't fathom who would want to hurt her, and the events of last night seemed more like a bad dream than reality. She'd heard of obsessed fans—people who developed an unhealthy fixation on public figures—but she didn't have any of those. Or did she?

She let out a sigh and forced the tension from her shoulders. She had to be safe now. She still felt bad that she had left her manager to deal with her family and the police, but at least her concert tour was basically over. Only tonight's concert would have to be canceled.

Kendra wasn't sure what story her manager would fabricate about why she had dropped out of sight, but she was relatively certain that whatever was printed in the newspapers was likely to be a work of fiction. He wouldn't want to tell the American public that she had gone into hiding because she'd had a panic attack—even if it had been justified.

Perhaps that's what scared her the most: the fact that both the police and her grandfather believed that she was the target of the bomb at her concert. She understood why her grandfather wanted her to let the FBI handle everything, but she also knew she couldn't live like that again. She couldn't live under the microscope they would put her under. If he thought she would be safe hiding out in Pinewood, certainly she would be.

Her grandfather had insisted on taking several precautions, beginning with having her drive her classic Mustang from LA to Phoenix instead of the new car she'd bought the year before. He'd explained that her new car had a GPS tracking system, as did her cell phone, which was why she now had a disposable cell phone in her purse. Her regular one was turned off and tucked in one of her dresser drawers at home. She had also started using cash so no one would be able to track her credit card activity.

Already, her appearance was quite different from her public image. Her long blonde hair was pulled up in a ponytail that fed through the back of her baseball cap, and her face was clear of makeup. Even the most devoted fans would have to look twice before seeing any resemblance between the woman she was at the moment and the successful singer she had built herself into.

She checked her rearview mirror to make sure, once again, that no one was following her. Relieved that there weren't any cars in sight, she focused once more on the town ahead. The little town wasn't much more than a few businesses on the main road and a lot of vacation homes.

Parking lots were empty and snow covered, except for a pickup truck in front of the only diner in town. If memory served, the owner was one of the few people who lived in Pinewood year round. Sure enough, smoke curled from the chimney of the little cabin right behind the diner.

Kendra smiled to herself as she considered that she was finally about to find out what real privacy was all about. She tried to remember the last time she had been alone, really alone, and couldn't come up with a single memory. Someone was always tagging along behind her to keep her on schedule or to make sure no one got too close to her.

She came to a stop sign, her car skidding a bit as she turned onto the dirt road that led farther up the mountain. Part of her hoped the snow would continue until she wouldn't have a choice but to stay for a while. She knew the weather was unpredictable here, especially during the month of February.

Her car struggled upward, the snow getting deeper as she climbed higher up the mountain. Realizing that her car wasn't likely to make it up the steep hill in front of her, she turned a block early, intending to circle around and come in the back way. She edged down the road parallel to her family's cabin, pleased that the car was now able to make steady progress. She turned at the next crossroad, and the vehicle immediately slid toward the center of the road. Kendra tried to compensate, but she angled too sharply, and the car came to a rumbling stop at the side of the road.

"Great," Kendra muttered to herself. She tried to ease the car forward but to no avail. Then she shifted into reverse. The car rocked back a few inches, but when she tried to move forward again, the wheels simply spun in the deepening snow.

She leaned her head against the wheel, exhaustion and frustration pushing her emotions to the edge. Tears threatened but were quickly conquered. Only another quarter mile and she would be safe and warm. That thought kept her going, giving her the strength to push the car door open and step out into the snow. Immediately, she looked down at her sandals and the snow that seeped between her toes. Then she studied the car tires. One look was all it took to realize that her car wasn't going anywhere.

She popped open the trunk so she could change into her tennis shoes. She stared at the contents as reality hit her. Her gym bag with her tennis shoes was indeed in the trunk of her car. Her other car. She was going to have to carry her things more than a quarter of a mile in the snow, wearing sandals. Remembering her grandfather's insistence that she check in as soon as she got to Pinewood, she got back into the car to call him, deliberately omitting the fact that her car was stuck in the snow and that her only decent pair of shoes was still in California.

With her cell phone still in hand, she circled to the back of the car once more. Realizing that she wasn't going to want to make a second trip anytime soon, she set her phone down and consolidated the groceries she'd brought with her and the most essential clothing and overnight items into one suitcase. Then she slipped her purse over her shoulder, lifted her suitcase with one hand, and grabbed her guitar case with the other.

* * *

"How can you not know where she is?" Sterling Blake demanded. He hadn't slept except in snatches on the long flight across the country. Then he had gotten off the plane only to find a message on his voice mail from Bruce Parsons telling him that Kendra had left her house before Bruce and Alan had arrived. He stood in the living room of his Malibu home and glared at the two men now. "You were sent to protect her."

"We talked to her manager," Bruce said, his voice tense. "Apparently, after she spoke with you, she left him a note saying that she needed a few weeks to herself, and she left the house."

"You've got to have some way to track her."

"We're trying," Alan said hesitantly. He was a younger version of his father, with dark hair and serious eyes. "We know she withdrew several hundred dollars from an ATM machine near her house, and there was a charge on one of her credit cards outside of Riverside."

"Which car is she driving?"

"The '69 Mustang," Bruce answered. "It doesn't have GPS capability, and she left her phone at the house."

"She's probably heading for the house in Palm Springs or her condo in Phoenix." Sterling shook his head, mystified about why his daughter would run away like this. "Send someone to both places in case she shows up. I don't want her unprotected."

Both men nodded and then quickly left the room.

* * *

Kendra's feet were frozen, her back and shoulders aching as she trudged forward. The snow was still falling steadily and would have been beautiful to watch . . . had she been sitting inside, watching it through a window. Instead, she could feel the flakes accumulating on her head and shoulders, melting through her baseball cap and into her hair. Her body shivered, her teeth chattered, and she tried not to think about the pain shooting through her bare toes.

The cabin was in view now, and Kendra smiled, or she would have smiled if she'd been able to feel her face. One painful step after another, she edged closer to the wooden structure. It was modest, she supposed, by her parents' standards, a mere six bedrooms, instead of the ten that her father had originally planned. Her grandparents had convinced him to scale back on the size and the luxuries, opting instead to build a second, smaller cabin across the street for when all of the extended family visited at the same time.

She could vaguely remember when the construction had begun on the big cabin the summer of her fourth birthday. The summer of her father's first Oscar-winning performance.

The security had started then—the constant presence of household staff and bodyguards. The big Hollywood star couldn't take any chances with his family's safety. Looking back now, she realized those early days hadn't been all that bad. The security during her childhood hadn't been anything compared to what had come in her teenage years.

Kendra pushed aside the thoughts of her childhood home and how smothered she had felt there. Had it not been for her father's demanding acting career and the stifling atmosphere of her home in Malibu, she doubted she would have spent so much time with her grandparents growing up. Without them, she might never have discovered the gospel and the joy it could bring her.

Sometimes it was hard to believe that her father had been raised Mormon, but even though he had abandoned most of the practices long before she was born, one thing was certain: family still came first for him.

A twinge of guilt shot through her as she considered how worried he would be. She thought of how she must look right now, snow-covered and frozen, and was suddenly glad he couldn't see her. For now, she would have to trust her grandfather to somehow assure her dad that she was okay without revealing her location. He mentioned this morning that he was going to tell her father that she had called him to let him know what had happened. Where the conversation would go from there, she couldn't be sure.

Kendra crossed the yard to the cabin and carefully climbed the steps to the front porch. She set the suitcase down in the snow and then struggled to fish her key out of her purse, despite the numbness in her fingers. Her hand trembled as she finally managed to grasp hold of the key and slide it into the lock.

She pushed the door open, barely remembering to grab her suitcase off the porch as she hurried inside. The furniture in the expansive living area had been replaced since she'd been here last. Several oversized chairs were clustered near the fireplace, and two loveseats were angled in the other corner of the room, facing the armoire that housed the television and DVD player. A few logs and some newspapers were stacked beside the fireplace. Kendra immediately reached for the thermostat beside the door and turned on the heat. Then she dropped her things on a loveseat and crossed the room to start a fire.

Her fingers were cold and red, and it took her a few minutes to accomplish what would normally have been a simple task. As soon as she was confident about the leaping flames, she closed the screen and plopped into the closest chair. She kicked off her soaking wet sandals and then realized that she would feel infinitely better if she were wearing dry clothes.

She shrugged out of her coat, pulled some dry clothes from her suitcase, and changed right there in the living room. She didn't worry about the mess she made in the process. All she could think about was getting warm.

Reaching for her grandmother's afghan off one of the loveseats, she curled up in a chair by the fire and pulled it over her legs. The smell of burning wood lingered in the air, and the warmth of the fire seeped into the room. Slowly, the shivering stopped, and her chattering teeth quieted. As the feeling began to return to her hands and feet, she settled back into the chair and let herself drift off to sleep.

Chapter 7

Charlie navigated the unfamiliar roads through the steadily falling snow. He hadn't thought to check the weather reports before starting out. This was Arizona. He had never really considered that only two hours north of the Phoenix desert, he would find a full-blown winter snow storm, and now he found himself wondering exactly how much accumulation was expected here in the mountains.

He glanced down at the handmade map Elias had provided for him after he'd realized Google Maps and MapQuest couldn't find the place. Now he could understand why. Street signs were in short supply and, rather than addresses, the properties were referred to by lot number. Without knowing where the cabin was, it was unlikely anyone was going to find it without help from someone who had been there before.

Charlie flipped on the radio and searched for a local station, hoping for a clue as to how much snow Pinewood was supposed to get. A foot of snow had already accumulated on the ground, and Charlie was immediately grateful that he was still driving the beat up four-wheel-drive he'd bought after returning home from his mission.

He made his final turn, the rear wheels sliding as he did so. Then he looked down the narrow road and wondered if he was lost. The snow on the road was pristine, and there weren't any vehicles parked outside the cabins that his map identified as belonging to the Blake family.

He edged his vehicle down the narrow road and parked near the cabin that he hoped was his temporary quarters. He climbed out of his SUV, trudged through the snow to the front door, and tried the key Elias had given him. The key turned smoothly, and Charlie narrowed his eyes.

If he was in the right place, then where was Kendra? He breathed in the smell of burning wood and turned to look at the cabin across the road. Then he saw it: the smoke coming from the chimney.

* * *

Kendra heard the knocking but didn't bother to open her eyes. Dustin or her butler would answer the door. When the knocking continued, she forced her eyes open and looked around. It took her a few seconds to get her bearings, to remember where she was and why she was there.

Her heartbeat immediately quickened as questions raced through her mind. Had she been followed? Had that bomb backstage really been meant for her? And who would want to hurt her?

Fear pulsed through her, irrational and strong. She pushed herself out of the chair, her grandmother's afghan pooling at her feet as she slipped on her shoes. She didn't consider the snow on the ground or her lack of transportation as she started for the back door, already planning her escape.

Then she heard a man's voice penetrate the closed door. "Kendra, are you in there? It's Charlie Whitmore. I'm a friend of your grandfather's."

Kendra stopped and turned to look at the front door as though staring at it would explain everything. Then the rest of Charlie's words sank in. Her grandfather had mentioned that a friend of his was staying in the little cabin.

Obviously, if Charlie had been in Phoenix yesterday getting the keys from her grandfather, he couldn't have been involved in the incident at her concert. Not to mention, her grandfather must trust this guy or he never would have suggested Kendra come up here by herself, knowing that he was around.

Still cautious, she drew in a deep breath and slowly crossed the room. Pulling the curtains back, she peeked out the window beside the door. The man standing in the falling snow was younger than she'd expected, probably only a couple years older than she was. His hands were tucked into his ski jacket; his Georgetown University sweatshirt visible beneath it. He pulled a hand free of his pocket and brushed at the snow accumulating in his short blond hair.

Again, Kendra wondered what he could be doing here, debating for a moment if she should really open the door. He turned toward the window and saw her. The corners of his lips twitched as though he was fighting back a grin.

Suddenly feeling ridiculous for being so paranoid, Kendra stepped back, pushed her hair back from her face, and tried not to think about the fact that she still didn't have any makeup on. Her curiosity humming, she forced herself to pull the door open.

"You must be Kendra," Charlie said the moment she opened the door. "I'm Charlie Whitmore, a friend of your grandfather's. I don't know if he mentioned that he's letting me stay in the cabin across the street."

"Yes, he mentioned it."

"Sorry to drop by on you unannounced," Charlie continued, his tone more professional than friendly. He motioned inside. "Do you mind if I come in?"

Kendra hesitated. The manners her nannies had ingrained in her demanded that she let him in, but she didn't know this man. She was also now acutely aware of how disconcerting it could feel to be without a bodyguard. When Charlie fought back a shiver, her manners won out over her trepidation. She let her confusion show on her face as he walked inside. She closed the door behind him. "How do you know my grandfather?"

"Actually, it's my father who knows him. I guess they met in DC a few years ago."

Her earlier conversation with her grandfather replayed in her mind, and she looked at him suspiciously. "Is your dad FBI too?"

"No." Charlie shook his head, and a smile played on his lips. "Actually, he's a U.S. senator."

Kendra stared at him blankly.

"Senator James Whitmore from Virginia," Charlie expanded.

"Sorry." Kendra shrugged. "I'm afraid I don't really follow politics."

"I guess outside of DC politicians aren't quite as well known," Charlie said wryly. "Maybe you've heard of my brother, Matt Whitmore. He's a baseball player. Just got traded back to the Florida Marlins."

"That name does sound familiar."

Charlie chuckled softly. "Well, one thing's for sure. If everyone in the West is like you, I definitely shouldn't have to worry about the paparazzi anytime soon."

"Seems to me that's a good thing," Kendra commented, her shoulders relaxing slightly. "I know how uncomfortable it is to be followed around because of who your family is instead of who you really are."

Amusement lit his eyes. "I have a feeling you would have people following you around even if your dad wasn't an actor."

She gave him a tentative smile. "So what are you doing here in the middle of winter?"

"I actually just finished up a case and needed some time away. I saw the smoke coming from the chimney but didn't see a car outside. I thought I'd stop by and make sure everything was okay."

"Everything's fine." Kendra nodded. She glanced around the room and noticed the clothes strewn across the floor and her suitcase lying open, the contents spilling out of it. A prickle of irritation started to form that no one had cleaned up the mess. Then she realized that she was the only person here. Apparently, being alone meant she had to pick up after herself. Color rose to her cheeks as she bent down and gathered the wet clothes. "My car got stuck in the snow."

"Really?" Surprise sounded in his voice. "I just got in a few minutes ago, and I didn't notice any cars on the side of the road."

"I tried coming in the back way. It didn't work out so well." She moved to the kitchen table and laid her wet clothes over the back of a chair.

"Were you planning on staying up here long?"

She turned back to face him. "Two or three weeks."

Charlie seemed to consider her answer for a moment, his expression serious. Then he motioned outside. "I was just going to head down to the store. Do you need anything? It might be a few days before we can get back down the mountain for supplies."

Kendra immediately glanced down at her feet and then looked back up at Charlie. Her grandfather obviously trusted this man, and he seemed honest enough. Deciding that she didn't have much choice but to trust him, she nodded. "Actually, I would love a ride to the store. I came up here on the spur of the moment, and I definitely forgot a few things."

Charlie's gaze swept down to see her open-toed sandals and her pink nail polish. His serious expression melted away, and humor lit his eyes. "Like boots?"

"Yeah." Kendra managed a laugh. "I'm sure Mrs. Burgess will harass me about this for the next five years."

"Mrs. Burgess?"

"The woman who runs the general store," Kendra explained. "If you want to know anything about anybody here in Pinewood, ask Mrs. Burgess. That woman has a memory like an elephant."

Charlie grinned. "Sounds like she's quite a character."

"Oh yeah." Kendra slipped her coat on, pleased that it was nearly dry. Then she glanced out the front window, suddenly realizing how long she must have been sleeping. Several more inches had fallen since she'd tracked her way into the cabin. She glanced over at Charlie, her voice wary when she asked, "Are you sure your car can drive in this?"

"It has four-wheel drive," Charlie told her. "We shouldn't have any trouble if we leave now, but I'm not sure how bad these roads will be by tonight."

Kendra retrieved her purse from the couch. "In that case, let's go."

Charlie reached for the door. "Do you have your key?"

Kendra nodded. She started to follow him outside, but then Charlie turned to face her. He seemed to debate for a moment and then motioned down toward her sandals. "Your feet are going to be frozen if you try to walk through the snow. Do you want me to carry you?"

Kendra's eyebrows winged up. "You aren't serious."

"Or I can give you a piggy-back ride."

"Now I feel like I'm back in third grade."

Humor filled his voice. "You used to wear sandals during snow storms when you were in third grade?"

"We didn't get a lot of snow storms in Southern California," Kendra said dryly.

"Come on," Charlie said, squatting down in front of her so he could lift her onto his back. "I promise not to drop you."

"This is silly," Kendra shook her head even as a giggle escaped her.

"No sillier than walking through a foot of snow wearing sandals." Charlie reached for her hand, his fingers engulfing hers as he pulled her closer.

Kendra considered how cold her feet had been after walking in the snow the last time and let logic win out. "Oh, all right." She reached her arms around his neck and let Charlie support her weight as he stood up and grabbed her legs to hold her in place on his back.

She caught the subtle scent of his cologne and felt his damp hair brush against her cheek. Her heart knocked against her ribs, and a tremor shot through her. Then she looked down at the slippery path Charlie had to take to reach his car, and the unexpected spurt of attraction took a backseat to practicality. "Be careful on the stairs."

"I'll be careful," Charlie promised as he boosted her up a little higher on his back. "You just hold on."

Snow blew into her face, flakes catching on her lashes and in her hair. Kendra held on tight as Charlie carried her effortlessly to the rugged SUV he'd parked across the street. As soon as he reached the vehicle, he shifted so she could stand on the running board then pulled the door open and helped her inside.

A moment later, Charlie climbed in on the driver's side, started the car, and cranked the heat. "What else do you need from the store besides shoes and socks?"

"The basics, I guess. Like I said, this trip was pretty spur-of-the-moment."

"With your career, I'm surprised you can do anything spur-of-the-moment."

"It isn't easy," Kendra muttered.

Chapter 8

Charlie was feeling more than a little pleased with himself about his good fortune. Apparently, Elias had been right about using his family background as a starting point to get to know Kendra, although he had been somewhat humbled to find that, while he was something of a local celebrity in Washington DC, the rest of the country apparently didn't know his name.

He'd felt like a name-dropper when he'd tried to find some common ground with her. He imagined that Lisa would have been quite indignant to find someone who didn't know who he was, even if that someone was a famous singer. The familiar pang settled deep in his gut as he tried to focus on the present.

Undoubtedly, even a casual acquaintance with Kendra would make his job significantly easier. Charlie also didn't discount the fact that the roads up the mountain were likely to be closed by tonight, if not sooner.

The fact that Kendra was planning on staying here for a few weeks was an added bonus. He knew that the Los Angeles Police Department was already chasing down some leads to try to determine who had set the explosive backstage at her concert. He wasn't terribly optimistic that the culprit would be ferreted out in the next few weeks, but he could hope that Kendra would agree to protection before she decided to leave Pinewood.

A few weeks would certainly give the LAPD time to figure out how to proceed with the case before Kendra decided it was time to get back to her life in the fast lane. If he was right, she would be ready to leave the quiet, isolated cabin long before the snow melted.

Kendra had been quiet on the drive down, except for making a request that they stop by her car so she could get the rest of her things.

Charlie had made the instant decision to dispense with that task first. He figured it wouldn't hurt to have the extra hour of snowfall to cover up his tracks.

Taking pity on her lack of appropriate footwear, Charlie had insisted on getting her things out of her car for her. Her belongings had been thrown haphazardly into the trunk, and he could only guess that she had repacked some of her things before hiking the rest of the way to her cabin.

He spotted her cell phone nestled under a pair of jeans and wondered if she realized it was missing. He took the time to make sure the phone was off and then went with impulse and left it behind. He doubted anyone could track the GPS signal with the phone turned off, but he decided not to give Kendra the chance to turn it on and give away her location. After loading all her things into his SUV and starting down the road again, Charlie was relieved that she hadn't seemed to notice its loss. Her focus, instead, had been on some of the more unexpected items he had gathered for her.

Charlie fought back a smile as he thought of the beat-up stuffed dog that had spilled out of a canvas bag, along with a few paperback novels. Color had flushed into her cheeks when he'd handed her the bag and she'd noticed his grin. He hadn't expected that she would get embarrassed about something so trivial, and he found himself realigning his image of her.

He supposed he'd never bothered to wonder what Kendra was really like, previously content to believe that her public image was accurate. After living his own life in close proximity to the spotlight's glare, he knew that public images were rarely much more than a two-dimensional snapshot of a three-dimensional person. He should have known better.

He certainly hadn't ever read anything about her being an avid reader, yet she'd packed a tote weighed down with an eclectic variety of books. Besides a couple of popular bestsellers, he'd also noticed a copy of *Great Expectations*, a few Jane Austen novels, and a ragged copy of Booker T. Washington's autobiography. Added all up, he figured her well-read and guessed that she was a bit of a romantic.

Kendra clutched the tote in her hand as the SUV bounced over the road, and he pulled into the parking lot of the general store. Charlie climbed out and circled to open her door. As soon as she stood up on the running board, he reached out and put both hands on her waist.

Her hands came up and instinctively gripped his shoulders for balance as he lifted her up and over the few feet of snow between the edge of the parking lot and the wide covered porch that spanned the front of the store.

Charlie's hands lingered at her waist for a moment, and he was unexpectedly satisfied when he noticed a blush rise in her cheeks. Attraction, strong and clear, rushed through him. He acknowledged it, felt his pulse quicken, and then reminded himself that he had no business feeling anything for Kendra Blake. He'd already learned the hard way not to trust anyone who wanted to live their life in the limelight, especially a beautiful woman. He gave her what he hoped was a casual smile and then released her and pulled the store door open.

The moment they stepped inside, Kendra called out a greeting to the woman sitting in a chair beside the cash register.

Mrs. Burgess looked up, her green eyes sharp, her wrinkled face splitting into a grin as she identified her visitor. She set down the paperback she had been holding and pushed out of her chair.

"Kendra Blake! How are you?" Mrs. Burgess looked past Kendra to see Charlie beside her. "What are you doing in town? And who is this handsome man you brought to meet me?"

"This is Charlie Whitmore." Kendra glanced at Charlie and added, "Charlie, this is Eleanor Burgess."

"Good to meet you, Charlie." Mrs. Burgess shook his hand briskly and then turned back to look at Kendra. "I didn't know you were dating someone." Her eyes narrowed. "How come I didn't know you were dating someone?"

Charlie laughed, and for the first time since he had knocked on Kendra's door, he felt himself relax. To his surprise, the tension he noticed in Kendra seemed to ease as well.

Kendra gave a little shake of her head and said, "We aren't dating."

"You aren't?"

"Nope, afraid not." Charlie shook his head.

"Well, why aren't you?" Mrs. Burgess demanded. "Two single, good-looking kids like yourselves. You need to stop worrying so much about your careers and start paying more attention to the important things in life."

Charlie glanced over at Kendra. With her hair pulled back in a ponytail and her face free of makeup, she looked like she was still a teenager. He noticed her fighting back a smile, and she winked at him before turning her attention back to Mrs. Burgess. Her voice was like an innocent schoolgirl's when she asked, "You mean, there's more to life than making money?"

"Money!" Mrs. Burgess thumped her hand on the counter for emphasis and narrowed her eyes again. "Why, money is the root of all evil. Says so in the Bible too."

"I think I read something about that." Kendra gave her a casual shrug and a grin. Then she moved forward and kissed her on the cheek. "I've missed you."

"You're a bad girl, Kendra Blake."

"You must have me confused with my sister."

Mrs. Burgess hooted with laughter. "That sister of yours always says the same thing when I scold her for anything." Her laughter faded when she noticed Kendra's shoes, or lack thereof, for the first time. "Where are your shoes, girl?"

"Let's see." Kendra seemed to consider for a minute, and when she spoke, there was both warmth and humor in her voice. "I think they're in the trunk of my Mercedes, but I might have left them at my house in Malibu or maybe at Daddy's house in Palm Springs." She paused for a second. "Or they could be in my place in Phoenix."

Mrs. Burgess stood up and wagged a finger at her. "Don't you play little rich girl with me, young lady. There's no excuse for coming up into this weather unprepared."

Kendra bit back on a smile. "Yes, ma'am."

Charlie watched the banter between the two women, a little surprised to see Kendra with her guard down. She didn't look like the disinterested rich kid who had grown up in the spotlight, nor did she look like the pop star whose photograph was constantly on the covers of magazines. Instead, she looked like a normal girl chatting with the store owner as though they were family.

Apparently determined to solve Kendra's wardrobe problem, Mrs. Burgess took her hand and started to pull her toward a small clothing section at the back of the store. "Let's see what we can find for you to wear."

Charlie called after them. "I'll take care of my grocery shopping while you deal with the shoe problem."

He couldn't help but grin as Mrs. Burgess lowered her voice fractionally and told Kendra, "Nothing like trying on shoes to send the men running."

Charlie shook his head as he grabbed one of the little carts next to the door and started browsing. If Kendra planned to stay for a few weeks, he had to assume that Elias would want him to stay for the duration. He wasn't crazy about misleading her about why he was here, but for now, those were his orders. As soon as he got back to his cabin, he would put the call into Elias and give him an update.

Charlie glanced out the store window and considered for a minute. Realizing that coming back into town for supplies would be difficult until after the storm had passed and the roads were cleared, he tried to decide what supplies he might need.

He'd been so eager to see if Kendra was really at her family's cabin that he hadn't done an inventory when he'd first arrived. Instead, he'd dropped his bag in one of the bedrooms and had headed straight to her place.

Better be prepared, he told himself. He started in the household section, picking up some matches, a lantern, a flashlight, and a bag of charcoal. He hoped he didn't have to cook outside, but he suspected a summer town like Pinewood was probably low on the priority list when it came to winter power outages.

After filling up one cart with emergency supplies, Charlie moved to the grocery side of the store and began making his selections. He heard Kendra's laughter ring out. Maybe, if he could convince her to have dinner with him, he would have an excuse to keep an eye on her. And just maybe, he could find out why she was refusing protection.

* * *

Kendra put the hood up on her newly purchased parka and stepped out of Charlie's SUV, her purse in one gloved hand and her tote in the other. The shopping spree had depleted most of the cash she had on her, especially since she had followed Charlie's example and bought enough supplies to last her for at least a week or two. If she decided to stay longer, she would have to talk to Mrs. Burgess about setting up an account with her rather than risk using a credit card.

Charlie moved to the back of the vehicle, opened the rear door, and hefted a box of supplies. "If you'll unlock the door, I'll get this stuff inside for you."

"You don't have to do that."

"It's not a problem." Charlie shrugged. "That way you won't have to keep tracking snow through the house."

"That's true." Kendra offered him a smile. Then she started up the steps and retrieved her key to unlock the door. To her surprise, when she started to slide the key into the lock, the doorknob shifted. Testing it, she turned it to find that it was already unlocked.

She looked at it a moment, puzzled. Had she forgotten to lock the door? She tried to bank down the uneasy feeling that instantly surfaced. Before she could turn to look for any signs of an intruder, Charlie's hand came down on her shoulder.

His eyes were intense, as though he, too, were sharing her thoughts, her questions. His voice was low, barely louder than a whisper when he said simply, "Wait."

Kendra nodded obediently. Then she watched him as he moved back to the front of the porch and studied the yard. She looked out, wondering what he was looking for. She could see their tire tracks on the road and the faintest outline of the footprints Charlie had left when he had walked across the street to her cabin earlier.

Was it her imagination, or were there also smaller tracks on the road? Perhaps from a sled or a snowmobile?

Charlie turned back to her. "Have you seen anyone but me since you got here?"

She shook her head. The directness in his eyes had her fumbling, and the truth, at least part of it, tumbled out of her mouth. "No one but my grandparents knows where I am."

"Is it okay if I check out your place before you go inside?" Charlie asked softly. "It may sound silly, but it would make me feel a lot better if I know you're safe."

Kendra's head bobbed up and down, and she swallowed hard. If Charlie was worried too, maybe her concerns weren't just from her imagination running away with her.

Charlie handed her his car keys. "Why don't you go wait in the car. I'll be right out."

Again, Kendra nodded. She started back down the stairs, slipping on the second step and having to carefully regain her balance. Then she hurried to Charlie's SUV and climbed back inside. Her tote fell onto the floor, and she absentmindedly pulled her favorite stuffed animal free and clung to it.

When she looked up at her front door, she saw Charlie glance back at her, making sure she was safely inside the vehicle. Then he slowly pushed the door open and disappeared inside.

Chapter 9

Charlie entered Kendra's cabin and quietly closed the door behind him. He set down the box of supplies he'd been carrying just inside the door and reached for the gun he kept holstered at the small of his back. His eyes swept the room, and he listened for any sound that was out of place.

The fire still flickered in the fireplace, though it had diminished to a dull glow, no longer providing any warmth in the room. Kendra's belongings were still strewn across the room, but nothing appeared to have been moved since they left.

It's probably nothing, Charlie assured himself, even though he'd felt the odd chill run through him when he'd realized her door was unlocked. He remembered asking her if she had her key, but since Kendra had been the last one out of the cabin, he couldn't be sure if she had thought to lock the door or not. But he also didn't remember seeing those faint snowmobile tracks on the road when they'd left earlier.

Then again, now that he thought of it, he had been more concerned about getting Kendra to his truck without her freezing her toes off than he had been about making sure everything was secured properly. That pretty face of hers was proving to be a distraction, and he didn't have time for that right now.

He was probably overreacting by making her wait for him outside. Regardless, though, it wouldn't hurt to err on the side of safety. He would just check out the cabin to make sure everything was as it was supposed to be, and then he could laugh off this little panic attack and tell Kendra that his protective side was showing because she was staying here alone.

He slipped his boots off, partially to mask the sound of his steps and partially to keep from tracking moisture across the floor. He checked out the main level first: the living room and kitchen, the three bedrooms, two bathrooms, the mudroom, and various closets. When he was satisfied that the back door was locked tightly and that there wasn't any sign of anyone having been inside the mudroom recently, he turned back down the hall and headed up the stairs.

The third stair from the top creaked loudly under his weight. He froze for a moment, listening once again as he lifted his weapon a little higher. The loft overlooked the living room below, and three doors opened off of it. Cautiously, Charlie entered the first room to find a bedroom and a private bathroom. His methodical search revealed that the other two rooms were identical to the first, and all of them were empty.

A sigh escaped him, and he holstered his weapon. He took a moment to steady himself before heading back to the door, slipping his boots back on and motioning to Kendra that it was all clear.

Kendra climbed out of the car and moved toward him, her face pale. He'd scared her, Charlie realized. He wasn't sure if that was a good thing right now or not. He wanted her to understand the dangers she was facing—otherwise, how could she defend against them?—but he also needed her to trust him.

He moved toward her and pasted on an apologetic smile. "I'm sorry about that. I thought I heard something inside."

"Is everything okay?"

"Yeah, everything's fine." Charlie reached for her hand, pulling her gently up the steps and toward the front door. "Why don't you go inside and warm up by the fire. I'll get everything else from the car."

"Are you sure you don't need any help?"

Charlie shook his head and nudged her inside before going to unload. He made several trips, each time depositing his load near the door. When all of her belongings were finally unloaded, he took off his boots and helped her carry her groceries into the kitchen and set them on the counter.

"Thanks so much for your help," Kendra said, and Charlie was relieved to see that most of her color was back. "I don't know how I would have managed to get supplies if you hadn't been here."

"I'm glad I could help," Charlie told her. "I'm going to go get my stuff put away, and then I thought I'd make some dinner. Any chance you want to join me?"

Kendra looked at him blankly. "Join you?"

"Yeah." Charlie nodded, amused by her expression. If he didn't know better, he would have thought that she wasn't used to having men ask her out. Not that he was asking her on a date, exactly. "Come have dinner with me."

"Oh, okay," Kendra said, still looking somewhat stunned.

"Great." Charlie stepped toward the front door. "Why don't you come over around five? That way, it will still be light out when you walk over."

Kendra simply nodded. Then Charlie pulled on his boots and walked out the door.

* * *

A bomb had gone off at her concert, she was hiding away from the world in a snowbound cabin, and all she could think about was her upcoming date. At least, she thought it was a date.

Kendra shoved cans into the kitchen pantry, her conversation with Charlie replaying over and over in her mind. She cringed as she thought of how she had acted. She'd felt like a tongue-tied schoolgirl who had just been asked out on her first date. In a way, the description wasn't all that far from the truth. Though she hadn't been a schoolgirl for some time, she couldn't remember the last time she had been out on a date.

How long had it been? Two years? Three? She shook her head as she tried to remember when she had broken up with Steve DeFoe, her boyfriend of almost two months. The memory of those two months nearly caused her to reconsider going to Charlie's for dinner.

Steve had been so charming, so attentive when they'd first started dating. Then he'd turned possessive. When he had first started complaining about her bodyguards and their lack of privacy, Kendra had been sympathetic. Then the complaints had escalated into arguments, both with her and with those tasked with protecting her.

When he'd shown up at her house in the middle of the night, demanding that she let him in, Kendra had realized Steve wasn't who she thought he was. The argument that ensued had turned nasty, and ultimately, Kendra had ended the relationship. Steve's temper had exploded then, and she didn't even want to think about what might have happened had her bodyguards not been nearby.

At first, she'd felt bad about the fistfight that had ensued between Steve and Alan Parsons, but then Steve had started giving interviews and spinning lies. After seeing the incident splashed in the tabloids and dealing with the constant media pressure in the weeks following the breakup, Kendra had resigned herself to the fact that dating simply wasn't worth the effort.

As she considered what it would be like to date like a normal person, without all the bodyguards and security, without any of the paparazzi or hovering fans, Kendra found herself smiling. Then another thought struck her, and her excitement waned.

Perhaps this wasn't really a date. Maybe Charlie was just being friendly. Kendra moved into the living room and stared out the window at the cabin across the street. Her lips slowly curved up into the beginnings of a smile. Whether dinner tonight was a date or simply a friendly gesture, it wouldn't hurt for her to get to know Charlie a little better.

* * *

"You already saw her?" Elias Washington's voice came over the phone.

"Yeah." Charlie nodded to the empty room. "I invited her over for dinner tonight. I thought maybe I could find out why she's refusing protection."

"I don't have to explain to you that gaining Kendra's trust will go a long way in helping our investigation."

"I kind of figured," Charlie said. "By the way, the weather reports say that this storm is supposed to keep dumping snow for another day or two. Do you have any idea how long it normally takes to get the roads plowed up here?"

"Pinewood is a summer town. They don't plow the roads up there," Elias told him.

"Then I guess it's a good thing I picked up enough supplies in town to last a couple of weeks. If we really get another foot of snow tonight, even my four-wheel drive isn't likely to make it down the mountain anytime soon."

"Do what you can to stay close to her. I want nightly updates."

"Anything else you want me to work on while I'm up here? I have a feeling I'm going to have a lot of down time."

"I've already e-mailed you the case file from the bombing at Kendra's concert," Elias told him. "Also, Rick Michaels, in the LA office, was hoping for some more help with investigating the latest serial killing. Sometimes it helps to have a fresh set of eyes read over the case files."

"I doubt I can do much from up here, but I can at least take a look."

"Good," Elias said. "And, Charlie?"

"Yeah?"

"Be careful."

"I will. I'll talk to you tomorrow." Charlie hung up the phone and walked to the window. Staring out at the snow, he considered what he had to do. His first priority was to keep Kendra safe, and he supposed that meant getting to know her. He didn't really like the idea of misleading her about why he was here, but this certainly wouldn't be the first time he'd had to stretch the truth. Over the past two years with the Bureau, he had learned how to skim over details, to twist the facts so he could lead people to think what he wanted them to.

All he had to do was not volunteer too much information. He could play the role of the vacationing lawyer, the guy who needed to get away and hide from the world for a few days. And just maybe he would be lucky enough to gain Kendra's trust and figure out why she was running from all the people who wanted to help her.

Chapter 10

The streets were busy outside Kendra Blake's condominium as the Phoenix rush hour peaked. He watched the constant flow of people into and out of Kendra's complex and studied each vehicle that passed into the gated community. Of all of the places she could hide, he thought this would be her first choice. He didn't know what to make of the fact that she hadn't arrived yet.

She had said once that she felt safe here. He couldn't understand why, except that the general population didn't know that she owned the upstairs unit. She also seemed to like being close to her grandparents' place, the ancient little house located several miles away.

He had considered that she might hide there, too, but he'd checked it out earlier in the day and hadn't seen any sign of her. That had been after he'd broken into her condo to make sure it was really empty. Bypassing the front gate had been pathetically easy. There wasn't a security guard, and the lock on Kendra's front door had been easy enough to pick.

Now all he could do was wait and stay out of sight. It was only a matter of time before he would find her. Finally, the day he'd been waiting for was nearly here.

* * *

Kendra took a deep breath and then raised a hand to knock on the door. There wasn't any reason to be nervous, especially now that she understood why Charlie had invited her to dinner. The explanation was simple, really. She was the only person he could talk to within a ten-mile radius.

She clasped her hands together and took a little step back when the door swung open. Her mouth instantly went dry. His long-sleeved T-shirt stretched over his broad shoulders, and his quick grin sent butterflies to battle in her stomach. He might have asked her over for a friendly dinner, but that didn't negate the fact that Charlie Whitmore was one handsome man.

"Hi, there." Charlie stepped back, motioning inside. "Come on in."

"Thanks." Kendra stepped over the threshold and took a look around as she waited for her stomach to settle.

The cabin was just as she remembered it: a simple A-frame structure, the entire front wall made up of tall windows. Two sofas were angled in the open living area so that anyone sitting on them could enjoy both the view out the front windows and the warmth from the wood stove. The curtains were open, revealing the steadily falling snow. The smell of burning wood lingered in the air, combining with the faint scent of Charlie's aftershave and the mouthwatering aromas coming from the kitchen.

"Here, let me take your coat."

"Thanks." Kendra slipped her coat off and then leaned down to take off her boots as well. After she set them by the door, she turned and asked, "Do you need help with anything?"

"I think everything is set. The chicken just needs to cook for a few more minutes." Charlie draped her coat over the side of a chair to dry and looked over at her, a sudden look of concern crossing his face. "You aren't a vegetarian, are you?"

A giggle escaped her. "No, I'm not a vegetarian."

"Good." Clearly relieved, he started toward the kitchen, glancing back as though making sure she was following him. "Can I get you something to drink?"

"Just some water would be great. Thanks." She slid onto a stool by the kitchen counter as Charlie walked behind it and retrieved a glass from a cabinet. After he filled it with ice and water, he set it in front of her. "You know, you really didn't have to go to all of this trouble."

"It wasn't any trouble." Charlie lifted the lid off the pan on the stove and stirred. "Every time I feel like I need to get away from civilization, I forget one very important thing."

"What's that?"

"I like people."

Kendra grinned. "I know what you mean."

Charlie replaced the lid on the pan and looked up at her, his blue eyes direct. "So you said you're planning on staying up here for a couple of weeks?"

"Maybe longer." Kendra shrugged. She imagined that between the incident at her concert and her sudden disappearance, her name was already being splashed all over the news. Charlie didn't seem to know anything about her reasons for being here, so she kept her answer neutral. "I was actually thinking about hiding out here for a while so I can work on some songs for my next album. It seems like I never have any time to write anymore."

"Do you like to write your own songs?"

Kendra's smile was instant, a dimple flashing in her cheek. "I love it. It's my favorite part of what I do."

Charlie smiled in response. "You must be good at it. I can hardly turn on the radio anymore without hearing you sing to me."

"Really?" Kendra studied the man across from her, amused by his choice of words. "Do you like it when I sing to you?"

Charlie laughed. "I guess I do."

Before Kendra could respond, a phone rang. Charlie pulled his cell phone out of his pocket and glanced at the caller ID. He looked at Kendra apologetically. "Excuse me for a minute."

Kendra nodded, her eyes dropping to stare at her water glass.

"Hey, Amy." Charlie's greeting was warm, and Kendra found herself envious of the woman on the other end. What would it be like to have a man like Charlie greet her with that same friendly, familiar tone on a regular basis?

He was quiet for a minute and then spoke into the phone once more. "Don't worry. I'll make sure I'm there, but I can't really talk right now. Can I call you back later?" He hesitated for a moment and then nodded. "Okay. Bye."

Charlie put his phone back in his pocket before looking back at Kendra. "Sorry about that."

"That's okay," Kendra said. Then she surprised herself by asking, "Was that your girlfriend checking up on you?"

"No, I don't have a girlfriend." A look of vulnerability flashed in his eyes but quickly vanished. He busied himself at the stove for a minute, and then his eyes met hers once more. "That was actually my sister. She's trying to plan a big anniversary party for my parents next year."

"Really?" Kendra felt her cheeks heating, and she told herself she didn't have any reason to be embarrassed. After all, it was a normal curiosity for her to wonder if he was involved with someone. "Do you have any other siblings? You mentioned a brother earlier."

"No, just an older brother and younger sister." Charlie stirred the chicken again and then turned off the stove. "What about you? Do you have brothers and sisters?"

"Just my younger sister." Kendra's lips curved up. "You might have heard of her. Sienna Blake."

"Right, the actress." Charlie nodded. "You have quite a talented family."

"Sounds like I could say the same thing about you."

Charlie simply shrugged and then picked up a hot pad. He carried the food to the table and looked up at her. "Dinner is served."

"It smells wonderful," Kendra said when he lifted the lid, not quite able to hide the surprise in her voice. "You know, I didn't peg you for a guy who likes to cook."

"It's my sister-in-law's doing," Charlie admitted. "I spent a few weeks living with them in Florida to help out when she was pregnant with her second kid. She was determined that at least one Whitmore learn their way around the kitchen—besides my mom, that is."

"Your brother and sister don't cook?"

"Not unless you count burnt toast."

Kendra laughed as she took her seat. Charlie retrieved a tossed salad from the refrigerator and sat beside her.

"Do you mind if I offer a blessing on the food?"

Surprise showed on her face, but she shook her head. She folded her arms, bowed her head, and listened to Charlie's simple prayer. When he was done, she looked up at him, astonished.

"You're Mormon?"

"Yeah," Charlie said, clearly surprised by her question. "How did you know that?"

"The way you blessed the food." Kendra shook her head as this new development played through her mind. "I'm Mormon too."

"Seriously?" Charlie asked with the same tone of bewilderment that she had used moments before. "I didn't know that."

Kendra's shoulder's lifted. "I think that may be the only area of my life the press hasn't exploited."

"Have you always been a member?"

"More or less. My grandparents used to take me and my sister to church when we visited them, which was a lot when we were growing up," Kendra told him. "Then when I got older, I realized I didn't really like my parents' lifestyle, and I finally got their permission to get baptized."

"How old were you?"

"Fifteen."

"You must face a lot of challenges being LDS in the music world," Charlie commented as he passed a serving spoon to Kendra.

When Kendra simply shrugged, he changed the subject. "I was kind of surprised when your grandfather called to tell me that you were coming up here. I thought you were on another one of your concert tours."

Kendra's hand briefly tightened on the spoon. She scooped some of the chicken and rice mixture onto her plate before lifting her eyes to meet his. "Actually, I just finished my tour and needed a break." She motioned toward the window. "Of course, I may end up with a longer break than I had planned for."

"I know what you mean." Charlie nodded. "I didn't expect to find this much snow here in Arizona."

"You sure came a long way for a few weeks off," Kendra said. "Didn't you say that you live in DC?"

"Not anymore. I live in Phoenix now."

"Really?"

Charlie nodded. He hesitated, as though trying to decide how much to tell her. "I love my family, but I needed to get out of their shadows for a while."

Kendra's eyes lifted to meet his. Slowly, a smile bloomed on her face. "I guess we have more in common than I thought."

Chapter 11

Charlie looked over the police report from the bombing at Kendra's concert and shook his head. He had hoped to find some obvious clues as to who had set off the explosive, but clues were apparently scarce in this case. The backstage security had been tight, surprisingly so. The band members, caterers, and concert staff had all worked Kendra's concerts before. None of the fans with backstage passes had been given access to the area near the stage, which meant they could eliminate that group of people.

The interview with Kendra's personal security guard had revealed little, except that he had been hit from behind during one of Kendra's songs. Other than that, no one had seen or heard anything out of the ordinary.

A little frustrated that the police hadn't uncovered more information, he set Kendra's file aside and began reading through the case files of the Malibu Stalker. His gut churned as his mind absorbed the gruesome details. Charlie had chosen this career because he'd wanted to make a difference, but trying to get into the mind of a serial killer was one part of the job he wished he could avoid.

As Elias had said, each victim fit the same physical description. And each woman had been killed with a single bullet through the heart.

The crime scenes had also been eerily similar. Each woman had been wearing a blue dress when she was killed, and each body had been found next to a backyard swimming pool, a red rose lying on the ground beside her.

He grabbed a notepad out of his laptop case and began jotting down the basic information about each victim. The first had only been twenty-one years old when she was killed three years earlier. The oldest and most recent victim, supermodel Joslyn Korden, had been twenty-four.

All six women had been staying in Malibu at the times of their deaths, and no fingerprints had been found at any of the crime scenes. Nor had there been any sign of forced entry. He thought about this for a moment, considering the implications. Had all of these women known their killer, or had they all been careless in letting a stranger get too close to them?

Charlie glanced through the victims' photos, each face reinforcing what he'd already learned. They were all young, blonde, and beautiful. He thought of Kendra's conversation with Mrs. Burgess and her mention of her house in Malibu. His teeth clenched together as he realized that Kendra also fit the profile of the women being murdered. Every one of these women looked a lot like her.

He took a deep breath and blew it out as he tried to focus once more on the words in front of him. The psychological profile described the Malibu Stalker as intelligent, familiar with security systems, possibly with a former police or military background. His victims were chosen for their physical appearance, presumably because they reminded him of someone he was obsessed with. He went to great lengths to set the scene, each crime scene nearly identical to the others. His obsessive tendencies wouldn't be readily apparent, and it was possible that the killer was functional, even appearing normal, in everyday activities.

Beyond that, most of the information described common demographics of known serial killers: white male, lower to middle class, probably between twenty-five and thirty-five years old. Following that description was the classic disclaimer stating that the demographics were based on past cases and that a certain amount of deviation was possible. In other words, it could be just about anyone.

Charlie shut down his computer and crossed to the front windows. He stared out into the darkness, the only visible light coming from the cabin across the street. The snow had stopped for the moment, but according to the latest weather reports, another storm was expected to hit them within the next few hours.

His concerns heightened after reading the case files, Charlie retrieved his weapon from the nightstand where he had left it and pulled on his jacket. He stepped outside, listening to the stillness. His breath plumed out in front of him, and he could taste the snow in the air. According to his watch it was only ten o'clock, but in the quiet of the mountains, it felt much later.

He stared at Kendra's place, wondering if the light in the front window meant she was still up or if she had left it on to give her a sense of security.

He hated the fact that she would probably be safer if it appeared that no one was home. *It could be worse,* he supposed. Right now, apart from the single light, only the smoke coming from the chimney and the variety of tracks in front of the cabin indicated that anyone was there. If her car had been parked out front, there would be no question as to her presence.

She hadn't seemed terribly concerned about her safety over dinner, causing Charlie to believe that she trusted her grandfather's assurances that no one would be able to find her here. He heard the first notes of a song ringing out in the quiet. He didn't recognize the tune, but he found himself approving of the catchy melody. Charlie leaned on the railing and thought back to his evening with Kendra.

He still couldn't quite believe that she was Mormon, and he wondered at the odds of her being assigned someone to protect her who shared her religious beliefs. Not that she knew he was here to protect her, of course. Other than her religious beliefs, she really hadn't revealed much about herself other than basic information he could have uncovered simply by typing her name into Google.

Now, he found himself wondering what made her tick. Was she playing the guitar late at night because it helped her relax, or did she think of it as work? Were the songs she wrote born from her own experiences or from her dreams? And why had she turned to her grandfather for help instead of her own parents? He knew they didn't share the same religious beliefs, but was she close to them?

As much as Charlie had needed to step outside of his father's shadow for a while, he knew that if he ever ran into a problem he couldn't handle alone, his parents would be the first people he would turn to for help. Even though he preferred to shelter his parents, especially his mother, from the dangers of his job, they had been the ones he'd relied on for support after his former partner had gotten shot.

Charlie closed his eyes as he thought of the way Brian had pushed him aside, had essentially taken the bullet that had been meant for him. He hated knowing that Brian was still cooped up in a rehab center trying to regain use of his legs, knowing that he might not ever succeed.

With a sigh, Charlie moved back inside and tried to realign his thoughts. He needed to leave the past where it belonged and concentrate on what was important in his future, like finding out exactly who Kendra Blake really was so he could make sure she stayed safe.

* * *

She had disappeared, both physically and electronically.

Kendra's phone was turned off, and he hadn't been able to detect any activity on her computer. He typed in a search for recent internet articles on Kendra, only to find that the incident at her concert was still dominating cyberspace.

His plan had worked, perhaps a little too well. Kendra had understood his message. She understood now that she wasn't safe in front of all those people. But why hadn't she gone somewhere that he could find her? He knew her hiding places. He knew where she would feel safe.

His jaw clenched as he considered what could have caused her to disappear so completely. Someone was helping her. She had turned to someone else, someone besides him.

He pushed away from his computer desk and stared up at the wall in front of him. Photographs of Kendra covered every inch of space on the wall, some clipped from magazines and others taken from his own camera. He focused on a picture of her smiling down at him, humor in her eyes.

She was laughing at him. She thought she could hide.

Fury bubbled up inside him, and he slammed his open hand against the wall. She would be his. She didn't have a choice.

This was her destiny. And his.

* * *

Kendra stared out at the blanket of white that seemed to go on forever. Tree branches hung low under the weight of the snow, their green only visible in patches. Snow was no longer falling, but clouds still loomed overhead.

She looked down at her watch, amazed, and a little embarrassed, that she had slept through the entire morning. Of course, her body was still on concert schedule, late to bed, late to rise. She stretched her hands over her head, not surprised by the stiffness in her back and her shoulders. She could hardly expect to spend hours hunched over her guitar without her body protesting a little.

She was still amazed by the way the music had flowed the night before, playing in her head in a way it hadn't in a long time. She knew her emotions fed into that. Her need to put the past few days into perspective had given her creative energy a boost.

She had expected the anxiety to surface first, to demand an outlet, but surprisingly, it was her sense of freedom that had dominated her thoughts when she'd sat down with her guitar the night before. She couldn't ever remember feeling so in control of her own life, so *liberated.*

The day before had started out so badly, and yet, somehow, everything had taken a turn for the better. Charlie had played a part in it, treating her like a person who had the right to make her own choices, even expecting her to exercise that right. She wondered if he had any idea what that meant to her.

She thought back to the way he had insisted on walking her home the night before. Why was it that she hadn't resented the gesture from him? Had it been someone on her security team, she would have felt stifled, trapped. But Charlie had walked her home, the paragon of a perfect gentleman as he'd made sure she was safely inside before leaving her alone.

Perhaps that was it. The fact that he had left her alone, that he had trusted that she would be okay without hovering over her the way all of the other men in her life had. Of course, the only men who had truly been in her life were her father and the various security men he had assigned to her. The few people she had dated during high school and those first couple of years after graduation had never lasted beyond a week or two. The only exception had been Steve, and that certainly hadn't turned out well. She supposed Steve had been right about one thing. Most guys didn't have any interest in going out with someone who already had half a dozen men following her around, watching her every move.

No one is watching me now, Kendra reminded herself as she dressed and headed downstairs in search of some breakfast. She looked down at her guitar that was leaning against the loveseat and at the scattered sheet music she'd left there the night before. She was oddly pleased, both by the signs of a successful evening and by the fact that no one had come along to shuffle the clutter out of sight.

She rubbed her arms against the chill in the room, noticing for the first time that the fire had gone out in the fireplace and that the heater was less than adequate in this big cabin. Putting breakfast on hold for the moment, Kendra picked up some newspaper and twisted it before setting it on the grate. Realizing that the stack of newspaper was going to have to last her, she used only two sections before she lifted a log and put it in the fireplace.

She struck a match, holding it under the newspaper until the flame grew. The flames licked at the side of the log until the wood finally caught fire. When Kendra was satisfied that it wouldn't go out, she put the screen back into place. Looking down at the last two logs next to the fireplace, she was faced with the reality that she was going to have to get some firewood before the day was out, or she was going to freeze.

After tidying up her mess from the night before, she grabbed an apple from the kitchen and wondered if her grandparents kept a stack of wood anywhere outside. She took a bite of the apple and crossed to a hall closet in search of some of her grandfather's work gloves.

She smiled when she not only found a pair of gloves she could use but also a knit hat and scarf her grandmother had undoubtedly made. She put them all on, along with her winter coat. Then she slipped her boots on and headed out the back door. Icy wetness seeped through her jeans and into the top of her boots as she trudged through nearly two feet of snow.

She thought she remembered a woodpile off the back porch, but with the deep snow, she couldn't identify where it was. Holding tightly to the railing, she walked down the steps and began searching along the back of the cabin. Her grandparents must have put the wood somewhere near the door, right?

When she didn't find anything but snow along the back wall, she circled toward the front door. She made it all the way to the front porch before her foot struck something buried beneath the blanket of white.

"Ow," she muttered to herself.

Leaning down, she began pushing the snow aside. Her hands were nearly to the ground when they finally hit something solid. Sure enough, she had found the wood stack. Brushing more snow aside, she could only shake her head in frustration. The wood stack consisted of five pieces of wood. Five. That wouldn't even last her through tomorrow.

With a sigh, she picked up the first two pieces and hauled them up onto the front porch and into the cabin. She considered her limited options as she deposited them by the fireplace. She might be able to gather some stray branches outside for firewood, but with the depth of the snow, she would likely end up with frostbite before she found enough to make it worth the effort.

She could try to go without a fire in the fireplace, but she already knew from last night that the heater in the cabin wasn't quite able to ward off the chill. The cabin had been built as a summer vacation home, not a snowbound hideaway. Even the fireplace was more for aesthetics than warmth, unlike the wood-burning stove in Charlie's cabin, which could heat most of the cabin without the aid of an electric heater.

Maybe if she was lucky, Charlie would have some wood at his cabin he'd be willing to part with, at least until they could get back into town for more supplies. She went back outside to get the rest of the wood and heard someone calling her name. She turned around, instantly smiling when she saw Charlie heading toward her.

"Hey!" Charlie called out again. "Do you need some help?"

"Hi, Charlie." She waved vaguely at the pitiful stack of wood. "I was just bringing in some wood."

Charlie looked down at the remaining logs. "Looks like you're about done."

"Actually, I just started."

"I guess your family doesn't normally come up here during the winter." Charlie grimaced. He leaned over and handed a log to Kendra before picking up the last two logs and turning toward her front door. "The wood stack at the other cabin didn't have much to it either."

Kendra opened the door for Charlie, her hopes dashed that she could beg some wood off of him. She stomped her feet before she stepped inside to shake most of the snow off of her jeans. Charlie followed suit, brushing at the ski pants he was wearing before moving inside to set the wood down on the hearth.

"There are a couple of fallen trees down the road. I thought I might go chop one of them for firewood, but I was hoping you might have a sled or something I could load it up on. I'd rather not dig my truck out if I don't have to."

"Actually, I think there are a couple of sleds in the storage room." Kendra motioned down the hall.

Charlie followed her into the wide mudroom that housed the washer and dryer along one wall and an assortment of supplies and recreational equipment on the other side. Two sleds were leaning against the wall in the corner.

Kendra pointed to them. "Will these work?"

"Yeah, those will be great."

"Is there anything I can do to help?" Kendra asked.

"Help?" Charlie looked at her, bewildered.

"I don't think you'd want to trust me with an axe, but I can probably help you load the logs onto the sleds."

"I was planning on using a chain saw," Charlie said. "But yeah, if you want to help, that would be great."

She reached for her scarf and gloves. "I'd feel guilty if I let you do all of the work, especially since I'm hoping that you'll share some of the wood."

"Yeah." Charlie looked at her, his expression serious for a moment before he added, "I'm willing to share."

Chapter 12

"What do you mean, you know where she is but you won't tell me?" Sterling Blake demanded, his fingers gripping his phone tightly. "She's my daughter, and I have the right to protect her."

"She's a grown woman, Sterling," William countered. "It's time you respect that and let her make her own decisions."

"Dad, how can you say that? You, of all people, know how dangerous it is for her to be without a bodyguard, especially right now."

"I understand perfectly, but you need to let me handle this my way. If you send her some of your bodyguards, you might very well be leading the bomber right to her. And I never said she didn't have protection."

"What?" Confusion filled Sterling's voice.

"Look, I agree with you that she needs someone looking out for her right now. That's why I put her in protective custody."

"How in the world did you get her to agree to that?"

"I have my ways," William said cryptically. "Trust me, son. I won't let anything happen to your little girl."

* * *

Charlie handed Kendra another log and shook his head in amazement. He had expected her to act more like Lisa. On the surface, the two women had a lot in common. They were both beautiful, and they both came from money. He thought they'd both sought out the spotlight, but now he wasn't so sure about Kendra. He supposed it would be more accurate with her to say that she was used to the spotlight, and he was starting to think that she tolerated it more than she searched for it.

He knew it wasn't fair to put Kendra in the same category as his ex-fiancée, despite the similarities. Lisa had been cold and calculating in her pursuit of him. As much as it pained him to admit it, Charlie knew he had let himself get caught, let himself see what she had wanted him to see. Since breaking off his engagement, the demands of his job had given him an excuse to steer clear of the dating game. Deep down, though, Charlie knew that he was really afraid of repeating the same mistake again, of finding himself involved with someone who cared more about his name than she did about him.

Glancing over at Kendra, he realized that she had already knocked down some of the walls he'd built, and now he found himself once again wondering who she really was. She had been helping him load and haul wood for nearly two hours. Despite the deep snow and the freezing wind, she hadn't complained once. She definitely wasn't acting like the prima donna he had originally taken her for.

"I think that's about all we're going to be able to fit on the sleds for this load," Kendra said as she shifted yet another thick log into place.

"In that case, let's head back to my place, and I'll start splitting logs. I'd like to get some of the wood inside tonight so it has a chance to dry out." Charlie secured the chain saw on top of one of the stacks of wood and grabbed the rope attached to the sled nearest him.

He fell into step beside Kendra, slowing his pace to match hers. When they'd taken the first of three loads to his cabin, he'd half-expected her to say that her sled was too heavy for her. Instead, she had moved forward with a slow, steady progress.

Now, at the end of the third load, he noticed her breath coming a bit more heavily, pluming out in front of her in the cold. They were nearly to his cabin when he noticed her shiver. Then he noticed her jeans. From the top of her boots all the way up past her knees, the denim was soaked through.

"You must be freezing."

She just shrugged, but Charlie didn't miss the way she clamped her teeth together to keep them from chattering. "Is there an axe at your cabin, or do you need me to find Grandpa's?"

"No, I found one." When they reached his cabin, Charlie pulled his sled off to the side of the road and then reached for Kendra's. "I can take it from here. Why don't you go inside and get warmed up."

"Are you sure you don't need any more help?"

"I've got it," Charlie assured her.

"Can I at least make you some hot chocolate?"

"That would be great."

"Okay." Kendra stepped toward her cabin. "I'll see you in a little while."

Charlie nodded. He watched her make her way back to her cabin, noticing the way she shivered again. Then she turned and looked back at him, giving him a timid smile, and he felt an odd sensation seep through him. He managed to smile back, waiting until she slipped inside before turning back to the work at hand.

He set a log on an old stump that had been fashioned into a chopping block, grabbed the axe, and reminded himself that Kendra Blake was just part of a job he needed to do.

* * *

Elias looked up when a knock came on his office door. He waved in Ray Underwood, one of his senior agents. "What's up?"

"I think we have a bigger problem than we thought," Ray told him. "I just got off the phone with LAPD. They told me that someone has gained access to Kendra Blake's laptop. There was a high-tech spyware program running on it."

"Have they been able to trace it?"

"Not so far." Ray shook his head. "Whoever this guy is, he's good. The IP addresses change regularly, and he only gets on for a few minutes at a time—just long enough to download the new data."

"Then they need to focus on how this guy got the spyware on her computer," Elias concluded. "It sounds like they're dealing with an insider. That would explain how someone gained access to both her laptop and the backstage area."

"That's what the detectives in LA think."

"Let them know that we're willing to offer assistance if they need it. And make sure they keep us in the loop."

"I'll stay on top of it," Ray assured him before turning to leave the room.

* * *

"Here, let me hang that up for you." Kendra reached for Charlie's coat as he shrugged out of it. He had already brought in a stack of wood through the back door, leaving it in the mudroom to dry out.

"Thanks." Charlie handed the coat to her, tugged off his gloves, and then leaned down to take his boots off so he wouldn't track snow into the cabin.

She hung his coat up on the rack that was mounted to the wall near the washer and dryer and then motioned to the door. "Come on into the kitchen. I'll get you that hot chocolate I promised."

"Sounds good." He followed her out of the storage room and down the hall.

Kendra glanced over her shoulder at him. "You must be exhausted. I didn't think you were going to split all of that wood today."

"Another storm is supposed to be coming in tonight, and it's supposed to be a big one. I didn't want to get caught unprepared."

"It looks like it already started." Without thinking, she reached up and brushed at the snow in his hair.

He froze at her touch, his eyes locking on hers for a moment. She felt her cheeks heat and quickly snatched her hand back. "I'm sorry. You just . . ." She stumbled over her words and felt her breath catch in her lungs. "You have some snow in your hair."

Charlie's eyes stayed on hers, but he reached up and tousled his hair, causing the rest of the snow to rain down over his shoulders and onto the floor. Then he used his fingers to comb his hair back into place.

"I, uh, I'll get you that hot chocolate." Kendra quickly turned toward the kitchen and reached for a thick mug that was sitting on the counter. She concentrated on measuring out the hot cocoa mix and pouring the steaming water from the kettle. When she turned back to hand him the mug, she was surprised to see Charlie still staring at her.

He reached out and took the hot chocolate from her. "Thanks."

"You're welcome." She motioned to the pot she'd put on the stove earlier. "Are you hungry? I was about to make some dinner."

Charlie's eyebrows lifted, and the familiar humor sparked in his eyes. "Can you cook?"

Kendra's lips curved into a smile. "I picked up a few things in Young Women's."

"Young Women's?"

She nodded, noting his confusion. "You know, those activities they hold at church every Wednesday night for the youth."

"Sorry. It's still sinking in that you're LDS."

"Is it that hard to believe?"

"Just odd." Charlie shrugged. "I mean, what are the chances that we'd both come up here to get away from life and find another Mormon doing the same thing?"

"I guess it is a pretty big coincidence," Kendra admitted, now wondering if her grandfather had sent her up here with ulterior motives. Maybe he'd wanted her to meet Charlie. Or more specifically, he had wanted her to meet an eligible bachelor who happened to be Mormon.

"So how is it that your grandparents are LDS, but your parents aren't?"

"My dad was raised Mormon."

"But he isn't active?"

She shook her head. "Not during my lifetime."

"What about the rest of your family?"

"My mom has never really had any interest in religion," Kendra admitted. "As for my sister, she's still trying to figure out if it's possible to pursue a career in Hollywood and be an active member of the Church at the same time."

"Acting is a tough business."

Kendra looked at him thoughtfully. "Not many people think so."

"Not many people know what it's like to live with the paparazzi constantly following you."

Kendra considered Charlie's background, her eyes lifting quizzically. "Did you have that growing up? I mean, being the son of a senator?"

"A little bit," Charlie admitted. "I never got it as bad as my brother did."

"Because he's a baseball player?"

"That and he's the oldest." Charlie took a sip of his hot chocolate. "It never seemed to bother him much. Besides, in politics, the press tends to die down when it isn't an election year."

"I guess that's true." Kendra rubbed her arms against the chill in the room, glancing over to see that the fire was dwindling. "Would you mind putting another log on the fire?"

"No problem." Charlie walked to the fireplace and shifted the screen aside. "Your fire sure doesn't put out much heat, does it?"

Kendra shook her head. "My dad liked the look of a fireplace instead of a wood stove, so we ended up with the pretty version instead of the functional one."

Charlie put another piece of wood on top of the dwindling flames. "I gather your grandfather is more practical."

"Oh, yeah. He insisted on having a wood stove in his cabin. He said it was cheaper to put in than a regular fireplace, and it would cut down on their electric bills when they wanted to visit up here in the winter."

"I doubt your father worries much about utility bills."

"Very true," Kendra agreed as she put some water in a pot and started adding the ingredients for her favorite soup. She put everything on to simmer as Charlie crossed back to the kitchen.

He motioned to the stove and asked, "So what's for dinner?"

"Cheddar chowder."

"I don't know that I've ever had that before, but right now, anything hot sounds good." Charlie gave her an odd look and then added, "Thanks for your help today with the wood."

"It was fun." Kendra gazed over at the snow that was beginning to fall. It reminded her that she was isolated here, that the snow was keeping anyone from finding her. She looked back at Charlie, suddenly grateful she wasn't all alone the way she had planned. "I think I could get used to the peace and quiet up here."

He motioned to the front windows. "That's good, because with all of the snow we're getting, it looks like we're going to be stuck here for a while."

Nerves fluttered in her stomach, not in fear but in anticipation. "In that case, how are you at backgammon?"

Charlie fought back a smile. "I am a master at backgammon."

"Oh, really?" Kendra's eyebrows lifted in challenge. "I guess we'll just have to see about that."

Chapter 13

Detective Dan Eadelton entered the interrogation room and took a good look at Zack Prescott. He was dressed casually in jeans and a T-shirt, his pretty-boy face beaded with perspiration as he sat in a molded plastic chair next to a scarred wooden table. The moment the door opened, Zack turned to face him with a combination of fear and confusion apparent in his eyes.

"Do you know why you're here?" Dan asked, dropping a thick file on the desk.

Zack swallowed hard. "I already told that other detective that I didn't have anything to do with what happened to Joslyn. I never even met her."

"Joslyn?"

"Joslyn Korden." Zack looked at him, and his confusion heightened. "Isn't that why I'm here? Because you wanted to ask me more questions about the explosion at her photo shoot?"

"Actually, I wanted to clarify a few things in your witness report about the incident at Kendra Blake's concert the other night." He took his time sitting down, but his mind was working at lightning speed.

He was familiar with the Korden case. A small bomb had detonated during Joslyn Korden's photo shoot ten days earlier. Joslyn had gone into hiding following the incident, and her body had recently been discovered. Since the FBI believed she was the victim of a serial killer, only the investigation into the bombing had remained under LAPD control. Now Dan found himself wondering if the Korden case and the Blake case could be related.

No one was hurt when the small bomb detonated in a storage room while Joslyn's photo shoot was going on. The explosion at Kendra Blake's concert certainly hadn't been intended to hurt people en masse. Could these bombs have both been intended to scare these women? Were they some kind of initial step in this serial killer's ritual? And could this man sitting before him have had anything to do with the six women who had already been slain?

His pulse kicked up a notch, and he had to force himself to stay calm as he settled into his chair and opened his file. As though he didn't have any place better to be, he drew a pen from his pocket and shifted his notes in front of him. "It says here that you were on stage when the explosion went off backstage at Kendra Blake's concert."

"That's right."

"What about before the concert?" he asked. "Did you notice anything unusual?"

Zack shrugged a shoulder. "Kendra seemed kind of nervous before the show, but other than that, I didn't notice anything."

Dan stared at him, his face carefully expressionless. Then he looked down at his files. "Were you on stage for the whole concert?"

"Yeah."

Dan's eyebrows drew together. "That's interesting. Two of your fellow dancers mentioned that you disappeared for a few minutes between numbers."

"Just for a few seconds. I went to the bathroom during one of our off numbers." He sat up a little straighter.

"So you had just enough time to knock Kendra Blake's bodyguard unconscious and set a bomb backstage."

The muscle in Zack's jaw jumped. "That's crazy! I didn't have anything to do with that. I would never try to hurt Kendra."

"Well, Zack, as much as I'd like to believe you, you're the only name that's come up at both crime scenes," he improvised. He scratched his chin as though considering. "Makes me wonder if it's just a coincidence or if you have something to do with all of this."

"I already told that other detective that I wasn't anywhere near the studio that day. And there were a lot of people around when I left the night before."

"Tell me about what happened at the studio."

"There really isn't much to tell. I worked at Grant Photography for a few months as a photography assistant until I got the gig with Kendra Blake," Zack told him. "Grant was shorthanded for Joslyn's photo shoot, and he knew I was in town for the Grammys, so he called and asked if I would work it."

"Did you work it?"

Zack shook his head. "I helped set up the day before, but I had to be at rehearsals and sound checks on the day of the shoot, so I couldn't be there."

"I see." Dan considered this newest information. If the two bombings were connected, then it would be easy enough to confirm that Zack had been at rehearsals during Joslyn's photo shoot like he said he'd been. He shuffled his notes back into the file and stood up. "I'll need to talk to a few people so I can corroborate your story."

"I'm telling you the truth," Zack insisted. "I didn't have anything to do with any of this."

"I hope not, for your sake." With that, Dan turned and left the room.

* * *

Charlie's cell phone rang the moment he walked into his cabin. He checked the caller ID, unsurprised to find an FBI prefix displayed. "Whitmore."

"Charlie, I'm afraid we've had some new developments," Elias said in a brisk tone.

"What's going on?"

"We're still looking into it, but a detective with LAPD thinks he uncovered a link between Joslyn Korden and Kendra Blake."

Charlie's blood ran cold as he thought of how Joslyn Korden had died. "What kind of link?"

"A few days before Joslyn's murder, a small bomb exploded during her photo shoot."

"You think it's the same person who set the bomb at Kendra's concert?" Charlie managed to ask as he lowered himself onto the couch.

"Our analysts are helping the LAPD go over the forensics reports right now, but the preliminary findings suggest that both bombs may have been set by the same person," Elias told him. "If that's the case . . ."

Dread settled in the pit of Charlie's stomach. "You think the Malibu Stalker might be after Kendra."

"It's possible," Elias told him. "The bombing is unique to Joslyn Korden. None of the other victims had anything similar happen to them before they were killed. We don't know if the serial killer changed his MO for some reason or if Joslyn's murder and the bombing are completely unrelated."

"Joslyn's also the only high-profile victim. Maybe the bomb was set to rattle her somehow," Charlie commented. "If that's the case, he could be using the same tactic on Kendra."

"Maybe. We know that Joslyn went into hiding after the bombing." Elias hesitated for a moment. "You realize that if we're right, Kendra obviously doesn't understand what she's dealing with."

"Maybe it's time she learns. If she knows how serious this threat is, she might agree to a full protection detail."

"I don't want to take the chance that she'll get spooked and take off."

"Where would she go?" Charlie asked, glancing at the snow still falling outside. "Her car's stuck, and there's no way she's getting out of here without help."

"And it would only take one call to her father to get whatever help she might need," Elias reminded him. "From what William Blake has told me, Sterling isn't very happy about being kept out of the loop."

"He doesn't know where she is?"

"He knows she's in protective custody, but he doesn't know where," Elias told him. "We've gone over the security that was backstage at the concert, and we've had a chance to talk to her bodyguard, who was injured. All the evidence is pointing in the same direction. It's very possible that whoever set the explosive is someone she knows."

"But you just said you think a serial killer may be behind this."

"We're still considering all possibilities," Elias said. "Including the possibility that the Malibu Stalker takes the time to gain the trust of his victims before he kills them."

"I was actually wondering if that was the case. None of the victims' homes showed any sign of forced entry," Charlie mused, "and that would also explain why there's so much time between murders."

"Exactly," Elias agreed. "There doesn't seem to be any specific pattern of when the murders take place, but there are usually at least a couple of months between them, which brings us back to the possibility that the killer takes time to get to know his victims."

Charlie considered this newest information, an unsettled feeling churning through him. He needed to help Kendra understand the danger, but how could he do so without spooking her? Could he explain that if she returned to her normal life, she could be running right into the arms of a murderer?

"What if I tell Kendra that I saw articles online about the Malibu Stalker? I could let her know what she's dealing with without saying I'm FBI. It might make her reconsider letting us protect her."

"I don't know, Charlie. She still might get spooked and try to run home to her family," Elias cautioned.

"Unless she can't call home," Charlie said, thinking of her cell phone still sitting inside her car. "Her phone's in her car. I can go get it; make sure she doesn't try to contact anyone without me knowing about it. Neither of our cabins has a landline."

"That's probably not a bad idea, no matter what you tell her. How's the weather up there anyway?"

"Another storm front's over us right now. There're already two feet of snow on the ground, and it looks like we're about to get a few more inches," Charlie told him. "Even I would have to work at it to get out of here."

"Are you okay on supplies?"

"Yeah, I'm good." Charlie nodded. "I'll give you a call tomorrow, after I talk to Kendra."

"Good luck."

"Thanks," Charlie said, already planning his next encounter with Kendra.

* * *

Kendra stared at the open novel without reading a word. Her mind wasn't on the latest murder mystery she'd brought with her. Rather, it was on the man across the street—the man who was quickly consuming all of her thoughts.

It was silly, really. She hardly knew Charlie Whitmore and now, after only two days, she couldn't stop thinking about him. *How much more cliché can this get*, she asked herself. Girl runs away to the woods to get away from life. She meets a handsome stranger and falls in love. Not that she was in love with Charlie or anything, but the word *handsome* certainly fit him. The fact that he was also LDS was certainly an added bonus.

For a moment, she let herself wonder what it would be like to date someone who had the same religion she did. Then she immediately realized that she barely knew what it was like to date at all. Still, the romantic in her dreamed that some day she would fall in love with someone who could take her to the temple. Someone who would give her the gift of love and friendship and show her what it was like to have the priesthood in her home.

Kendra shook her head and tried to bring herself back to reality. This wasn't the time or the place to start a relationship, and she definitely wasn't looking for one right now. She had work to do, music to write, before her manager pushed her back out on tour.

The spring awards season would be heating up soon, and that meant fittings and rehearsals, public appearances, and radio interviews. She didn't know if she'd be able to fit it all in, especially when she wasn't sure who had set off the bomb at her concert, and more importantly, why.

All she knew for sure was that security would be oppressive when she went back. Her chest tightened at the thought—the inevitable increase in bodyguards and the decrease in privacy.

She set her book aside and reached for her guitar. Leaning back comfortably on the loveseat, she strummed a few notes. She didn't think about what she was playing. She just let the music come, let it take her wherever it wanted to go. When words started echoing through her mind to meld with the music, she reached for a pencil and paper and scribbled a few notes down.

An hour passed by unnoticed and then two. Her fingers shifted over the strings, her voice stroking over the words she'd written. When at last she was satisfied, she read through the words once again. She wasn't surprised to find she had written a song about hope and friendship, a song about searching for love.

* * *

His feet were freezing despite the two pairs of wool socks he wore under his snow boots. Charlie had walked to where Kendra's car was parked shortly after the sun came up in the hopes that he could secure her cell phone before she was up and around. After hearing her play her guitar late into the night, he imagined she would sleep through most of the morning.

The task of breaking into Kendra's car hadn't gone as smoothly as he had originally hoped. It had taken him twenty minutes of fighting with the lock before he'd managed to pop open the trunk. Picking locks had seemed so much easier at Quantico when he'd taken the class at the FBI Academy.

Regardless of the time it had taken him, he now had Kendra's cell phone in his pocket, and her car was locked up tight as though no one had ever been there. Unfortunately, if Kendra decided to go search her car herself for her missing phone, the evidence would be right in front of her in the form of his footprints. As much as he hated it, the deep snow made it impossible to go anywhere without leaving a trail, especially now that the storm had passed and there wasn't any fresh powder to hide where he'd been.

He turned the corner and looked down the street. Even from this distance, he could see the trail that he and Kendra had created between their cabins. If anyone did manage to locate the Blake cabins, it wouldn't take long to realize that someone had been coming and going from both of them.

Charlie stared at the footprints, trying to retrace his steps as he headed back to his cabin. On the way, he noticed another cabin on the side of the road, its yard and porch hidden under the untouched blanket of snow, a pickup truck parked in the driveway.

Curious as to who might be staying there, he looked up at the chimney only to see that there wasn't any evidence of a fire inside. There also weren't any lights on. For a moment, he wondered why a vehicle would be up here if no one was home. Puzzled, he moved closer and brushed some of the snow away. Underneath was a protective cover draped over the truck. Apparently, the owner only used the vehicle when he was vacationing in the mountains.

With a sudden flash of inspiration, Charlie brushed the snow off the vehicle so it would look like it had been used recently. Then he continued up the driveway and onto the porch of the cabin. After kicking some of the snow away from the front door, he walked back through the yard. He continued on to the next cabin and repeated the process. One by one, Charlie left deliberate footprints and signs of life at each cabin on the street before finally doubling back to his own.

He climbed up onto his front porch and looked down the street, pleased with the results. Now, except for the smoke coming from the chimney, it looked like all of the cabins on the street had people staying in them. In fact, the spot where Charlie had parked his SUV was actually just as close to the cabin next door as it was to his.

Charlie moved inside to thaw out. The wood stove gave off enough heat to warm the whole cabin, but Charlie immediately moved closer to it. He shrugged off his outer clothing, laying his gloves and socks on the bricks beneath the wood stove so they could dry.

When he looked out the window to see if there were any signs of life at Kendra's place, he noticed a light snow beginning to fall. Apparently, the storm wasn't over yet.

Chapter 14

Kendra wrapped both hands around her cup of hot chocolate, reveling in the warmth of the steam rising from it and the rich scent. She blew lightly on the dark liquid before taking her first sip. She smiled as the heat seeped through her, and she carried the mug with her to sit by the fire.

She had stirred the fire to life before indulging in a long, hot shower that morning. Now she was ready to curl up and enjoy her hot chocolate and a good book, assuming her mind would cooperate and let her read instead of think about Charlie.

The corners of her mouth lifted as she remembered the three games of backgammon they had played the night before. He had actually been a challenging opponent, even though he hadn't succeeded in winning any of the games. He had come close once, threatening her enough that she had resorted to taking a quick break in the middle of their third game to warm up the caramel cake she'd bought at the store the day before.

Maybe it was true that the way to a man's heart was through his stomach. Dessert had certainly succeeded in distracting him last night.

He hadn't mentioned anything about seeing her today, and she wondered if she would have to come up with an excuse to go over to his cabin again. Not that she didn't want some time to herself, too, but she had enjoyed bantering over their games last night and having someone to talk to, someone who really listened.

She had nearly told him about what had sent her into hiding, but she hadn't wanted to ruin such a perfect evening. In her mind, it had been perfect: Dinner with just the two of them, the fire flickering romantically in the background. Their conversation had been simple and easy; no one hanging over her shoulder to listen in, no one interrupting to ask for an autograph or a picture. She wondered if her parents could understand how much she had missed out on by growing up under so many restrictions.

Kendra settled into her chair, but instead of picking up her book, she simply stared into the fire. She wished she could call and talk to her parents, to assure them that she was okay. Unfortunately, she didn't know how to contact them without leaving an electronic trail that would lead right to her. Even though she only had her new cell phone with her, she had little doubt that someone on her father's security team was tracking the GPS locators on all of their incoming calls.

That lesson had been learned the hard way when she was sixteen and tried to take off to the beach without her bodyguards. She had tried calling from a friend's phone, only to have Alan show up five minutes later to bring her back home.

Her thoughts were interrupted by a knock at the door. She looked through the window and saw Charlie standing on the porch.

She answered the door, her light mood fading when she saw the serious expression on his face. "Hi, Charlie. Is something wrong?"

He didn't answer her question, instead motioning inside. "Do you mind if I come in?"

Kendra stepped aside and waved him in. He stood there just inside the door, not making any motion to take off his coat or boots to indicate he planned to stay for more than a minute or two. She looked up at him, prepared to ask again what was wrong. Before she could, he looked down at her and their eyes met.

"Kendra, I just saw the news on the internet." Charlie said, his voice vibrating with both surprise and concern. "It said that a bomb exploded at your concert a few days ago."

Kendra immediately tensed.

"What happened?" Charlie pressed.

Kendra took a step back and moved to sit down on the loveseat. She took a steadying breath before lifting her eyes to meet Charlie's. "Do we have to talk about this?"

"Look, it doesn't take a rocket scientist to figure out that you came up here right after it happened." Charlie shrugged out of his coat now, tossing it haphazardly over the stair railing. Then he looked at her again, his blue eyes intense. "Who are you running from?"

"I'm not running," Kendra insisted. "I just needed to get away for a while."

"Aren't you worried about the Malibu Stalker?"

Her eyebrows drew together. "Who?"

"The Malibu Stalker." Charlie reached into his inside coat pocket and drew out a folded computer printout. His hand wasn't completely steady when he dropped it into her lap. "The guy the police think is after you."

An unprecedented sense of fear filled her as she scanned the printed words and read about the past crimes of the man the press had nicknamed the Malibu Stalker. When she looked up at Charlie, her chin quivered as she tried to fight the sudden urge to cry. "You think someone is trying to kill me?"

"I don't know," Charlie said, his voice soft, his eyes still serious. "But that's what the cops think."

Kendra brought her hand up over her mouth. Panic, fear, and terror all melded together as she fought back a sob.

"Hey, I'm sorry." Charlie sat down next to her and reached for her hand. "I thought the reason you were hiding up here was because you knew about all of this."

Kendra shook her head and swallowed hard. She didn't want to cry in front of Charlie, but right now, she couldn't get past the facts he'd laid out in front of her.

Someone wanted to *kill* her.

That thought circled through her mind as Charlie reached his arm around her and pulled her close. The first tears spilled over, and her body quivered as the emotions bubbled up inside her. She curled into him as he stroked her back and spoke quietly to her. She barely heard the soft reassurances he murmured, but his tone was comforting as the full force of her tears continued.

When she finally quieted, Charlie simply held her. Even though her mind was still consumed with the reality he had painted, she drew comfort from Charlie's strength.

He shifted slightly so he could see her face. Then he reached down to wipe a tear from her cheek. His voice was gentle when he spoke. "Do you want me to see if I can get in touch with the police or the FBI for you? They can probably offer you some kind of protection."

Kendra shook her head. "I don't want to think about that right now."

"Why not?"

"I've lived my whole life with people following me around to keep me safe," Kendra said, wondering how she could possibly explain. "After the fire backstage, my dad was going to send me more bodyguards. I know he would have pestered me about my safety until I gave in and moved back home where he wants me."

"I gather you don't want to move back home," Charlie surmised.

"It isn't just that." She sighed. "When I lived there, I felt like I was going to suffocate if I didn't find some time to myself. I need some time to live my life without an audience, some time to just breathe." She looked at him quizzically. "Does that make any sense?"

Charlie nodded. He stared at her for a moment as though lost in his own thoughts. Then he asked, "Don't you think you should at least talk to the FBI? It wouldn't be the same as moving back home or having your dad force bodyguards on you."

"Maybe not, but I need some time to think about it." She stared up at him, warmth settling through her as he continued to hold her by his side. A ghost of a smile crossed her face. "I'm glad you're here."

"Me too." His hand lifted, gently brushing her hair back behind her ear.

Their faces were close, tears still moist on Kendra's eyelashes. Her heartbeat quickened when his gaze skimmed down to her mouth. The sudden image of kissing Charlie Whitmore sent a thrill up her spine along with a skittering sense of panic. The hand on her shoulder was gentle, but his eyes were dark and intense. Then he shifted slightly, creating a safe distance between them.

"Have you eaten lunch yet? I could fix you something."

She shook her head, still feeling like she was under a spell. "I'm not really hungry."

Before he could respond, the rumble of an engine sounded outside. Charlie sprang up with a speed that surprised her and rushed to the window.

It took a moment for Kendra to understand the source of his concern, to remember that they were snowed in and that whoever was out there might be the person trying to hurt her, the person who wanted to kill her. Her voice was shaky when she asked, "Who is it?"

"I'm not sure." Charlie shifted by the window so he could look out without being seen. "It could just be someone out snowmobiling."

She let out a shaky breath and moved to the other side of the window so that she, too, could peer out without being noticed. Her heartbeat quickened when she saw a man turn his snowmobile into her driveway.

"Do you know him?" Charlie asked.

Kendra had to take another breath before she managed to focus. Then she made herself take a good look at the man in the driveway. He pulled off a helmet, his mop of brown hair spilling out wildly. "That's Jed Burgess, Eleanor Burgess's son."

"Stay here," Charlie said in a commanding tone. "I'll go see what he wants."

"Okay." Kendra's head bobbed up and down in agreement. "Be careful."

He glanced over his shoulder then and gave her a nod of encouragement. "I will."

Chapter 15

Charlie controlled the urge to reach for his weapon. From what Kendra had told him after their trip to the general store, he knew that the Burgess family had lived in Pinewood for years. The fact that Jed Burgess was a white male between twenty-five and thirty-five years old didn't mean he was a serial killer. Then again, there wasn't any evidence that he wasn't one either.

The moment the door opened, Jed looked up, his eyes hopeful. Then he saw Charlie, and his disappointment showed before he managed to control it.

"Hi, there," Jed greeted him as he dismounted the snowmobile and stood facing Charlie. "You must be Kendra's friend."

"That's right." Charlie tried to keep his voice casual as he moved down the steps. "I'm Charlie Whitmore."

"Good to meet you." Jed tugged off his glove and offered a hand. "Jed Burgess."

Charlie shook his hand and let his curiosity show on his face. "What brings you up this way?"

"Just following orders." Jed opened the storage compartment on the back of his snowmobile.

Charlie tensed, his right hand lifting slightly in case he really did need his gun. Then Jed pulled a white pastry box out of the storage compartment and turned to offer it to Charlie. "My mom was worried that you and Kendra might not be able to get out with all of this snow. She wanted me to deliver this cake and pass along her phone number in case you needed anything."

"That was nice of you to bring this by. I'll make sure Kendra gets it."

He nodded and passed the box into Charlie's hands. Then Jed looked up at Kendra's front door. "So I guess you and Kendra are dating?"

Charlie banked down on his conflicting emotions and tried to consider how best to handle the probing question. "You could say that."

Jed mounted his snowmobile and gave him a subtle nod. "You're a lucky man."

"I guess I am," Charlie managed.

Jed motioned to the box Charlie now held. "One of Mom's business cards is inside. We're supposed to get another eight to ten inches of snow tonight, but if you think of anything you need, I can run a delivery up here before the storm hits."

"I appreciate that, but I think we're okay for now." Charlie stared at the man in front of him. Logically, he doubted that Jed Burgess was the man responsible for six murders in California. He decided to trust that logic for a minute. "I wonder if I can ask you and your mom a favor though."

"What's that?"

"Kendra and I came up here to get away from the paparazzi. People may come through town looking for us."

"And you don't want us to tell anyone that you're here," Jed finished for him.

"Yeah." Charlie nodded. "Most people wouldn't be able to find this place without directions."

"Isn't that the truth." Jed let out a short laugh. "Don't worry. Your secret is safe with us."

"There's one more thing," Charlie added. "Could you let me know if anyone does show up looking for Kendra?"

"No problem." Jed patted his jacket pocket. "I don't have a pen on me, but you can give Mom a call and leave your phone number with her. We'll watch your back."

"Thanks a lot." Charlie waited until Jed started the engine and turned the snowmobile back down the road.

The man seemed harmless enough, but just to be safe, Charlie would have Elias run a background check on him. It should be easy enough to prove whether Jed had been in LA on the dates of any of the murders.

After Jed disappeared from view, Charlie moved back to Kendra's front door. She was safe for now, but he doubted he would get much sleep tonight until he could eliminate Jed as a suspect.

Charlie had a feeling that thoughts of Kendra would keep him up even if he didn't have any potential suspects to worry about. He had been prepared for her tears. He'd provoked them deliberately. What he hadn't counted on was the way he'd felt when he held her.

Somehow he had to get back on level footing, especially until he could tell her why he was really here. He pushed open the door to find her waiting nervously by the window. He banked down the urge to go to her, to gather her close. "Jed was just delivering a cake for us from his mom."

"Oh." Kendra's eyes followed him as he moved to the kitchen and set the box on the counter.

Charlie lifted the lid to reveal a German chocolate cake. He pulled the business card with Mrs. Burgess's phone number out of the box and tucked it into his pocket.

"What was that?" Kendra asked, following him into the kitchen.

"Just Mrs. Burgess's phone number. Jed gave it to me in case we need him to bring us any supplies."

"That was thoughtful of her."

Charlie nodded and considered for a moment. "How well do you know Jed?"

"Not very well, actually," Kendra said. She opened her mouth as though she was going to say something else, but then she stopped and simply shrugged her shoulders.

"What?"

"I know this isn't very nice to say, but he always gave me the creeps. Every time I came into town, he just stared at me, but he never said anything." Kendra shrugged again. "I used to think he was just shy, but then he'd stop by and talk to Grandpa every time I came to town, and he didn't seem shy at all."

"Did he ever give you a reason to be scared of him?"

"Not scared, exactly." Kendra blew out a breath. "Uneasy is probably a better way to describe it. I always felt like he was staring at me, especially when I wasn't looking."

"He probably just didn't know how to act around such a beautiful woman."

Color crept into her cheeks, and her eyes dropped to the floor.

Despite the seriousness of the conversation, Charlie found himself amused to see her embarrassed over such a simple compliment. His voice was light when he added, "Face it. Women like you can make men nervous just by breathing."

Kendra just shook her head. Then she looked down at the cake, and her expression softened. "She remembered."

"Remembered what?"

"My favorite kind of cake."

Charlie looked up at her, trying to gauge her mood. She looked uncertain and still a little scared. She also looked like she didn't want to be alone.

"At least we have dessert for tonight," Charlie said casually. "Is it my turn to fix dinner?"

"Is that your way of inviting me over for dinner?"

"I guess so." Charlie managed to smile at her. "But tonight I get to pick the game."

The corners of her mouth lifted. "Does that mean you don't want me to bring my backgammon game over to your place?"

"That's exactly what I'm saying." Charlie nodded. "I'm sure I have a deck of cards around somewhere. How are you at gin rummy?"

Her eyebrows lifted. "I can hold my own."

"Tell you what." Charlie moved toward the door. "I have to check in with my office, but after that, I'll come back over and we can hang out. I'll even bring over the steak I bought the other day, and we can fix it for dinner. That way you won't have to go out in the snow."

"I'd like that," Kendra said. Charlie started to turn away, but Kendra reached for his hand. "Charlie?"

"Yeah?"

"I'm sorry I got so emotional earlier, but thanks." She looked up at him, her eyes still red from crying. "Thanks for being here with me."

Charlie stared down at her and felt himself wavering between his developing feelings for Kendra and his sense of propriety. He gave her hand a squeeze. "I'll see you in a little while." Then, before he could do something stupid, like lean in and kiss her good-bye, he turned and walked out the door.

* * *

Kendra picked up the printed article Charlie had given her and read it again, taking her time and absorbing the details. There weren't any photos of the victims, but she knew who Joslyn Korden was. She had even met her a few times at charity events.

How was it that she hadn't realized Joslyn was a victim of a serial killer, especially when the serial killer was targeting women who looked like her and lived in Malibu, where she had been raised?

That question circled in her mind, but she could come up with only one answer. She had been so busy living her own life that she hadn't bothered to keep up with what was happening outside her own little world. Certainly her father would have known about the Malibu Stalker, but undoubtedly, he would have tried to shelter her and her sister from the cold hard reality that young women like them were being murdered. His viewpoint was that if they didn't know about it, there was no sense in bringing it to their attention. Of course, Sienna didn't have blonde hair like Kendra and the victims. But while her sister had inherited dark hair from their mother, Kendra had little doubt that Sienna had been sheltered from the information as much as she had.

She couldn't begin to imagine what kind of person would do something like this. Why would anyone want to deliberately kill someone, to take another's life, simply because they could?

The article revealed very little about any suspicions of who the killer might be, and Kendra could feel a huge weight settling on her shoulders as she considered her options. Moving back in with her parents would likely ensure her safety. It would also guarantee that her life would never move forward. Just the thought of living inside her childhood home, of dealing with the oppressive security measures her father had in place, made her stomach clench.

She wanted to be safe, but she also wanted to live. In the past three days, she'd felt like she was just beginning to discover who she was. She could make her own choices and tend to her own needs. Already, she had realized how much she liked keeping her own hours and eating when and what she wanted. She enjoyed cooking and the sense of satisfaction that came from preparing something herself and liking the results.

Even writing her music with no one around was a gift she refused to take for granted. She took pleasure in the clutter her work created and the knowledge that she was responsible for cleaning up her own messes.

No, as safe as her father could keep her, she knew she would suffocate if she moved back home. She thought of Charlie, of his suggestion of talking to the FBI. She tried to convince herself that she could work with them, but she knew from her grandfather's days with the Bureau that their protection would only last for a short while unless she entered the Witness Protection Program. With her fame, she doubted she would be a candidate anyway.

The bottom line was that, eventually, she would have to deal with her father and the security force he was constantly thrusting on her. Kendra let out a sigh. It didn't matter if it was the FBI or her father's security team. Once she gave her freedom to someone else, she was afraid she would never find a way to win it back again.

She moved to the window and stared outside at the thick clouds looming overhead. The wind lifted some of the powdery snow, blowing it along the road, creating drifts against the pine trees on either side. Charlie's SUV was still parked along the road, but it was completely covered in snow.

The snow gave her comfort for now. As long as it lasted, whether it was days or weeks, she would be safe. As long as the roads were impassible, she could continue to hide, continue to find herself again, to discover who Kendra Blake was when the spotlight was turned off. But then what?

As much as Kendra was enjoying her freedom and Charlie's company, eventually she would have to face reality. She thought of her house in Malibu, the house that her father insisted she buy if she was going to live on her own. It was too big for her taste and too much of a showplace to be a real home. Not that she knew what a real home was.

Her parents had given her and her sister both love and all the material things they ever needed throughout their childhood, but the family house in Malibu wasn't anything like the kind of homes she read about in books and had seen in the movies. Besides the constant presence of security personnel, her parents kept a full household staff, and from childhood, she and her sister had been taught not to touch anything outside of their bedrooms and playroom.

In many ways, Kendra had found what she considered her dream house in Nashville. It was much smaller, a lovely four-bedroom tucked away in a nice neighborhood not too far from the recording studio. Smaller still was the two-bedroom condo she had purchased in Phoenix. The condo had been her first purchase after she'd taken over her own finances from her parents. She had planned for it to be a getaway, a place for her to disappear when she needed a taste of normalcy. Unfortunately, she rarely found time to spend there.

The sudden realization that the women killed by the Malibu Stalker all lived in California struck her. She thought back to the night when she had turned to her grandfather for help and realized that his insistence that she leave California had been inspired. If she could just leave Malibu behind permanently, maybe she would be able to find both her safety and her freedom.

Chapter 16

Charlie pulled out his phone the moment he stepped through his front door. Elias answered on the second ring.

"Hey, Charlie. I was just about to call you."

"What about?"

"The LA office finished their analysis on the two explosives. They were definitely set by the same person."

"That wasn't the news I was hoping for," Charlie told him. "Can I get you to run a background check for me? The name is Jed Burgess. His primary residence is here in Pinewood."

"What's his story?"

"His mom runs the general store here in Pinewood," Charlie began. "He stopped by Kendra's place today, and from what she told me, he's shown some interest in her in the past."

"You really think some guy living in the Arizona mountains could be a serial killer in Malibu?"

"I doubt it, but it's worth taking a look at him," Charlie said, feeling suddenly foolish to think that Jed Burgess could possibly be involved with the murders in California. "It should be easy to eliminate him from the suspect list since he lives here. If we don't find any evidence of him being in California near the dates of the murders, we'll cross him off the list."

"All right. I'll put Ray on it, and one of us will get back to you."

"Thank you, sir."

"One question though," Elias said. "You said he paid Kendra a visit. I thought you said the roads weren't clear enough to drive on."

"They aren't. He came up the mountain on his snowmobile," Charlie told him. "And he never saw Kendra. I was at her house when we heard him pull up so I went out and talked to him."

"Kendra didn't find that odd?"

"Like I said, she doesn't feel comfortable around the guy. She was pretty upset. I had just shown her an article about the Malibu Stalker."

"Did she agree to protection?"

"Not yet, but I think she's considering it." Charlie rubbed a hand over his face. "From what she said, her hang-up comes from the heavy security her dad has always insisted on. Sounds like she's been feeling caged in for some time."

"Then it's a good thing Sterling Blake doesn't know where she is right now."

"Yeah, and I think it's best we keep it that way for the time being."

"Definitely," Elias agreed. "Keep me in the loop with your situation up there, and I'll get back to you about Burgess."

"Thanks."

Charlie hung up the phone and then dug out the business card in his pocket. He dialed the number for Eleanor Burgess. Six rings later, he was about ready to hang up when Mrs. Burgess's voice came on the line.

"Mrs. Burgess? This is Charlie Whitmore."

"Charlie! How are you and Kendra doing up there? Do you know if my boy dropped that cake off yet?"

"He did."

Before Charlie could add his thanks, she started speaking again. "You know, I always hoped Kendra would take a shine to my boy, but the girl was never in town long enough for him to work up the nerve to talk to her, much less ask her out on a date." Mrs. Burgess sighed into the phone. "Oh well. At least she's got you up there to help look out for her."

"Yes, she does," Charlie said, not quite sure what to think about Mrs. Burgess's revelation. Then he clued in on her last sentence. "Did you see the newspaper articles about Kendra?"

"Couldn't help but see them, but don't you worry. I won't tell any of those reporter people where she's hiding," Mrs. Burgess promised.

"I'd appreciate it if you'd give me a call if anyone comes looking," Charlie told her.

"Don't you worry about a thing. I'll make sure no one comes calling unexpectedly. Of course, with all this snow, I don't think you'll have anything to worry about for a while."

"Thanks, Mrs. Burgess," Charlie said. "And thanks for the cake."

"You're welcome. You just give me a call if there's anything else I can do for you."

"I will. Thanks."

* * *

He was nervous. Charlie let that thought work its way through his brain before he tried to decipher the reasons behind it. He was man enough to acknowledge his developing feelings for Kendra, even though he knew the timing was wrong for him to act on them. He was also experienced enough in dating to recognize that the attraction was mutual.

What he didn't have experience with was being attracted to a woman who was off limits. He knew he couldn't do his job properly if he started thinking of Kendra as more than just a person who needed his protection. He just hadn't expected his protective instincts to turn so personal.

He had dated Lisa for more than six months, but not once could he think of a time when she had cried in front of him. Not once had she ever really *needed* him. In just a few days, he could feel the attachment between him and Kendra growing, and it scared him. If she had been a needy sort of woman, he could have brushed it off. In fact, that would have made him want to put some distance between them.

But Kendra wasn't needy in that clingy sort of way. She just needed someone to confide in, someone to trust. Charlie felt both privileged and terrified that she had chosen him to be that person.

Just another few days, he told himself. A few more days and the storms would be over, the roads would be passable, and, if all went well, Kendra would agree to protection. Then he could tell Kendra the truth. That he was her protection.

He shifted the bag of groceries he'd brought with him and reached up to knock on the door as snow began falling once more. The footsteps sounded immediately, and Kendra didn't try to hide the relief that showed on her face when she opened the door.

Charlie walked inside and shut the door behind him. He looked down at her, not quite able to gauge her emotions. "How are you doing?"

"Still a little shaky, I guess, but other than that, I'm okay."

He set down the grocery bag and took off his coat and boots. Then his eyes met hers, and he had to fight the urge to reach for her hand. "I'm really sorry that I upset you."

"It's okay." Kendra managed a smile. "As scary as it is to think that someone would really want to hurt me, it's better that I know about it."

Charlie nodded and then picked up the groceries once more. He started for the kitchen and put the food on the counter. Then he turned to face her. "I know you haven't had much time to think about it, but do you have any idea about what you're going to do now?"

"You mean now that I know someone is trying to kill me?"

"Yeah."

"I don't know." Kendra walked into the living room and sat down on the loveseat. She looked a little disappointed when Charlie sat opposite of her instead of taking the seat next to her. "I doubt anyone would look for me here, especially right now with all this snow."

"What about your dad? Won't he think to look here?"

"Maybe after awhile." Kendra shrugged. "I thought about calling him myself to let him know I'm doing okay, but I know my dad. I'm sure he has someone tracking the GPS signals on all of his incoming calls. The minute I call him, he'll know where I am."

"And if he knows where you are, he'll send his bodyguards to find you and take you home," Charlie finished for her.

"Exactly."

"Do you really think he's tracking all his incoming calls? I know it's possible, but I doubt your dad has the kind of equipment necessary to do that."

"He doesn't, but Bruce and Alan do."

"Bruce and Alan?"

"Parsons." Kendra nodded. "They've been working for my dad since I was a teenager. Dad hired Bruce's firm right after a threat came in against me."

"You've been threatened before?"

"Dad doesn't know that I know about it," Kendra admitted. "Alan let it slip one time after I tried to go to the beach without any bodyguards. Apparently, someone sent a bunch of letters to me, and it freaked Dad out. That was when my dad hired the Parsons."

"How old were you when that happened?"

"Sixteen," she told him. "I remember a couple of months after Dad hired them that Alan used the GPS signal on my phone to find me. Then, a few weeks later, I turned my phone off so they couldn't track me down. I used my girlfriend's phone to call and let my dad know that I was okay and that I just wanted to go out with some friends for a while. Five minutes later, Alan showed up to take me home."

"It sounds like this Alan guy takes his job pretty seriously."

Kendra nodded. "His dad owns the company. Sometimes I think my dad trusts Bruce and Alan more than he trusts me."

"I'm sure he's just worried," Charlie told her.

"You know, I probably should check in with my grandfather so I don't have to worry about the Parsons trying to track me down. I'm sure he can get a message to my parents." She reached for her purse on the end table and dug through it for a minute before she shook her head. "I think I might have left my phone in my car."

"Do you want to borrow mine?" Charlie asked and pulled his phone out of his pocket.

"That would be great. Thanks."

Charlie handed his phone to her. As he watched Kendra dial the phone number from memory, Charlie found himself smiling. He had a feeling that he was about to see a very accurate picture of exactly who Kendra Blake really was.

* * *

Kendra smiled the moment her grandfather's voice came over the phone. "Hi, Grandpa."

"Kendra? I was hoping you would call," William told her. "I was starting to worry about you."

"I'm sorry I didn't call you back sooner. I think I left my new phone in the car, and I haven't wanted to go out in the snow to dig it out."

"If you aren't using your phone, I guess you met my friend up there."

"Yes," Kendra answered, once again suspicious of her grandfather's motives. "In fact, Charlie's planning on making me dinner tonight."

"I see." William seemed to consider for a minute. "You know, I don't know if I adequately interrogated him before letting him get to know you. He is a returned missionary, isn't he?"

Kendra rolled her eyes and looked over at Charlie. "Grandpa wants to know if you went on a mission."

He nodded. "I served in Quebec."

"Yes, he's a returned missionary." Kendra smiled into the phone. "Better now?"

"A little." William chuckled. "You can't blame me for worrying. I hadn't planned on setting you up with a new boyfriend, but maybe I should have."

The image of Charlie holding her earlier flashed into her mind, and she could feel the blush rising in her cheeks. She shifted on the loveseat and tried to push aside the hope that had swelled in her, concentrating instead on the current status of their relationship. Then she realized that her grandfather was fishing for information. "Are you trying to interrogate me?"

"I'm just making conversation."

"Right," Kendra said with a hint of sarcasm in her voice. "Look, I'll call you again in a week or so. Can you just let everyone know I'm okay?"

"I will, but you be careful."

"I will," Kendra said. "I love you."

"Love you too, pumpkin."

As soon as Kendra hung up, she handed the phone back to Charlie and caught him trying to smother a grin. "What?"

"It's just that your grandpa is a lot like mine."

Her eyebrows lifted. "Really?"

"Yeah." Charlie nodded. "He can give you the third degree in fewer than sixty seconds, but the minute you have his approval, you feel like all is right with the world."

Her smile bloomed. "That's exactly how it is. He's still raw about the fact that most of his children have fallen away from the Church. Out of seven kids, only two are still active."

"That would be tough."

She nodded. "I think he and Grandma have pinned their hopes on converting their grandchildren, even if they have to do it one at a time."

"It seems to have worked with you and your sister."

"Yeah, it has." She let out a little laugh. "I think back to growing up, and the one thing I loved more than anything was going to visit my grandparents. I just always knew what to expect, you know?"

"Yeah." Charlie nodded, and his eyes met hers. "I know."

Chapter 17

His patience was going to pay off, he assured himself. He tugged off his gloves, plugged his iPod into its docking station, and turned up his music. He closed his eyes and let the music sweep over him. She was singing to him, and he could already imagine what it would be like if she were here right now.

Impatience clawed at him, but he fought it back. Kendra wouldn't be like the others. She was the one he was waiting for. She would understand that they were meant to be together. This time, everything would be different.

Kendra might be out of reach for a few more days, but he could wait that long. He had waited for years already.

* * *

Her bedroom was blindingly bright when Kendra managed to force her eyes open. After hearing the wind howl with the storm last night, she hadn't expected to awaken to sunlight streaming through the windows. She had no idea what time it was, nor could she be sure what time she'd finally gone to bed the night before. She only knew that Charlie had stayed most of the day yesterday, not leaving her alone until after ten.

She stared up at the ceiling as she remembered the events of the day before. She still couldn't quite wrap her mind around the facts laid out in the news article Charlie had given her. Rather than focus on the fear that threatened, Kendra thought of her time with Charlie. She couldn't figure out what it was about him that made her let her guard down. Not since high school could she remember having any friends with whom she could really share confidences and who accepted her for exactly who she was.

As much as she hated to admit it, she hadn't done much to keep those high school friends from being driven away over the years, first by the strict security her father had imposed and then by the demands of her career. Occasionally, she would still hear from old acquaintances, but those times were usually just a quick phone call that included the inevitable request for concert tickets.

Charlie was the first person in years who didn't seem to want anything from her. Yesterday they'd talked for hours about his family and hers. He told her about his mission in Canada. She told him about the strain of being on the road.

Somewhere in this adventure of running away, she'd found a precious gift. She'd found a friend.

A sense of anticipation rushed through her, and she forced herself to acknowledge that she was hoping Charlie would become more than just a friend. Admittedly, he hadn't really done anything to indicate he was romantically interested in her, but she certainly couldn't have been the only one who'd felt a spark between them when he held her. The intense look that sometimes came into his eyes had to mean something beyond simple friendship.

Her mind still churning, Kendra sat up in bed. When the down comforter shifted off of her, the sudden chill surprised her. She quickly pulled a quilt from the bed and wrapped it around her before heading for the bathroom. She flipped on the light switch, but the bathroom remained dark.

She stared at the light fixture for a moment, shaking her head as she guessed that the light bulb must have burnt out. Turning away from the bathroom, she headed out of her room and down the hall. That's when she noticed the light she'd left on the night before was also out. She reached for the hall light switch, flipping it on only to see that it didn't yield the desired results either.

"Great," Kendra muttered under her breath. "My first sunny day here, and *now* I lose the electricity."

Gripping the blanket tighter, she turned back to the bedroom and gathered up some clean clothes. Uncertain of how long the electricity would be out, she decided to use what she could of the hot water before it was too late. She showered in record time—under three minutes—and managed to keep the hot water for almost all of it.

She quickly dried off and changed into a pair of jeans and a long-sleeved T-shirt. Still chilled, she grabbed a hooded sweatshirt and put it on too. After donning a pair of wool socks she'd bought at the general store, she wrapped her wet hair in a towel and went into the living room to check on the fire.

After stirring it back to life, she retrieved the comforter off her bed, curled up on the chair nearest the fireplace, and wondered how the pioneers survived without hair dryers.

* * *

Charlie heard the knock at the door and forced himself awake. Three seconds was all it took for him to push the sleep from his brain and realize that it had to be Kendra who had woken him. The realization that the electricity had gone out sometime during the night took nearly twice that long.

He had been up until nearly four in the morning reviewing case files and trying to find a common link among the victims, apart from the obvious factors of physical description and location. Now he wondered if the batteries on his laptop and phone had charged before the power went out.

Already dressed in the sweatpants and T-shirt he'd slept in, he raked his fingers through his hair and jogged to the front door. A pitiful amount of heat was still coming from the wood stove in the front room, and it obviously needed a fresh log or two to get it going again.

Charlie pulled open the front door to find Kendra bundled up and standing on his front porch, the hood of her parka covering her hair. "Hey, there." Charlie stepped back from the door and waved her inside. "Come on in."

"Did I wake you?" Kendra asked. "Normally you're up before me."

"I put in a late night last night. I had some work I had to finish up." Charlie raked his fingers through his hair again and turned to deal with the fire. "What time is it anyway?"

"Almost eleven," Kendra told him, her eyes narrowing. "I thought you were on vacation. How come you had to work?"

Charlie stoked the fire and closed the stove before turning to face her. "It was just some research for a case I've been working on." He gave a casual shrug. "You know how it is. The new guy always gets the grunt work."

"Oh," Kendra said, shifting her weight.

"I'm sorry." Charlie motioned to the couch. "Did you want to sit down?"

"Sure." Kendra nodded. She sat and rubbed her arms against the chill.

Charlie sat on the couch beside her, noticing that her hair didn't look completely dry. "I gather your electricity is out too."

"Yeah." She nodded. "I've never had this happen during the winter before."

"Me neither." His stomach grumbled, reminding him that he hadn't eaten since dinner the night before. "I'm starving. Have you eaten yet?"

She shook her head. "It was too cold in my cabin to even think about food."

"Once the fire gets going, it'll warm up in here." Charlie stood up and crossed to the kitchen. "It's been awhile, but I can probably fix some ham and eggs on the stove."

Her eyebrows lifted. "Without electricity?"

He pointed at the wood-burning stove. "On that stove."

"You can really cook on that thing?" Kendra asked skeptically.

Charlie nodded and lifted the kettle off the electric stove. He filled it with water and dug out a skillet. He then put them both on the wood stove to heat. "I stayed at a cabin for a few weeks after I finished law school. It was pretty rustic. There wasn't a regular stove, so I didn't have much of a choice but to learn how to cook on the old-fashioned kind."

She smiled at him. "Sounds like it was an adventure."

"I guess you could call it that," Charlie said, still sensitive about the events that had led him to that mountain cabin a couple of years ago.

Kendra must have sensed his change in mood because her smile faded. "Are you okay?"

"Yeah, just thinking." Charlie started to brush off those memories, but something in Kendra's expression made him reconsider. "I actually went to that cabin to get away for a while after my old girlfriend and I broke up."

"Had you been together long?"

"Not really," he said as he struggled against the familiar feelings of failure. He crossed into the kitchen, giving himself a minute to organize his thoughts. He retrieved the ham and eggs out of the refrigerator and then walked back to where Kendra was still watching him with interest. He didn't know why he felt compelled to explain his failed relationship to her, but he let himself continue. "I guess it was what you'd call a whirlwind romance. We were only together about six months before we got engaged."

Her eyebrows lifted, but she remained silent.

Charlie dropped the ham in the skillet and forced himself to face her. "I thought everything was perfect. Then I started making career plans, and Lisa realized I wasn't who she thought I was."

"Who did she think you were?" Kendra asked hesitantly, almost as if she were afraid to pry but couldn't stop the question from popping out of her mouth.

Bitterness filled his words. "A rising politician, the heir apparent to my father's career."

She seemed to consider his answer for a moment before she asked, "I gather you aren't interested in politics?"

"Not at this point in my life anyway." Charlie shook his head. "She wanted to be a politician's wife. As soon as she realized I didn't fit the bill, we broke up."

"Well, I'm sure it's better that you broke up with her instead of ending up with some social climber who wanted to change you into someone you're not," Kendra said, sympathy humming in her voice.

"How do you figure I broke up with her?"

"I don't know." Kendra's shoulders lifted, understanding and compassion showing in her expression. "I just assumed that you wouldn't want to stay with someone like that."

"You know, you're the first person to realize that I was the one who decided to break up."

"Really?" Her eyes narrowed. "I would think it would be obvious to anyone who knows you."

"You would think," Charlie said, not quite able to hide the hurt in his voice. "Then again, you didn't see Lisa storm out of our engagement party."

Kendra winced. "Ouch. That must have been rough."

"Not as rough as it would have been had we gotten married before she realized that I . . ." Charlie broke off, appalled that he'd nearly finished his sentence, that he'd nearly admitted that he was an FBI agent.

"That you what?"

Charlie kept his eyes on her, a slice of guilt sneaking through him as he deliberately evaded revealing the truth. "That I had other priorities in my life."

Kendra's shoulders lifted, and she looked at him sympathetically. "I've never dated anyone for very long, but I imagine it would be really tough to get over a break-up like that, especially if you were talking about marriage."

Charlie's eyes narrowed, and he looked at her quizzically. "What's the longest you've ever dated anyone?"

"Two months," Kendra told him ruefully. "And quite honestly, it was a disaster."

"What do you mean?"

"I guess you could say that heavy security and possessive tendencies definitely don't mix."

"Keith Kerringer was possessive?" Charlie asked, referring to an actor Kendra had been linked to a year or two ago.

Kendra laughed. "I never dated Keith. That was just the paparazzi selling magazines." Then she shook her head. "The possessive ex was Steve DeFoe. Things ended pretty badly considering that he came to see me in the middle of the night and ended up in jail."

"On what charge?"

"Assault and trespassing." She shook her head. "Alan came to my rescue when Steve showed up at my house in Malibu. They got into a fight, and Alan insisted on pressing charges."

"Sounds like we both picked real winners," Charlie said dryly. He flipped the ham in the skillet and opened the egg carton before glancing back over at her. "How long ago did you break up?"

"It's been a long time, probably two or three years."

Charlie's voice was incredulous. "You haven't dated anyone since then?"

Kendra shook her head. Her voice was casual, but embarrassment crept into her cheeks. "I've been focused on my career. Or at least my father has wanted my focus to be on my career."

"And now you're here in the mountains trying to figure out what you want in life?"

She managed to smile. "Pretty much."

Charlie judged her mood, realizing this might be the right time to come clean with her, to ask her if she would accept FBI protection. "In that case, I have a very important question to ask you."

Kendra's posture immediately tensed, and Charlie altered his plan. He gave her a playful smile and asked, "How do you like your eggs?"

Chapter 18

Kendra stood beside the fireplace in her cabin and shivered. She looked at Charlie, who had followed her inside. Then she sighed as she considered her options. Mrs. Burgess had already called Charlie to check on them and had revealed that the power was out all over the mountain. She also gave them the bad news that the road leading up to their cabin was closed down and that it was unlikely that even snowmobiles were going to make it through for at least a couple of days.

Since trying to make it down the mountain in Charlie's SUV was out, that left only two options. She could stay at her cabin and hope the fireplace would give her enough heat to keep her from freezing, or she could follow Charlie's suggestion and move into his place until they regained electricity.

The simple fact was that the wood burning stove in Charlie's cabin gave off sufficient heat to keep the whole cabin warm as long as the doors were kept open. It also provided a cooking method. As Kendra had discovered earlier, the fireplace in her parents' cabin wasn't likely to provide enough heat to allow her comfort during the day, much less when the temperature dropped after the sun went down. She also couldn't imagine trying to cook over the open flames.

She turned to face Charlie. "Are you sure you don't mind me crashing over there with you?"

"Kendra, it's no big deal," Charlie assured her. "But since we don't know how long we're going to be without power, you should probably bring most of your stuff with you. We aren't going to want to keep walking back and forth in the snow."

"Good point." Kendra motioned to the back of the cabin. "I'm going to gather up my clothes. Would you mind packing up some of the groceries?"

"No problem."

Forty-five minutes and three trips later, Kendra set her guitar down in Charlie's living room and edged closer to the stove to warm up. While she had gathered her things, Charlie had cleaned out both of their refrigerators and put their food in an ice chest out on his back porch to keep everything cool. He had then put some meat and vegetables in a pot on the stove to simmer.

Kendra rubbed her hands together to warm them and gratefully turned when Charlie approached with two cups of hot chocolate.

"Here, this should help warm you up."

Kendra's eyes lit up as she grabbed the thick mug and took her first sip. "You're my hero. This is exactly what I needed."

Charlie chuckled. "You definitely aren't hard to please."

"Let's hope you still think that tomorrow after you've been stuck with me for a while."

"I think we can manage," Charlie said wryly. Then he motioned to her guitar. "Maybe now that you're staying over here, I'll really get to hear you play."

Her eyebrows lifted. "Did you want to hear me play?"

"I listen to you play every night." Charlie settled down on the couch beside the fire and looked up at her.

"You can hear me all the way over here?"

"Just the guitar," Charlie told her. "But feel free to sing me to sleep. I won't mind." His grin flashed. "Really."

"Oh, you won't, huh?" Kendra plopped down on the couch next to him. "I have a feeling the next day or two will definitely be an adventure."

"If nothing else, you're going to get to know me better than you probably wanted to."

Kendra cocked her head to one side and considered for a moment. Then she shook her head. "I don't know about that. I think I'm going to like getting to know you better."

Charlie's grin faded, and his voice lowered. "I hope so."

* * *

Her words echoed in his head, his earbuds firmly in place as Kendra's songs played over and over. The animal was fighting to break free again, that part of him that he was trying desperately to tame—or at least control. His fingers curled into fists, his short fingernails biting into the palms of his hands until twin trickles of blood oozed free.

He knew he should feel pain, but he was numb. Nothing was going to make him feel again until he had her. Nothing.

* * *

Charlie looked over at Kendra, who was sitting by the fire, her fingers fiddling with her guitar strings. He finished putting away the last of their dinner dishes and then walked into the living room. Already, the wood stove had warmed the living area, and the bedroom doors were open wide to let the heat seep into them as well.

Kendra had unpacked her things in the bedroom closest to the living room before settling down on one of the couches. Even though the room had warmed significantly, she still had a blanket wrapped loosely around her shoulders and another one draped over her legs. The only light in the room came from the lantern he'd bought, the flickering flames casting shadows over her in the otherwise dark room.

She played a few chords and then started playing a melody, one that Charlie had heard only vague snippets of during Kendra's late-night sessions. She stopped a couple times, scratching down some notes in the notebook beside her. Then, once she seemed satisfied, she began again, and this time her voice joined the melody.

Charlie lowered himself onto the couch opposite of her and simply stared. She was so beautiful, her hair flowing over her shoulders, her face free of makeup. Her voice stroked over the unfamiliar words, huskier than it normally sounded on the radio.

When she segued into the next song, Charlie realized that she was completely absorbed in her music. He doubted she even remembered he was there. She made it halfway through the second song before she stopped abruptly and shifted to write something in her notebook again. Then she picked up where she'd left off.

She repeated the same song several times, sometimes making changes as she went. Then, finally, she seemed satisfied. She set her guitar aside and rolled her shoulders restlessly. That's when she looked over and saw Charlie staring.

Even in the darkness, Charlie could see her cheeks flush.

His voice was soft. "That was nice."

"Thanks." She pulled her blanket tighter around her shoulders and curled her legs up underneath her.

"I gather that's one of your new songs," Charlie commented. When she nodded, he asked, "How long does it take you to write one?"

"It depends. Sometimes I can get one down in an hour or two." Kendra shrugged. "Others can take as long as a couple months."

"It must be a lot easier to write when you're away from everything."

She couldn't stop the grin. "I've been averaging a song a night since I got here. I've never had the music flow so well before."

"You've never had this kind of freedom before."

"I know." Kendra stared out the window for a minute. "I keep wondering how I can find this kind of freedom after I leave here. When I think about what could be waiting for me at home, I don't want to even think about going back."

"Have you thought any more about talking to the FBI, maybe letting them protect you?"

Kendra sighed. "Every time I think about it, I remember how smothered I felt before I came here." Her eyes met his. "I just don't think I can live like that again."

Charlie took a deep breath. "If the Malibu Stalker finds you, you may not live at all."

She fell silent for a minute. Then she nodded slowly. "Which is why I'm not going back to Malibu."

"What?"

"If all of this guy's victims lived in Malibu, then I'll steer clear of there until they catch him," Kendra told him. "I can move back to my house in Nashville, or I have a condo in Phoenix I can stay at."

"That's not a bad idea, but you should really still have some kind of protection," Charlie said gently. "If this guy has keyed in on you, moving won't necessarily stop him from coming after you. Serial killers tend to be obsessive. They don't stop until they get what they want or until they are arrested."

Her eyebrows drew together in concentration. "Sounds like you know a lot about this kind of stuff."

Charlie shrugged and chose his words carefully. "I should. We study a variety of criminal cases in law school. Serial killers are definitely among the scariest."

An unexpected edge came into her voice. "Well, I'm sure I'll sleep well tonight now."

"I'm sorry, Kendra," Charlie said, wondering if he had pushed too hard. "I'm just worried about you."

"I know." She managed to keep her voice steady, but Charlie could see the tears glistening in her eyes. Immediately, a stab of guilt shot through him.

"Hey, I really am sorry," Charlie began, shifting to take a seat beside her. "I didn't mean to scare you."

"I know," Kendra managed. Then she leaned into him, and Charlie automatically wrapped his arm around her shoulder. She took a deep breath, as though fighting against her emotions. "I guess I just keep hoping that all of this will go away, that the police will find out who the stalker is so I can feel safe again."

"They'll find him," Charlie assured her, praying his words were true. He tried not to think about how well she fit beside him, but he couldn't manage to resist lifting a hand to toy with the ends of her hair.

She looked up at him, those fascinating green eyes so full of trust. "I can't imagine what I would have done if you hadn't come up here. You've been a godsend."

Charlie managed to smile as he tried to ignore the attraction that sizzled between them. "I don't know about that. I think I'm the lucky one."

She shifted slightly so she could see his face better. "How so?"

"For one thing, this trip has given me the chance to get to know you," Charlie told her.

"I hope that's a good thing."

"Yeah, that's a good thing." He gave her shoulder a squeeze and then forced himself to pull away and stand up. "We should get some sleep."

Kendra nodded, but she didn't stand. Instead, she spoke, her voice hesitant. "Charlie?"

"Yeah?"

"Do you think you could . . ." She trailed off for a moment. Then she took a deep breath and asked, "Would you mind giving me a blessing?"

"I'd be happy to give you a blessing," Charlie responded automatically. The question had caught him off guard, but he found himself touched by the simplicity of her request and by her obvious faith. He circled the couch so he could stand behind her, trying to recall the last time someone had asked him to exercise his priesthood. He found himself a little nervous when he realized that he hadn't given anyone a blessing outside of his immediate family since he had completed his mission almost eight years ago. "What's your full name?"

"Kendra Elizabeth."

He uttered a silent prayer for inspiration as he laid his hands on Kendra's head and began. He was hesitant at first, his words awkward. Then he felt the Spirit flow through him as he offered Kendra a blessing of comfort and peace. He assured her that her Heavenly Father loved her and that He was mindful of her needs and the innermost desires of her heart.

Charlie's voice caught with emotion when he continued to tell her that the Lord had put people in her life to help her with her current challenges and that, with faith, she could overcome all obstacles placed before her.

As soon as Charlie finished, Kendra looked up, her face streaked with tears. She offered him a watery smile and whispered, "Thank you."

Charlie nodded, not trusting his voice as he stepped to her side.

Kendra reached for his hand and gave it a squeeze. "You know, it was really nice being able to ask for a blessing without having to pick up the phone first. I've always wondered what that would be like."

Charlie looked at her a little confused before remembering that she had grown up without the priesthood in her home. "I guess that's something I always took for granted."

She nodded and gave him a sleepy look. "Good night, Charlie."

"Good night." He picked up the lantern and followed her to her bedroom doorway to make sure she could see okay. Then he moved into the next room and turned down his covers. He set the lantern on the bedside table and knelt down on the floor.

As he began his nightly prayer, he found himself plagued with old doubts and unresolved questions. He thought of the woman he'd planned to marry more than two years before and of the events that had transpired before he'd realized Lisa didn't love him as much as she loved his social status. Even though he understood that all women weren't like that, logic hadn't helped him get past the hurt enough to start dating again.

His early years of dating had been so fun and carefree, and he desperately wanted to find someone he could be that way with again. And he found himself asking for guidance on what to do about Kendra. When he had blessed her, he knew that he had been put here with her for a purpose. Now he needed to know what that purpose was. His questions poured out, and he prayed that he would find the answers soon. He especially hoped that he could find a way to tell Kendra the truth about his being with the FBI.

When he finally ended his prayer, he climbed into bed beneath the stack of blankets, his thoughts once again dwelling on the intriguing woman lying in the next room.

Chapter 19

Charlie slept restlessly and woke early with a new resolve. He needed to keep a professional distance between himself and Kendra. He kept letting himself get pulled into the illusion that life was normal and that they were both free to pursue a relationship, but as fascinating as he found her, Kendra was a target and the possible means to finding the man who was responsible for six murders. It was high time he get his priorities straight and stop letting himself get distracted.

The last thing he needed was to get attached to another woman who wouldn't support his career choice. Kendra's lifestyle would never mesh with his, even if she was willing to date an FBI agent. Her life was concerts and television appearances. His was stakeouts and court dates. And in addition to all of that, the very nature of his job—protection—didn't sit well with her. It could never work.

Then he glanced through the open door of Kendra's room, and he felt his heart melt. Her petite frame was buried beneath a mountain of blankets, and only her head was visible. She was turned toward him, her dark eyelashes contrasting against her porcelain skin. Sometime during the night, she must have gotten chilled because there was now a knit cap covering her head that hadn't been there when they'd gone to bed.

He barely resisted the urge to move into the room to brush the hair off her cheek and feel the softness of her skin. His heart squeezed in his chest as he turned from her and forced himself to deal with the cold reality facing her. He moved to put another log on the fire before returning to the bedroom he had temporarily claimed as his own.

Instinctively, he flipped the light switch to confirm that the electricity was still out. He then retrieved his cell phone from the night table and checked the time. Seven thirty-five. He called Elias, keeping his voice low when he answered.

"Is everything okay?"

"Yeah, but I wanted to let you know that we lost electricity up here yesterday."

"Do you want me to send someone up there to pick you up? We can get ahold of a couple of snowmobiles if we need to."

"Actually, the road's closed at the main pass so even snowmobiles can't get through," Charlie told him. "Believe it or not, we're doing okay so far. Kendra is staying over at my place, and there's a wood stove here for heat and cooking."

"You're starting to sound like a Boy Scout."

Charlie couldn't help it. "Hey, I got my Eagle."

"Figures." Elias chuckled. "How's the girl holding up? Any progress with getting her to consider protection?"

"Still working on it." Charlie glanced at the door, realizing that Kendra could wake up any minute. "Any progress on that person of interest I mentioned?"

"Actually, I wanted to talk to you about that." Elias's voice turned serious. "We can place Jed Burgess in California at the time of at least two murders so far."

"Are you serious?"

"Yeah. Ray found hotel receipts lasting for about ten days each time," Elias told him. "Both times, he left right around the time the victim was killed."

"That's crazy. I didn't think it could really be him."

"Sometimes these cases break more by luck than anything else," Elias said. "Coramavich is heading up your way this morning to pick him up and bring him in for questioning."

Charlie thought about the ex-boyfriend Kendra had mentioned. He moved to the door and looked out to make sure Kendra wasn't in the hall. Then he closed the door and lowered his voice. "I actually have another name for you to check out. Steve DeFoe is an old boyfriend. Their break-up was two or three years ago. If it was three—"

"Then the timing could coincide with when the killings started."

"Exactly," Charlie said. "Anyway, assault charges were filed, probably in LA, right after the break-up. He got into it with one of the bodyguards."

"We'll check it out." Elias hesitated a moment. "Do you have a way to charge your phone if the electricity doesn't come back on soon?"

"Yeah, I have a car charger with me."

"I still want you to check in with me every night."

"That might be a bit difficult under the circumstances."

"Night, morning. Whenever works. Just keep me up to date."

"I'll do what I can." Charlie hung up and closed his eyes for a moment. Then he moved back into the hall and peeked into Kendra's room once more. Suddenly, the challenge of dealing with their basic needs seemed like the easy obstacle facing him. Keeping his distance from the beauty lying a few feet away was the one he wasn't sure he was ready for.

* * *

"Elias?" Ray Underwood put a hand on the doorjamb to Elias's office and waited for his boss to look up. "You have a minute?"

"What's up?"

"We've got a problem," Ray began. "I just got a call from Coramavich. He can't find Jed Burgess."

"What do you mean he can't find him? That town only has a population of about thirty during the winter months."

"Yeah, but with the electricity out up there, a lot of the locals have left town."

"What about his parents' place?"

"They were home, but he wasn't. His mother said he headed up to Flagstaff for a few days to visit some friends. She said she didn't know where he was staying. It's hard to say if she was covering for him or not," he told him. "When they checked out his place, the truck registered to Jed Burgess wasn't there, but his snowmobile was. Odds are he didn't go up the mountain in his truck since the road leading up to where Charlie is staying is still impassible."

"Did they check out the road?"

Ray nodded. "Yeah, and they said there wasn't any possibility of anyone making it past there until they get a plow in from Flagstaff to clear it out."

"When's that supposed to happen?"

"End of the week at the earliest."

Elias shook his head and muttered, "Great."

"Do you want me to call Charlie and let him know that Jed Burgess is still at large?"

"No, he's got enough to worry about."

"What about the other guy, DeFoe?"

"We pulled the arrest report. The incident happened three months before the first victim was found."

"Do you really think it could be him?" Ray asked skeptically. "If it is, that would mean that Kendra is the person the Malibu Stalker has been obsessing over this whole time."

"It's definitely a long shot, but right now, we're chasing anything and everything."

"So we've got two suspects," Ray said.

"Three if you include Zack Prescott, the dancer that the LAPD questioned. They're still checking out his alibis," Elias told him. "The LA office is doing a work up on the ex-boyfriend. They should have enough data to pick him up for questioning within the next day or two."

"They checked out the computers of the six victims. None of them had spyware like the program that was running on Kendra Blake's laptop."

"Maybe the spyware isn't related to the murders," Elias considered. "We still aren't sure the bombings at Kendra's concert and Joslyn's photo shoot have anything to do with the serial killer."

"I know. Right now, everything is just speculation," Ray said.

"Stay on top of it," Elias ordered. "William Blake is understandably concerned about his granddaughter, and I'd like to have some solid news to give him the next time he calls."

Ray nodded somberly. "Yes, sir."

* * *

Sterling Blake paced the room repeatedly, his hand in his pocket, his fingers wrapped around his cell phone.

"Honey, you're going to wear a path on that carpet. Come sit down."

"I don't want to sit down. I can't believe we haven't heard anything from her." Sterling had pulled in a few favors to postpone the filming of his new movie, but he knew he only had a few more days before he would have to go back to work. At least the movie was nearly finished. Three or four more days of shooting at the studio, and then he could refocus on what was really important right now. Finding his oldest daughter.

"Your dad said she called him a few days ago."

"Aren't you worried?"

"Of course I'm worried, but she's a smart girl. I'm sure she's fine."

"Why did she turn to my parents for help instead of us?"

Monica Blake tilted her head and gave him a knowing look. "What would you have done if she'd called us?"

"You know exactly what I would have done." Sterling stopped pacing long enough to face his wife. "I would have traced her call and sent the Parsons to bring her home."

"Like I said, Kendra is a smart girl. I'm sure she knew what your reaction would be, and she obviously isn't ready to come home yet." She pushed a strand of her dark hair back behind her ear. "If you keep forcing all this security on her, you're going to drive her away."

Sterling barely heard his wife's concerns. Instead, his mind was already mulling over possible options. "Maybe I should see if Alan can set up a trace on my parents' phone."

"Sterling, stop. If she needs our help, she'll call."

"I hate not knowing where she is or how to get in touch with her."

"I know." Monica stood up and crossed the room to lay a hand on his arm. "But for now, we have to accept that she's a grown woman and that she can take care of herself."

"If anything happens to her . . ."

"Nothing's going to happen to her," she assured him. "I'm sure you'll figure something out to make sure she stays safe."

Sterling nodded slowly. "Actually, I do have an idea."

* * *

Kendra rolled up the sleeves of the sweatshirt Charlie had lent her and started rinsing the dinner dishes as Charlie picked up a dish towel beside her. She smiled down into the sink, amazed at how easily they had fallen into a routine. The electricity had been out for four days, and somehow, Charlie had made the inconvenience an adventure. He included her in his numerous self-imposed chores, from digging his car out from under the snow to cooking meals and keeping up with the fire in the stove. They played games during the day and spent their nights talking in the dark. They had even started reading the scriptures together each morning.

Most of all, Charlie talked to her. Really talked to her. She couldn't remember anyone taking the time to get to know her like this or anyone who wanted to know more than what was right on the surface. He asked questions about her, her past, and her plans for the future. He was also genuine when he talked about his own family and about the various challenges they'd faced in the past.

In just a few short days, Kendra already felt closer to him than anyone else besides perhaps her grandparents and her sister. Even her own parents probably knew less about her hopes and dreams for the future than Charlie did now. She supposed part of that was because they shared the same religious beliefs, including a desire to someday marry in the temple.

It was odd, she realized, that she had been so desperate to find some time alone, and yet, now she couldn't imagine what it would have been like to not have Charlie to talk to, to confide in.

She wasn't quite sure how to define their relationship. Friendship, certainly, but perhaps the beginning of something more. Whether Charlie would ever act on that something more was the real question. Ever since he brought up the Malibu Stalker, he had been oddly careful not to touch her beyond a brotherly pat on the shoulder or an occasional brush of their hands.

At first, she thought she had misinterpreted his interest. She had been so sure he'd been about to kiss her that night, but since then, there were times she thought she had imagined that tender moment together. Then she would catch him looking at her, and that warm rush would wash over her again.

She had wanted him to kiss her, a fact that still surprised her. So much time had passed since she'd dated, certainly a lot longer than the tabloids would have led people to believe. Now she hoped Charlie would act on the attraction that continued to spark between them.

In fact, she found herself torn between hoping the electricity wouldn't be restored so she would have the excuse to spend more time with Charlie and wanting the power to come back on so she could once again enjoy the many luxuries it provided.

Amazing, Kendra thought now, *that so many basic needs are so dependent on electricity*. She was beyond grateful that Charlie had stocked up on oil for the lantern he'd bought and that he had proven to be quite adept at cooking on the wood stove.

Although preparing food was a constant chore, Kendra found that mealtime was her favorite part of the day. She liked working side by side with Charlie and sitting down across from him at the table as they shared that time together.

She smiled as she considered the way they had settled into their easy, almost domestic routine. They had breakfast together each morning, and then Charlie spent time reading through his stack of files while she worked on her music. After lunch each day, they played games or did various chores around the cabin. Then night came, and Kendra could revel in the quiet, undisturbed conversations they shared. Typically, he convinced her to play him one of her songs, not the popular ones he knew from the radio but whatever she was working on that day.

Normally, she didn't like to share her music until it was more polished, but she found she enjoyed playing for Charlie. He didn't seem to care that she often zoned out while she was fiddling with a new melody. At times, she even found herself bouncing ideas off him, surprised at how helpful his comments could be, even though he wasn't a musician.

She could feel herself drawing closer to him, falling for him in a way she hadn't expected. The more those feelings intensified, the more frustrated she became. *If only I had more experience with men*, she thought to herself. Of course, with her career it was unlikely things would work out with Charlie anyway. She supposed she should just enjoy the moment and not worry about the future until she really had to.

She thought about the way she had waited each day, hoping that Charlie would do or say something to give her a glimpse of how he was feeling.

Suddenly, her fingertips brushed his as she handed him a plate, and the resulting spark of attraction drew her back to the present.

Pulling the plug on the sink, she looked over at him and told herself to stop obsessing. Then she opened her mouth and couldn't stop the words from escaping. "Are you going to want to see me once we get out of here?"

Charlie shifted to face her. "What do you mean?"

"You know, get together." Her shoulders lifted. "Go out."

He looked down at her for a moment, as though debating what he should say. Then slowly, he nodded. "I would like to go out with you once this whole ordeal is over, but there's something I need to tell you."

"What?" Kendra asked, instinctively bracing against Charlie's serious tone.

"Kendra, the real reason I came up here was to—" The phone rang, interrupting whatever he might have said.

Charlie's jaw clenched, and he pulled his phone from his pocket. The moment he looked down at the caller ID, his whole body tensed. He looked down at Kendra, shook his head, and said apologetically, "I'm sorry, but I've got to take this."

Kendra nodded automatically. She watched helplessly as he flipped the phone open, barked out a hello, disappeared into the bedroom, and closed the door between them.

Chapter 20

"What?" Charlie snapped, not quite able to keep the frustration out of his voice.

"Can you talk?" Elias asked in lieu of a greeting.

"I can now." He glanced at the closed door and tried to steady his emotions. "What's going on?"

"A couple of things you need to know," Elias began. "First of all, we haven't been able to locate Jed Burgess. It looks like he may have left town because of the power outage."

"Great," Charlie muttered as he considered the possibilities.

"Coramavich paid a visit to his parents' place, and they said he went to Flagstaff, but they didn't know where he was staying."

"Any more details on whether he was in California at the time of the other murders?"

"Yeah. So far we can place him in the LA area for four out of the six," Elias told him. "We're still waiting on the last of his credit card records to see if we can place him there for the other two."

"What's taking so long to get the credit card records?"

"It was a mix up with the credit card company. They gave us access to the wrong account," Elias said with a touch of annoyance in his voice. "That should be cleared up today."

"You said you had a couple things to tell me. What else is going on?"

"The LA office did some digging on Steve DeFoe. It turns out he was at her concert the night of the incident."

"Really?" Charlie considered this newest information. "Did you track down the arrest record for DeFoe?"

"Yeah. It looks like the break-up with Kendra happened just over three years ago."

An uncomfortable thought weaved through Charlie's mind, one he hadn't entertained before, and one he hoped to put to rest quickly. "Did the break-up happen before or after the first murder?"

"It was before the first murder," Elias said, and Charlie could hear him rustling through papers. "A little more than three months before." Silence hung on the line for a moment, and then Elias voiced Charlie's fears. "You're wondering if Steve DeFoe is the Malibu Stalker? If he's killing people who remind him of Kendra?"

"I hope not, but the timing would fit." Charlie ran a hand over his face. "What if Kendra is the person the stalker is fixated on? If she is, it doesn't matter where she tries to hide; he's going to keep coming after her."

"Ray and I were talking about that earlier. The LA office is going to look into his whereabouts for the dates of all the murders. And, of course, we'll keep checking out Burgess, especially since we can place him in California for four of the murders."

"Again, what is Burgess's tie to Malibu? The only one I can think of is his association with the Blake family," Charlie said, his stomach churning as he spoke. "Think about it. Kendra has had heavy security most of her life, especially since she was a teenager. One of these guys fixates on her but can't get past the bodyguards to see or talk to her. He then takes out his frustration by finding substitutes."

"It would fit the psychological profile of the killer," Elias said. "If the Malibu Stalker has fixated on her, that might also explain why she's the only one with the spyware program on her computer."

"What spyware?"

"Apparently, someone managed to plant some kind of high-tech spyware on Kendra's laptop. We haven't been able to track down the guy who was monitoring it."

"It's sounding more and more like she could be the real target." Charlie let out a shaky breath. "Look, I've got to tell Kendra who I am."

"Do you think she'll accept protection?"

"I don't know." Charlie ran his fingers through his hair. "When I was talking to her earlier, she mentioned staying clear of Malibu for the time being."

"But if you're right, she may be the primary target," Elias commented. "Maybe it's time you convince her to hide out somewhere else for a while. Would she trust you enough to go with you to a safer location?"

"Are you asking me to trick her into going to a safe house?"

"It may be necessary for her own protection," Elias said. "You said yourself that she was planning on hiding out for a few weeks anyway. What are the chances she would go with you?"

"I don't know." Dozens of thoughts raced through his head, but at the heart of them all were his developing feelings for Kendra. He hesitated a moment. Then with a sigh, he admitted, "She thinks she has feelings for me."

"That's good."

"Not really. Not when I have to lie to her."

"Just give us another day or two. A plow is supposed to be coming down from Flagstaff to clear the road by tomorrow or the next day. If one of these leads doesn't pan out, we're going to have to convince Kendra to let us protect her somewhere else, especially since you're without power," Elias insisted.

"I just don't see her buying into it. She's Mormon. The only reason she's willing to spend the night in the same house with me right now is for survival," Charlie insisted. "I can't imagine she would be willing to set up house somewhere with me under normal circumstances. Maybe we should bring in a female agent."

"That will only work if she agrees to protection. And she trusts you," Elias reminded him, sending another wave of guilt through Charlie.

"Do you have someplace in mind?"

"Actually, I do. There's a cabin in Oak Creek Canyon I used a few years ago. It's secluded enough that no one's going to find you, but it's close enough to where you are now that we won't have any trouble relocating you."

"What story am I using?"

"A friend from work found out you didn't have electricity and offered to lend you his cabin in Oak Creek. Keep it simple," Elias told him.

"I'll see what I can do," Charlie said. As soon as he hung up the phone, he closed his eyes for a moment, praying she would agree to protection. If he was right, if she really was the person the stalker was obsessed with, she was in more danger than either of them could have imagined. Charlie was afraid to think about how she would react to the news and to the fact that he had been hiding the truth from her all this time.

Charlie stuck his phone back in his pocket and walked back out into the living room. Kendra was sitting on the couch, fiddling on her guitar. When she looked up, her expression was guarded.

Charlie thought of Elias's words and of his suggestion to use Kendra's feelings to let him take her somewhere safe. Moving forward, Charlie tried to convince himself that it was that suggestion, not his own selfish interests, that gave him the courage to sit beside her. He was on the job, and he couldn't fail.

Before he could find any words to say, Kendra asked, "Who was that on the phone?"

"That was my boss. He's a bit anxious for me to get back to work."

Trepidation crept into her voice. "So you'll be leaving soon?"

"Maybe." Charlie considered his words carefully. "They're supposed to clear the road in the next day or two. With the snow melting off a bit, I should be able to make it back down the mountain tomorrow or the next day."

"Oh." Kendra swallowed hard and looked away.

"I want you to come with me."

Her eyes whipped around to meet his. "What?"

"The case I'm researching will only take me an hour or two a day, so I can take another week or two before I have to get back to the office. But I do need to be somewhere that has reliable electricity. My boss has a cabin down in Oak Creek Canyon. He offered to let us stay there."

"You told him about me?"

"Not your name, just that I had a friend staying with me that I hoped could stay there too," Charlie told her.

"Really?" Confusion, hope, and a touch of vulnerability flashed in her eyes.

Charlie reached for her hand and gave it a squeeze. "Yeah. Really."

The spark between them flickered, and Charlie felt his emotions tangling. He pushed aside his guilt for the moment, letting himself get lost in the sweet simplicity of two people finding friendship, and maybe something more.

He accepted the inevitable fact that he would hurt her before this ordeal was over, but he wouldn't think about that now. Instead, he brought her hand to his lips. "What do you say? Will you come with me? I really don't want to leave you here alone." Her fingers briefly tensed in his before Charlie added, "Besides, I'd like the chance to spend more time with you."

Slowly, a smile bloomed on her face. "I think I'd like that."

Charlie's smile mirrored hers. "Good. Now, I think it's time for a rematch."

"Are you sure?"

"Absolutely." Charlie reached for the deck of cards sitting on the end table. "It's about time my luck changed."

"Okay." Kendra gave him a smug smile. "But remember. You asked for it."

Chapter 21

He slipped through the front door of her condominium, waiting motionlessly inside the door for a moment to make sure he really was alone. He already knew she wasn't here, but he needed some kind of connection until the day he would see her again in person. Listening to her music no longer helped fill the void, nor did staring at photographs of her.

His gloved fingers curled around the shiny silver key in his hand. Picking the lock had been easy enough the first time he had come here looking for Kendra, but he had decided that she wouldn't want him to have to break in. After all, they belonged together. She said so in one of her songs.

Making a key for himself had been simple enough once he'd taken the time to gather the right tools. And he wasn't worried about anyone seeing him and being suspicious; he belonged there. Besides, the neighbors would certainly get used to seeing him once he and Kendra officially became a couple. For now, though, he would keep his presence a secret.

He pocketed the key and moved slowly through the living room. A single framed photo rested on an end table. His lips curved up when he lifted it to eye level. Kendra and her baby sister. Kendra wearing blue.

The photograph still in his hand, he continued into the hallway and made his way to her bedroom. A thick duvet in bronze and cream stripes covered the bed, pillows in varying earth tones artistically arranged on top of it. He picked up a pillow and held it to his face, slowly breathing in the scent. Was that a trace of her perfume he smelled? Could it have lingered here since her last visit?

Setting the photograph on the bedside table, he slipped his shoes off and gently climbed onto the bed. He let himself relax against the sea of pillows and then stared up at the ceiling. Hugging a pillow to his chest, he let himself imagine. Soon Kendra would be here beside him. Soon she would be his.

* * *

Kendra stretched her arms over her head as she shook the sleep out of her brain. She didn't notice that she'd kicked off the top layer of her blankets during the night or that there was a whoosh of hot air blowing through the vents. Instead, she rolled out of bed and headed down the hall toward the living room to make sure the fire was still burning.

To her surprise, Charlie was stretched out on the couch, his Bible lying open on his chest and the lantern flickering on the table beside him. He stirred as she walked closer. His face was shadowed with a two-day beard, and even in sleep, there was a faint line between his eyes as though he were deep in concentration. She wondered for a moment if he was ever truly at peace. Then she noticed the splash of light spilling into the living room from the kitchen.

Electricity! The possibility of a hot shower sent a thrill through her, followed by the delight that she would be able to do laundry before she completely depleted her limited supply of clean clothes.

"Charlie! Are you awake?"

Charlie shifted and rolled onto his back, but he didn't open his eyes. "Hmmm."

Kendra grinned down at him as she sat on the edge of the couch beside him and nudged his shoulder. "Wake up. The electricity's back on!"

His eyes remained closed, but he shifted to make room for her, and his arm snaked around her waist to hold her in place.

"Charlie," she repeated, her voice growing thick as an unexpected warmth seeped through her. "Wake up."

Slowly, his eyes opened. Then he gave her a lazy smile, and his hand trailed up to stroke her back.

She didn't realize that she'd leaned closer until her lips were on his. She didn't think of anything except for the way Charlie's lips felt pressed against hers and the unexpected sense of acceptance and belonging.

She pulled back, embarrassment cresting even as she stared down at him. Then he shifted to sit up and pinned her with his deep blue stare. Before she could find any words, he stroked a hand down her cheek and leaned forward, hesitating for the briefest moment before he kissed her again. His fingers crept up into her hair, tangling in it as the kiss lingered and another wave of sensations crashed over her.

When he pulled back, he stared at her with a combination of confusion and something else she couldn't quite identify.

"You have an interesting way of waking a man up," Charlie said with the beginnings of a smile. "Not that I'm complaining."

A blush rose to her cheeks, and she scrambled to stand up. "I just wanted to tell you that the electricity is back on. I didn't mean to . . ."

Her voice trailed off. She didn't mean to what? Kiss him? Find that unexpected feeling of belonging in his arms?

Charlie stood as well and nodded at the hall. "Since we have electricity again, I'm going to go shave and grab a quick shower. Then I can go check if the road is clear yet."

"I thought you would want to stay here now that the electricity is back on."

He jerked a shoulder. "I could, but there's too big of a chance that we'll just get snowed in again."

"Oak Creek Canyon isn't much better than Pinewood."

"Yeah, but the roads get plowed in the canyon. That doesn't always happen here," Charlie reminded her. "Come on. My boss's cabin is supposed to be really nice. We can both get some work done, hang out, maybe even order a pizza."

"What about my car? Do you think we'd be able to dig it out?"

Charlie looked at her skeptically and slowly shook his head. "I doubt it can make it out of here yet, at least not safely. You can just drive down with me, and we can come back for it as soon as the snow melts off a bit more."

"At the rate the snow keeps coming down around here, I might not be able to drive my car again until spring."

"Worst case, I can get a tow truck to come in and bring it down the mountain for you. Once it's out on the freeway, we'd be able to drive it."

"I guess that's true." Kendra nodded. "I'll go ahead and get breakfast started."

Charlie gave her an odd look. Then he nodded. "Sounds good."

* * *

Charlie put the last of his clothes into his suitcase and zipped it closed. Then he took another look around his bedroom. He had already loaded his laptop and printer into his SUV, along with the groceries and supplies left over from his trip to the general store. He decided they'd need to stop by the store on their way out of town to do some snooping as to Jed Burgess's whereabouts. But he had one thing he had to do first. He had to tell Kendra the truth. The whole truth.

He still wasn't quite sure what had happened between them earlier. He had tried to rationalize that the only reason he had kissed Kendra was that he had been half asleep, but rationalizing that fact or the fact that she had kissed him first didn't negate the spark that had flashed between them or the reality that he wanted to kiss her again. Soon.

Perhaps it was selfish of him to come clean now and risk her kicking him out of her life and ultimately refusing his protection, but he couldn't keep pretending that he was someone he wasn't. The simple fact was that he was falling for her, and he didn't want to lie anymore.

And he couldn't very well stop by the store without making sure that Kendra wouldn't inadvertently mention that they were leaving or tell Mrs. Burgess where they were going.

He carried his suitcase outside and loaded it in his car. Then he trudged through the snow toward Kendra's cabin. His stomach tightened into knots as he climbed the front steps and strode across the porch to knock.

"Hi." Kendra waved him inside.

Charlie rubbed his arms against the chill in the room. The heater was going full blast, but Kendra hadn't started a fire, presumably because they were getting ready to leave. "Are you all packed?"

"Almost." Kendra took a step toward the hallway leading to her bedroom. "I'll only be a few more minutes if you want to wait here."

He reached for her hand and waited for her eyes to lift to meet his. "Actually, I wanted to talk to you first, if you don't mind."

Her eyebrows drew together. "Is something wrong?"

"Not exactly." He led her to the couch and sat down beside her. Then he took a deep breath. "There's something I need to tell you."

"Okay," she said cautiously.

"I know I let you believe that I came up here to get away from work for a while." Charlie's heart squeezed in his chest when she pulled her hand free of his and her expression became guarded. He took another deep breath and forced himself to continue. "Your grandfather actually sent me up here to make sure you were safe."

"What?"

"He was worried about you after what happened at your concert," Charlie rushed on. "Neither of us had any idea that the Malibu Stalker might be after you when he arranged for me to come."

Kendra stood up and took a step back. "So all this time you've been lying to me?"

"Kendra . . ." Charlie's voice trailed off as he stood as well. Before he could continue, a loud metallic bang sounded through the cabin.

Startled, her attention shifted away from him. "What was that?"

"I don't know." Charlie started toward the kitchen where the sound had originated, and now he could hear a loud hissing sound. He stepped past the kitchen counter to see a steady spray of water seeping out from under the sink. "It looks like a pipe busted. It probably froze while the power was out."

"Great," Kendra muttered. "What do we do now?"

Charlie pulled the cabinet open and searched futilely for a shutoff valve. "I can't turn off the water from here. Do you know where the main water shutoff valve is?"

"Yeah." she nodded and motioned toward the back door. "It's out there under three feet of snow."

Charlie sighed as he made his way down the hall. He grabbed a shovel from the mudroom, along with the wrench hanging on the wall that was clearly kept there for the purpose of turning on and off the cabin's water supply. "Point me in the right direction."

Kendra opened the door leading to the back porch and pointed at a tree on the edge of the property line. "It's about three feet in front of that tree over there."

He stepped out into the deep snow and turned back to face her. "You might want to throw a couple towels on the floor to soak up the water until I get it turned off."

She didn't speak, but she nodded before she turned and closed the door between them.

As soon as she disappeared back inside, Charlie trudged to the spot she had indicated and used the shovel to start clearing the snow away. He tried not to think about the look of betrayal on Kendra's face or what she might say once she had time to let his confession sink in. He focused on the task at hand, steadily shoveling snow from one spot in the yard to another.

After several minutes of working in the frigid cold, the shovel finally struck metal. Lifting the heavy steel covering away took another minute, but he finally managed to shift it aside so he could access the main water valve. Then he used the wrench to turn the water off completely. He tucked the wrench into his pocket and turned toward the cabin just as he saw a pickup truck lumber into the driveway.

Possibilities raced through his mind of who might be in that truck—none of them good. He dropped the shovel and ran toward the back door. His already rapidly beating heart picked up speed as he heard the car door slam followed by hasty footsteps on the front steps. His hand trembled as he pulled his weapon from its holster and leaped onto the back porch.

Surely Kendra would know not to answer the door to anyone. She knew that her safety was at stake, that she couldn't trust anyone right now. Then he heard voices, and his anxiety went into overdrive. What would he do if the Malibu Stalker had already found her?

He tried to focus on his training, on all the hostage scenarios he had studied while at the FBI Academy, but in the forefront of his thoughts was his concern about Kendra. He uttered a silent prayer, one he kept repeating over and over. She had to be okay. She just had to.

Cautiously but quickly, Charlie pushed the door open even as dread curled in his stomach. He made it down the hall in a few long strides, his weapon cold in his hand. When he saw Kendra calmly standing by the couch, a combination of relief and confusion pulsed through him. Then his focus shifted to the older man standing beside her, and his training took over.

"Hold it right there!" Charlie's voice was clipped and commanding.

The older man held his hands out to his side as Kendra's eyes widened and her mouth dropped open.

Kendra stared at his weapon for several long seconds before she lifted her eyes to look at his face. Finally, she managed to ask, "What are you doing?"

Before Charlie could answer, the older man spoke. "If I show you my temple recommend, will you promise not to shoot me?"

"Who are you?" Charlie demanded, his eyes an icy blue as he kept his weapon trained on the new arrival.

"Put that gun away!" Kendra insisted. "This is my grandfather."

Charlie's posture relaxed slightly, and slowly, he lowered his weapon. "Your grandfather?"

"That's right." Kendra's eyes were wide, her face pale. Then she shook her head in confusion. "Wait a minute. I thought you knew each other."

"Not exactly," Charlie started.

Her eyes narrowed, and she pointed at his weapon. "And what are you doing with that thing?"

Charlie glanced down at his gun briefly before he holstered it at the small of his back in a practiced move and tried to ignore the embarrassment that was quickly working its way to the surface. He didn't answer Kendra, but instead addressed her grandfather. "Sorry. I saw you pull up, and I didn't want to take any chances, not after everything that's been going on with Kendra."

"I can understand that." He nodded and then extended his hand. "William Blake."

"Charlie Whitmore." Charlie shook the older man's hand. Then he looked over at Kendra and saw that her mind was working through the fact that he and her grandfather clearly hadn't ever met before. She'd lifted a hand to her heart as though trying to steady its rhythm, and Charlie wondered if her heart could possibly be racing as fast as his was.

Kendra clenched her teeth as though trying to settle her emotions. Then she looked at Charlie, her voice vibrating with fury when she asked, "Who are you?"

A sense of trepidation shot through him when he realized Kendra hadn't completely understood what he'd tried to tell her a few minutes before. He sent Kendra an apologetic look, his eyes staying on hers as he said bluntly, "I'm FBI."

"What?" Kendra's mouth dropped open.

"That's what I was trying to tell you—" Charlie began.

"You mean, all this time . . . I thought . . ." Kendra trailed off. She shook her head, and color rose to her cheeks. Her expression filled with righteous indignation when she finally managed to form a complete sentence. "You were here because someone *paid* you to watch over me?"

"It wasn't like that," Charlie said weakly, and he shook his head.

Her voice was both frigid and commanding as she held up a hand before he could continue. "Don't."

Charlie grasped for words, any words that might erase the look of betrayal on her face. "Kendra, I care about you. I don't want anything to happen to you."

"Ken." William laid a hand on her arm. "It's not Charlie's fault. He was under orders not to tell you who he was."

"Which makes you as bad as him." Kendra sent her grandfather a withering stare before turning back to face Charlie. "So the only reason you came here was that I was your latest assignment. You must have thought I was an idiot to believe that it was just some great coincidence that we were here at the same time."

"That's not what I thought." Charlie could almost see the barriers Kendra was putting up between them, and a skittering sense of panic shot through him. "I didn't want you to think of me as a bodyguard."

Anger vibrated through her voice. "But that's what you were, weren't you?"

"Not exactly." He raked his fingers through his hair in an impatient gesture. "Let me explain."

"I don't need you to explain." Kendra's chin lifted, and her eyes cooled.

"Kendra—" Charlie started to apologize, but Kendra stepped back and shook her head before he could cross to her.

Before he could say anything further, another engine sounded outside.

"The road gets cleared, and now it's like Grand Central Station," Charlie muttered and moved to the window. He motioned to the man behind the wheel of a late-model SUV pulling up outside. "Do you know this guy?"

William walked to the window, pulled the curtain aside, and looked out. "He looks familiar. I think he's one of Sterling's bodyguards."

"Bruce?" Kendra started to move forward.

"Don't let him see you," Charlie warned.

Kendra sent him a withering stare, but she followed his advice and moved to the edge of the window, where she could peek out without being seen. She glanced over at her grandfather and shook her head. "It's Alan Parsons. My dad must have sent him. Perfect," Kendra muttered and then turned to face Charlie. "First I find out the FBI's been spying on me, and now this."

"Look, you can be mad at me later," Charlie said with an edge to his voice. "You said Alan was one of your bodyguards. Has he been here before?"

Her mind seemed to clear, and slowly, she shook her head.

William looked at Charlie skeptically. "How do you think he found her?"

"He followed you."

"Why would he follow Grandpa up here?"

"Your father wants you back home." William shook his head in disgust. "He's the one who insisted I check in on you now that the police think the Malibu Stalker might be after you. He must have had this Alan guy follow me."

"That doesn't matter right now." Charlie motioned to the door. "When he knocks, I want you to answer the door and pretend you haven't seen

Kendra. Tell him that she found out you'd assigned a bodyguard to her, and she took off."

His eyebrows lifted. "You want me to lie?"

"Sir, I'm sorry, but that's exactly what I want you to do. It's in your granddaughter's best interest."

Charlie watched the older man consider his request. Relief pulsed through him when William turned to Kendra and said, "Kenny, you go back into one of the bedrooms. Let's make this look believable."

"You're kidding."

"Honey, I just want you to be safe," her grandfather said softly. Then he jerked a thumb at Charlie. "And like it or not, I agree with Charlie. I certainly trust him a lot more than I do those boys your father keeps around him."

Kendra let out a frustrated sigh. Then she turned on her heel and stormed into the bedroom. Charlie let out his own sigh of relief when she closed the door with a quiet click rather than slamming it the way he had expected her to. He turned toward the front door and prayed that once the current dilemma was resolved, Kendra would let him explain. He didn't know what he would do if she refused to forgive him, if she shut him out of her life for good.

Chapter 22

Charlie tried to fight the sick feeling in his stomach as he watched Kendra climb into her grandfather's truck and slam the door. Alan had left within minutes of his arrival. The moment he was out of sight, Kendra's grandfather had started closing down the cabin, arranging for a plumber to come fix the broken pipe and packing his granddaughter's things into his truck. Kendra had remained in her room despite Charlie's efforts to talk to her through the closed door.

When she'd finally come out nearly an hour later, she'd effectively treated Charlie with icy silence. Now he could only watch as Kendra prepared to drive out of his life without any protection from the Malibu Stalker except the seventy-five-year-old man standing in front of him.

"Sir, I realize that you were FBI, but you've got to understand that she needs additional protection," Charlie said as Kendra's grandfather finished locking up the cabin.

"I do." William nodded and then turned to face him. "I also know that we're both in the doghouse with her right now."

"You know her better than I do. How do we fix that?" Charlie asked. "Elias has probably told you that we've already identified three suspects, one of whom we haven't been able to locate. I'm worried."

He nodded sympathetically. "I'll keep her close, and I'll see what I can do to make this right."

"I appreciate that," Charlie said. "I was planning on stopping by the store on my way out of town to see if Mrs. Burgess has heard from Jed, but I would like to follow you and make sure you get to Phoenix okay. Would you mind making a quick stop?"

"There's no need. I already stopped and talked to Eleanor on my way up here. She still hasn't heard from Jed."

"Is there anything else I can do to help?"

"Call Elias, and tell him I want a car outside my house. That will have to do until I can convince Kendra to let the FBI give her some help," William told him. "She may stay mad at me for a while, but I think my wife can talk some sense into her."

Charlie let out the breath he didn't realize he'd been holding. "I hope so." He dug his wallet out of his pocket and slid a business card free. "Here's my number. Please call me if there's anything else I can do."

William nodded. Then he stuffed the card into his pocket, walked over to his truck, and climbed in. Seconds later, the engine roared to life, and all Charlie could do was follow and hope that eventually Kendra would forgive him.

* * *

Kendra peered out the window to see the black sedan parked across the street. "The car's still there." She shook her head and turned to face her grandmother. "I can't believe Charlie and Grandpa did that to me."

Hannah Blake looked up at Kendra, her fingers steadily manipulating yarn and knitting needles. Her serene face was still largely without wrinkles, and her green eyes were nearly the same shade as Kendra's. "I'm sure they're only thinking about your safety."

"That's all anybody ever thinks about." Kendra huffed out a breath and dropped onto the couch beside her grandmother. "But nobody ever thinks about my life or the fact that no one ever lets me live it."

"I know it's hard, sweetie." She patted Kendra's knee and gave her an understanding look. "But from what your grandfather said, it seems they have reason to worry."

"Just like Daddy always had a reason to worry." Kendra rolled her eyes and settled back on the couch, letting her head drop back.

"But this is different," Hannah said gently. "This time there could be a real threat."

Kendra felt the fear curl in her stomach. "I keep hoping that Grandpa and Charlie are wrong."

"You already know that they aren't. I know that you don't want to hear this, but you need to let Grandpa's friends help you." When Kendra didn't respond, Hannah studied her intently. "What's bothering you the most? That this boy lied to you or that you believed him?"

"I was with him for eight days straight, and not once did I suspect his reasons for being there. I didn't just believe him," she said, misery filling her voice. She turned to face her grandmother and felt the tears well up in her eyes. "I really liked him."

"I see." Hannah looked at her in that understanding way of hers. "Did he like you?"

"I thought he did."

"But now you aren't so sure."

She shook her head. "Now I don't know what to believe. For all I know, everything was just a big act on his part."

"Seems to me that he was just trying to protect you."

Kendra shifted and faced her grandmother more fully. "Are you defending him?"

"I'm not defending anyone." She reached over and gave Kendra's knee another comforting squeeze. "But I want you safe. If Charlie Whitmore can keep you that way, maybe you should put your personal feelings aside for now."

"I don't know if I can."

* * *

Charlie read through the Zack Prescott interview and the background information that followed it. With several witnesses corroborating his whereabouts, the investigating officer believed that he could not have been responsible for setting the explosives at either Joslyn Korden's photo shoot or Kendra's concert unless he had somehow utilized a timing device. With the forensics reports still incomplete from the concert, LAPD had decided to err on the side of safety and had dispatched a surveillance detail to monitor Prescott's movements until they could rule him out conclusively.

Jed Burgess still hadn't been picked up, but Charlie was hoping that he would return home soon, now that the power was restored. Until then, Charlie hoped Kendra would tolerate the agent parked across the street from her grandparents' house.

He hated how things had ended between them and that he had been unable to soften the truth when he'd admitted he was with the FBI. He thought of the look on her face when the truth had sunk in. Accusation. Betrayal. Hurt. All the emotions he had hoped to avoid but somehow had known were inevitable.

He'd tried to talk to her after he followed her from Pinewood to her grandparents' house, but she'd disappeared inside the moment her grandfather had put his truck in park. Charlie had been left with no other option but to let one of his fellow agents take over protection duty.

For the past two days, it had taken every ounce of willpower he had to keep from driving past her grandparents' house. He wasn't sure he could hold out much longer.

"Charlie." Elias stepped into his cubicle and waited for Charlie to look up before he continued. "Go home and pack. You're going out on assignment."

"What?" Charlie stared at him. "I thought you wanted me to get caught up on the Malibu Stalker case."

"You can take all of that with you," Elias told him. "As of now, you're back on protection detail for Kendra Blake."

"What?"

"I just got a call from her grandfather. Kendra has agreed to let us protect her."

"Really?" Charlie asked.

"That's right. I've got you set up in a safe house nearby," Elias told him. "I have two agents taking her over there now."

Charlie nodded, trying to ignore the anticipation dancing in his stomach. He wondered what had changed Kendra's mind about accepting protection, and he had the distinct impression that her grandparents were largely responsible for her change of heart. He tried to push those thoughts aside and concentrate on the case. "Any news about Jed Burgess?"

"Nothing yet," Elias said. "Don't worry. We'll keep you in the loop."

"I'd appreciate it." Charlie stood and began packing up the files on his desk. Then he glanced back up at Elias. "How long are you planning on keeping Kendra at the safe house?"

"She agreed to one month."

"A month?" Charlie considered this, not sure what he had expected. Then reality hit full force. "Wait a minute. Are you expecting me to live there with her that whole time?"

"That's exactly what I expect. It will be more secure if we don't have a bunch of agents rotating through there. We'll work this case the best we can for the month she gave us. If we haven't caught the stalker before the month is up, all we can do is offer to help her however we can in setting up her own private security detail."

"Who else is on the detail with me?"

"We're stretched pretty thin right now, so it's only going to be you in the house during the day," he said. "Ray Underwood has volunteered to spend the nights over there with you, and he'll be bringing in your supplies."

"What about backup?"

"We've got it covered. The safe house is on a private road with only one way in, and there's a police station near the entrance. Our tech guys have already tapped into their security cameras to monitor the traffic going into the neighborhood."

"Is that really going to help? We aren't even sure who we're looking for."

"There are only six houses on that street, and we've already got a pretty good handle on who goes in and out of there. I've also assigned Angie Boyter to canvas the area for the first few days just to be safe."

"Thanks," Charlie muttered. He shuffled the files into his briefcase and clicked it shut. "I guess I'll see you later."

Elias nodded. "We'll get this guy, Charlie. It's only a matter of time."

Chapter 23

The feds thought they were closing in. They thought they could keep Kendra hidden from him. They were fools. Kendra would never stay secluded for long, even if she wanted to.

Already, his patience had paid off. He had been meticulous in his search for her, carefully taking the time to check out each of the locations she could have gone to stay out of the public eye, and now he knew exactly where she was. He knew if he waited long enough, he would get the chance to see her again.

Predictably, the fed parked down the street hadn't moved for the past two days. The men sitting inside the car changed every few hours, but the car or one just like it remained in place. He wondered if the FBI agents inside understood how pathetically obvious their stakeout was.

He supposed he should take pity on them. He knew what they looked like, how they thought. They, however, didn't have a clue what drove him. They couldn't possibly know how clever he was, how determined. It was only a matter of time before the feds gave up this fruitless effort of waiting for him outside Kendra's latest hiding place. If they didn't, he would give them something else to worry about, some other substitute.

When a silver sedan approached, he glanced down at his watch. The replacement was two hours early. Curious, he shifted in his seat and adjusted the binoculars that allowed him to see his target from a safe distance. An unexpected wave of anxiety crested when the two agents got out of their respective cars and approached the house where Kendra was hiding. It couldn't be . . .

His jaw clenched, and fury bubbled up inside him when Kendra walked out, flanked by the two men in dark suits. If they thought they could take her away from him, they were sadly mistaken.

He watched as Kendra got into the car and the two men loaded suitcases and Kendra's guitar into the trunk. Then they got back into their identical cars, as though using a decoy was a clever enough ploy to confuse him. He memorized the license plate number of the car Kendra was in and then waited as both vehicles pulled away from the house.

Tossing the binoculars aside, he started his car and pulled out onto the road, reminding himself that soon Kendra would be in his arms. Soon he would be able to kiss her and hold her the way he had dreamed of doing for so long. He thought back to the afternoon he had spent on her bed, dreaming of them together. It was time to make it a reality. He was ready, and he knew she was ready too. Her body—her heart—was practically begging to be his.

* * *

Kendra knew the exact moment Charlie stepped into the little three-bedroom rambler. She would have sworn something in the air changed and pulsed with a familiar energy. Doing her best to ignore it and the voices coming from the cozy living room, Kendra dutifully hung her clothes in the walk-in closet in the master bedroom.

The room was sparsely furnished with only a queen-sized bed and a dresser, but not much else would have fit anyway. The front door opened and closed repeatedly, presumably from Ray and Charlie unloading whatever luggage and supplies Charlie had brought with him. Ray hadn't given her many details about what to expect over the next month, but he had mentioned that Charlie would be the only agent staying with her full time at the safe house.

She was prepared to ignore him, unwilling to consider why he'd lied to her during their time in Pinewood. Her grandfather had said Charlie had been ordered to hide his profession from her, and in the back of her mind, she realized how skillfully he had danced around the truth. He had never actually said he wasn't with the FBI or that he was still working for a law firm. But a lie of omission was still a lie. And the truth still hurt.

Up until the moment when he'd announced that he was FBI, she had let herself get caught up in her growing feelings for Charlie. Now her emotions were tangled at the prospect of spending the next month with him. She couldn't think of the kisses they'd shared without flushing with embarrassment. Was it possible that he really cared about her, or had everything been an act on his part? Not knowing was driving her crazy, but she knew she needed more time before she would be ready to face him.

A door slammed closed, followed by the sound of an engine. Kendra peered out the window to see Ray pulling out of the driveway. She heard footsteps sounding in the hall and busied herself with the last of her unpacking. When those footsteps halted, presumably as Charlie went into one of the other bedrooms, Kendra felt her heart sink. Yes, she was prepared to ignore him. She simply hadn't expected him to ignore her first.

She glanced over at her guitar, considering whether she could motivate herself to write. With a shake of her head, she dug her copy of *Pride and Prejudice* out of her bag. Climbing onto the bed, she flipped the book open and began to read—well, tried to read.

The words blurred in front of her as her anger and embarrassment surfaced once more. The image of their last morning together crowded her mind, her stomach knotting at the realization that she had kissed him first.

But he had kissed her last. He had made her feel something, reminding her of forgotten emotions and stifled dreams. Because of Charlie, she had let herself imagine a life shared with someone else.

Her jaw clenched as footsteps sounded in the hall. She braced for a moment, listening carefully, waiting to see if the footsteps came toward her. She ignored the twinge of disappointment when she heard Charlie walk back down the hall away from her room.

One month, she reminded herself. That was all she'd promised to give the FBI. One month that she could work on her songs uninterrupted. One month for them to investigate and trap the Malibu Stalker. With her grandfather's help, she had already contacted her manager to update him on her plans. Her appearance at one upcoming charity event would have to be canceled, but she was determined to fulfill her commitment to the benefit concert for St. Jude's Research Hospital that would take place in about five weeks. Until then, she would remain under FBI protection.

The agent who had explained the process to her had seemed honest enough. He hadn't given her details of their plans other than his assurance that their top priority was to keep her safe and catch the man they believed was after her. His offer of a female agent to protect her had been tempting, but man or woman, the effect would be the same. She would still feel like she had a bodyguard.

She might end up feeling that way with Charlie, but as her grandfather reminded her, at least he shared her religious beliefs. If she was going to have to be in close quarters with someone, they might as well have some common ground. Not that she planned to actually speak to him, of course.

* * *

I can do this, Charlie assured himself. Of course, life might have been a bit easier had the FBI given them a more spacious safe house. But such luxuries were rare, he supposed, even when the person living there was famous. Kendra's celebrity status had actually been one of the main factors considered when choosing the remote location north of Phoenix.

The house itself was adequate enough for their purposes. There was a small study just inside the front door, and three bedrooms were clustered on one side of the house. The master bedroom occupied the back corner opposite the other two rooms.

Charlie hadn't been surprised to find that Kendra had claimed the master as her own. He would have suggested it had they arrived together, assuming that she would have actually talked to him. The living areas all connected, the decent-sized kitchen opening up into a great room that spanned the back part of the house. The open area beyond the backyard was all desert, with a mix of sagebrush and cacti growing on the hill that gently sloped away from the house. A concrete patio spanned the width of the structure.

He noticed the ring of large rocks that had been fashioned into a fire pit outside. A grill was angled near it, and Charlie was surprised to see that the patio furniture looked relatively new. The furniture inside the house was anything but. The kitchen table was small and round, the wooden chairs scarred. The couch and loveseat in the great room were well worn and mismatched. The entertainment unit was outdated and oversized, although the television and DVD player appeared to be relatively modern.

Charlie dumped his suitcase on the double bed in the bedroom he had chosen, the room directly across the hall from the master suite. He sorted his clothes into two piles, lights and darks, and then headed back down the hall to the laundry room located off the kitchen. Even though he had been back in Phoenix for two days, he had been so busy reading up on the Malibu Stalker cases that he had yet to find time to catch up on his laundry.

Now that he was babysitting Kendra, he decided he might as well take care of the basics. As soon as he started the first load, he headed back to the study. Ray had helped him set up his laptop and printer. His government-issued internet access keycard would allow him access to his work e-mail account and also scramble the IP address so no one would be able to trace his location.

The concern that someone had been following Ray after he'd left Kendra's grandparents' house weighed heavily on him. Ray had called in the local police for help, requesting they pull over the vehicle of interest for a routine stop, a ploy that would have identified the driver. Unfortunately, the car changed course right before the police arrived.

Aware that the stalker was believed to have some kind of military or law enforcement background, Charlie wondered if the man following Kendra had heard the dispatch and broken off his pursuit to preserve his anonymity. Charlie had been reassured that after the incident, Ray had followed protocol and taken additional precautions before bringing Kendra to the safe house, including switching cars in a secured underground garage.

Charlie logged into his e-mail account and began searching for the promised updates. The surveillance detail on Zack Prescott had reported three hours ago that everything was normal. Prescott had been spotted going into work after a lunch with friends shortly before one o'clock, which definitely placed him in California, not Phoenix. He also considered the possibility that the car Ray had spotted hadn't really been following them at all.

He unlocked his briefcase and pulled out the files on the other two prime suspects, Jed Burgess and Steve DeFoe. The possibility that Jed Burgess or Kendra's ex-boyfriend could be the man they were after terrified him. It led back to the fact that Kendra was the woman the stalker was obsessed with.

With a frustrated sigh, Charlie began studying Jed Burgess's information. Somewhere, there was a clue, something that would lead them to the man haunting these women. And if he was right, Charlie needed Kendra to forgive him enough to help him. If she was the key, she might just be the person they needed in order to unlock the secret of the Malibu Stalker's identity.

* * *

She read and reread pages in her book. She fiddled with her guitar. She wrote a terrible song about lies and revenge only to tear it into shreds. Every ten minutes, she glanced at her watch, wondering when Charlie would appear at her door to check on her. He was supposed to be protecting her, so how was it that he had arrived hours ago and hadn't once even peeked into her room to make sure she was indeed still alive and breathing?

She shifted her guitar, trying to find the right lyrics as she played through her newest creation once more. Then she caught the scent of meat cooking. Her stomach grumbled in protest, and her teeth clenched together. She couldn't even get something to eat without facing him. How had she thought she could do this for weeks on end?

Drawing a deep breath, she set her guitar aside and moved toward the door. She pulled it open to find Charlie standing on the other side, his hand lifted to knock.

A flash of discomfort crossed his face before he adopted the same professional composure he had worn when he'd appeared at her cabin almost two weeks earlier. His eyes met hers. "Dinner is about ready, if you're hungry."

Kendra simply nodded and then followed him to the kitchen. The table was already set for two, and Kendra could see why she hadn't heard him in the back part of the house for so long. He had clearly been busy in the kitchen. A simple white tablecloth covered the ugly kitchen table, and dinner rolls were nestled in a small bowl next to a larger bowl of broccoli salad.

Charlie motioned to the table. "Go ahead and sit down. I'll go get the steaks off the grill."

She waited until he disappeared through the sliding glass door before she took a seat and tried to tighten her grip on her shifting emotions. She managed to keep her focus away from Charlie when he set the steaks on the table and even through most of the blessing he offered. But when he added a plea for her safety, she felt herself weakening.

She kept her eyes on her plate, as though she could pretend Charlie wasn't sitting a few feet away, even though she couldn't mistake the faint scent of his aftershave. She cut into her steak only to discover that it was annoyingly perfect—medium, just the way she liked it. The broccoli salad tasted like it had come from a restaurant, a suspicion that grew increasingly stronger until she broke a roll open to find that it was still warm from the oven.

They ate in silence, Kendra only managing to finish half of the steak Charlie had grilled for her. Realizing that she couldn't eat another bite, she pushed back from the table and began rummaging through cabinets to find something to put her leftover steak in.

"There are some food-storage bags in the second drawer over there," Charlie said in an unexpectedly gentle tone.

Refusing to look at him, she pulled open the drawer, fished out a bag and slid the steak into it before crossing the kitchen to put her leftovers in the refrigerator. She rinsed her dish, slid it into the dishwasher, and started to leave the kitchen. She thought she was going to make it past Charlie without a confrontation until he stood up and stepped into her path.

"We need to talk."

She looked up at him now. "I seriously doubt we have anything to talk about. You lied to me so that I would be protected. Now I'm protected. You got what you wanted."

"I didn't want to mislead you."

"Whatever." She took a step toward the hall, only to have him shift to again block her path.

"Kendra, I'm sorry. I never wanted to hide my profession from you."

"But you did, didn't you?" She felt her chin tremble and struggled against her emotions. "I thought you were my friend. You made me think that you cared about me—the real me."

"I do care about you." His voice rose slightly.

"Yeah, as a way to advance your career." Kendra's anger erupted against his words, words that were certainly just a lie. Gathering her strength, she attacked before her embarrassment could beat her down any further. "I do have to give you credit on your acting skills, though. If you ever decide to change careers, let me know. I can put in a good word for you with my father."

The red haze of her emotions prevented her from seeing the recklessness that darkened his eyes. He took a step toward her. She instinctively took a step back. "I may have deliberately not told you who I work for, but I'm still the same person you spent all those days with in Pinewood."

"Don't give me that." She shook her head and took another step back so she could see him more clearly. She felt the wall behind her and wondered vaguely how she had ended up in a corner with Charlie staring down at her. "No one meets me and wants to know who I really am." Kendra's voice broke, and she took a steadying breath. "They only want to know what they can get from me."

"I can understand you being mad at me, but don't you dare stand there and accuse me of using you." He looked up at the ceiling and shook his head, even as the muscles in his jaw twitched. Then he let out a ragged breath, and his eyes met hers once more. "The only thing I want is for you to be safe." He held his hands out to his side and let them drop in a frustrated gesture. "Forgive me for caring."

Before Kendra could respond, the front door opened, and Ray walked into the room carrying a suitcase. He must have sensed the tension in the room because he didn't call out his normal greeting. Instead, he stared at them for a moment before motioning down the hall. "I'm going to go unpack."

Charlie simply nodded at him. Then he stepped back from Kendra and said, "I've got work to do," as he turned and left the room.

Chapter 24

Agent Neal Coramavich stood just outside the hotel room and nodded at his partner, indicating that he was ready. They could hear the television blaring, but the curtains were drawn, preventing them from seeing who was inside. They would try this the easy way first, but Neal's hand was already positioned to reach for his weapon quickly if needed.

Neal knocked on the door with three hard, quick raps. The television cut off, followed by the sound of approaching footsteps. The door creaked open, and the man inside looked at them inquisitively. "Can I help you?"

"Jed Burgess?"

"That's right." He nodded, confusion and a touch of concern showing on his face.

Neal pulled his badge from his inside jacket pocket and identified himself. "We'd like you to come with us, sir."

"Why?" Jed's concern flared into panic. "Is everything okay? My family?"

"Everything's fine. We just need to ask you a few questions."

Jed put a hand on his chest as though trying to steady his rapidly beating heart. Then he nodded. "Let me just get my shoes."

* * *

Charlie hated losing his temper. Absolutely hated it. He didn't know what he had expected from Kendra. He could even admit now that he had deliberately tried not to think about what to expect, but her accusations had gone far beyond whatever worst-case scenario he might have come up with.

Sure, he could have anticipated her being miffed at him for neglecting to tell her why he was really in Pinewood. He could even understand her feeling hurt or annoyed at him for the kisses they had shared. But nothing had prepared him for the accusation that he had mistreated or used her in any way because of her celebrity status.

He might have made a mistake in kissing her, but it wasn't like he had been alone in that little experiment. She'd kissed him first. The fact that he had kept his distance from Kendra up until that point should count for something.

He paced across the little office, annoyed that his pulse wasn't quite steady as he tried to get a grip on his anger. He paused by the window and looked out into the darkness. He needed to put some distance between himself and Kendra, and he supposed now was as good a time as any to do a quick check outside. He made sure his files were securely locked inside his briefcase and then turned to go. He stopped short when he saw Kendra standing in the doorway.

"I said I have work to do," Charlie said, a little more sharply than he intended.

"I just have to ask you one question." Kendra looked at him like a wounded puppy, and her voice was unexpectedly sincere.

"What?" Charlie bit off the word, annoyed both that she hadn't given him any time to compose himself and that her presence alone caused another wave of guilt to slice through him.

A faint blush rose to her cheeks, but she kept her eyes on his. "Why did you kiss me?"

His eyebrows lifted, and he was suddenly grateful that Ray was still getting settled in his room. "I would think that would be obvious."

She shook her head, and her voice was barely louder than a whisper. "Not to me."

He saw it now—the vulnerability and the hurt that was undeniably his fault. She'd told him that she never dated much, but he hadn't really considered that a woman like her, a beautiful, talented, famous woman, could really be that inexperienced with men. The naiveté he saw in her eyes told him that she had been completely honest with him in that most private part of her life.

Charlie swallowed. Hard. How could he explain that he'd made a mistake? How could he tell her he'd let himself get caught up in the moment, a moment he knew he should regret but desperately wanted to repeat?

He chose to leave several feet between them as he leaned back against the desk. She remained in the doorway, looking unexpectedly fragile. He shoved his hands in his pockets, fisting them there as his anger faded and a myriad of emotions replaced it. He wanted her to trust him and knew that nothing less than the truth would give her what she needed and what she deserved.

"I kissed you because I care about you," he said softly. "The real you."

Her eyes stayed steady on his, but Charlie could see the tears threatening. "I don't know what to believe anymore."

"Believe that I wanted to tell you everything. Believe that I never wanted to hurt you and that it was killing me to have to hide anything from you." He saw a single tear spill over, and his heart ached for her. She deserved to be happy, to be safe without worries, and he hated knowing that he couldn't give her those things right now.

He knew he needed to keep his distance, to put their relationship on a strictly professional level while he was protecting her, but when he saw the next tear spill over, he felt himself wavering. He knew it was a mistake when he pulled his hands out of his pockets, pushed away from the desk, and crossed to her.

Without a word, he slid his arms around her waist and pulled her against him. A second passed, then two, before her hands came up to encircle his waist. Then she clung to him as she fought off her tears.

Charlie held her while her breathing steadied and the little tremors working through her body faded. He wanted more than anything for the circumstances to be different. He wanted to be in a position where he could spend time with Kendra and have the freedom to explore the attraction between them. But he reminded himself that if she hadn't been forced to stay in one place because of the current threat against her, he never would have had any of this time with her.

Normal life for Kendra meant touring around the country, playing in concerts, and shooting music videos. With his job anchoring him in Phoenix, he was unlikely to ever have a real chance to date her. He started to pull away, only to find her staring up at him, tears still shimmering in her eyes.

She lifted a hand to his face and looked up at him expectantly. Their faces were close, and he leaned toward her instinctively, hesitating when his mouth was just a breath away from hers. He knew he should resist, knew that even a single kiss would complicate things between them further. Then she closed the distance between them. Her lips brushed against his, and he couldn't resist deepening the kiss.

His heart squeezed in his chest, and his emotions tangled as she consumed his thoughts. This was a woman to be cherished and treasured, a woman unlike any he had ever met. She was full of contrasts, of twists and turns that demanded to be explored: fragile one minute and daring the next. Charlie was overwhelmed with the need to understand her and have her understand him.

A door closed down the hall, and Charlie jerked back. He stared down at her, his breathing unsteady. How had this happened? How had Kendra managed to bypass his defenses? How had she managed to weave her way into his heart?

"Kendra, I'm sorry. I can't do this." He stepped free of her embrace and took another deliberate step back. "I can't focus on my job if we're together like this." He took a deep breath. "You understand that, don't you?"

The vulnerability was back in her eyes, but she nodded.

Footsteps sounded in the front hall, and Ray appeared in the doorway. "If everything's okay in here, I'm going to go check the perimeter of the house."

Again feeling the need to distance himself from Kendra, Charlie stepped toward the door. "I'll take care of it."

Ray's eyebrows lifted. "Are you sure?"

"Yeah, I'm sure." He glanced back at Kendra for a brief moment. Then he turned and left the room, hoping that focusing on defensive measures to keep Kendra safe would help him put his priorities back into perspective. As he donned his jacket and stepped outside, he let out a sigh. Like it or not, Kendra had destroyed the walls he'd built around his heart, and he had no idea what to do about it.

Chapter 25

Neal Coramavich stared warily across the table at Jed Burgess. He narrowed his eyes as he leaned forward. "You're telling me you were in Los Angeles on these dates to attend award shows?"

"That's right." Jed nodded. He tapped a finger on the four dates that investigators had placed him in California.

"I'm understandably confused," Neal said, shaking his head. "Why would someone who lives in Pinewood, Arizona, go to award shows in Los Angeles? How do you even get tickets?"

"About five years ago, a friend of mine wanted to go to the Academy Awards. His son was up for an award, but my friend had just had hip replacement surgery and couldn't drive yet. He didn't want his wife to drive all the way from Phoenix to LA, so he asked if I wanted to go," Jed explained.

"And this friend would be . . ."

"William Blake. His son is Sterling Blake," Jed told him. "Anyway, while we were there, I noticed how every time someone got up out of their seat, someone else came and sat down so there weren't any empty seats. I asked who they were and found out that there are people who go to the award shows to be seat fillers."

"Seat fillers?"

"Yeah, you know, to fill the seats so that on TV it always looks like there's a full house at the show."

"So you drive all the way to California to fill seats," Neal said skeptically.

"That's how it started. After a few shows, I got to know some people who work backstage. Those connections got me different jobs working at the shows, usually helping the backstage coordinators."

"Can you give me the names of the people you worked for?"

"Sure." Jed nodded agreeably. "Do you want their phone numbers too?"

"Yeah, that would be great." He pushed a pad of paper and a pen across the table, and Jed started jotting down the names and numbers. As soon as he finished, Neal asked, "Was Kendra Blake at any of these award shows?"

"Kendra?" His eyebrows lifted, but then he nodded. "Sure. She's always at them."

"Always?"

"Well, yeah." He nodded again. "She always goes if her dad's up for an award, which is just about every year, and she usually gets at least one nomination for the music award shows."

"Were you in LA for either of these two dates?"

Jed leaned forward and read the dates on the paper Neal shoved in front of him. "This date doesn't look familiar, but I might have been in California for the one in February. The Grammys would have been right around that time."

"I see." Neal tried to size up the man across from him and couldn't. He was offering information, apparently without censure, and he didn't act like a man who had anything to hide. Neal had no idea if he was really that good an actor or if he was really as clueless as he seemed. "Have you ever met Joslyn Korden?"

Now his eyebrows drew together. "The model?"

"Yes, the model."

Jed shook his head. "No, I can't say that I have."

"What about this woman? Lacey O'Riley." Ray slid a DMV photo in front of Jed.

Again he shook his head. "Who is she?"

"Can you look at these photos and see if you might have seen any of them?" Neal slid four more photos across the table as he considered the information Jed had already given him and twisted it to suit his purposes. "They might have been at one of the award shows you were at."

"If any of them were there, I didn't notice them," Jed said after studying the group of photos. "But like I said, the last few years I've been working backstage. I didn't really get a chance to see many people out in the crowd."

Neal nodded, gathered up the stack of photos, and slid all his notes into a file. "I'll be right back."

He walked out of the interrogation room and entered the viewing room adjoining it, where Elias was watching through the glass. "What do you think?"

"I think this guy is clueless."

"Yeah, but do you think he could be lying?"

"I don't think so. I don't think he's our guy, but I do think he's given us another angle to consider."

"The award shows?"

Elias nodded. "Five out of six of the murders were committed around the same time as one of those shows. See if there were any similar events on that other date."

"What about him?" Neal jerked a thumb toward the glass separating the two rooms.

"Make sure you have good contact information for him and then let him go."

* * *

Kendra rolled over in bed and stared at the faded blue-and-white-striped wallpaper. After her talk with Charlie the night before, she had unpacked her belongings in her bedroom and found herself working on lyrics as she let her emotions settle. Charlie had checked in with her after he'd finished looking around outside but then had left her alone with her thoughts. She suspected he needed some time alone as well.

Her chest was still tight with anticipation as she tried to figure out what to expect over the next few weeks. As unrealistic as it was, she wanted the illusion back. She wanted to pretend that she was safe and that Charlie was with her because he wanted to be. The way he had kissed her last night made her think that his feelings for her were genuine.

He must have withdrawn from her because his professional integrity wouldn't allow him to explore the sparks that kept snapping between them—at least, she hoped that was the reason. She didn't know whether to wish for this situation to drag on so she could stay with Charlie indefinitely or to hope that life would return to normal so she could see what would happen once he was free to shed his professional armor.

What would it be like, she wondered, *to feel safe and loved and content?*

She shook her head and blew out a breath. She tried to think of the last time she had really felt that way, quickly realizing that she had to go all the way back to her childhood. When she'd turned twelve, her father had decided it was time to teach her about the real world, about how everyone wanted something from people like the Blakes and that danger was everywhere and had to be combated.

Since then, she had never felt completely secure, and now she also didn't know whom to trust. She wanted to trust Charlie. She wanted to believe what he had told her the night before. But she simply didn't know if she could.

He had been the only bright spot in this whole ordeal, this nightmare that she'd put a time limit on. Ray Underwood had tried to be up front with her, explaining that a month might not give them the time they needed to track down the leads Charlie had turned up—leads he had uncovered by talking to her, by pretending to be her friend. That still grated at her, the way she'd thought he was such a good listener while, in reality, he had been interrogating her without her knowledge.

Still, she was realistic enough to consider that if he could figure out who was after her, this nightmare would finally end.

After she showered and dressed for the day, she walked down the hall and heard Charlie's voice.

"Do we have enough to hold him?" Charlie asked as she approached the office door. She glanced inside to see him holding his cell phone to his ear as he paced the narrow room. "Okay, then e-mail me the Burgess interrogation as soon as you get it." He paused again and then nodded to the empty room. "Thanks."

Kendra waited until he hung up before asking, "Were you talking about Jed Burgess?"

Charlie turned to face her, his shoulders tense and surprise evident on his face. He seemed to debate how much to tell her before he let out a sigh and nodded. "A couple of agents picked him up last night in Flagstaff."

"Why?"

"Because he was in California at the time of several of the murders."

Her eyes widened. "You think Jed could be the Malibu Stalker?"

"We had to at least check it out."

"That's crazy. I mean, he's a little weird, but I don't think he'd ever hurt anyone."

"Serial killers often look completely normal while living their everyday lives," Charlie told her. "It's my job to consider all possibilities in order to find the man behind these murders."

"I thought your job was to protect me."

"That too." Charlie nodded. "But it certainly won't hurt for me to stay in the loop and do a little research over the next few weeks."

"You don't really think it's Jed, do you?"

"He was in the right place at the right time to be our guy, but my boss doesn't think it's him." Charlie shrugged, cautiously shifting behind the desk, as though trying to keep a barrier between them. "I should be getting the report within the next hour or two."

She nodded absently and sighed. "Exactly what are we supposed to do here for the next month?" She waved a hand at the front window, looking out at the long driveway that led to the main road. The closest house was at least a half-mile away and was one of only a few scattered in this part of the foothills outside Cave Creek.

"I'll do my research. You'll write your songs." Charlie offered her a little smile. "You can beat up on me in backgammon and pretend to lose to me in gin rummy."

Her eyebrows lifted. "And tomorrow?"

"The same."

"Look, I understand you have your work to keep you busy, but as much as I love writing music, I'm starting to get cabin fever. I really need something to break up the monotony."

"Like what?"

"Going for a run, watching a movie." She shrugged. "Something."

"Kendra, this isn't like the Witness Protection Program, where they set you up with a new identity somewhere and you start a new life," Charlie said gently. "The whole idea is to keep you out of sight. Most people know who you are. Just going to the grocery store is a security risk."

"I understand that, and I'm not trying to be difficult. Really, I'm not," she said. "But I've already gone almost two weeks without being able to go anywhere or even work out. I'm going to go stir crazy if I just sit around here all day."

"I don't know what to tell you," he told her. "I thought all of this was explained to you when you agreed to protection."

She let out a little sigh and nodded. Then she switched gears. "What about a treadmill or an exercise bike? I'll pay for one."

Charlie seemed to consider her idea. "Actually, that's not a bad idea. I've got a decent treadmill at my apartment. Let me see if Ray might be willing to pick it up on his way over here tonight." His lips curved up into the beginnings of a smile. "It might help keep both of us sane."

"Thanks, Charlie," Kendra said. Then she asked, "By the way, where is Ray?"

"He left about an hour ago. He's only going to be staying over here at night so I can get some sleep."

Her eyebrows lifted. "So he's basically our night guard?"

"Pretty much. Unless we need him over here sooner, he's planning on spending his evenings with his family, and then he'll come over after his kids go to bed." He gave her a reluctant smile and then asked, "Since I made dinner last night, does that mean you're making breakfast?"

Humor danced in her eyes, and she wondered how such a simple question was able to put her more at ease than all his explanations had from the night before. "I guess I could do that." She paused and then added, "As long as you promise to help with the dishes."

"Deal."

Chapter 26

Charlie looked out the office window, surprised to see Ray pulling into the driveway even though it was only four o'clock in the afternoon. He also felt an unexpected wave of relief. Keeping tabs on Kendra was easy enough. Security equipment was set up outside of the safe house, and Angie had already called in to let him know that her surveillance hadn't shown anything unusual.

The challenge was trying to maintain a professional distance from Kendra. He wasn't sure what he had expected of her this morning, especially after he'd kissed her and then retreated so quickly, but he certainly hadn't expected her to act like nothing had happened between them.

The tension he'd been expecting had quickly dissipated, but every time he looked at her, he felt edgy. And he knew it was his own fault.

Charlie opened the door and walked outside to see that his treadmill was in the back of Ray's truck. "Hey, Ray. I didn't expect you to make a special trip to bring this over."

"Neal offered to help me load it up at your place, and I didn't want to pass up on his offer. I wanted to give you an update anyway." He jerked a thumb at the treadmill. "Do you want to get this unloaded first?"

"Sure." Charlie moved with him to the back of the truck, and together they muscled the bulky machine up onto the front porch. They were able to utilize the two wheels on the bottom to push it into the house. Kendra appeared as Charlie maneuvered the treadmill through the front hall. He glanced up at her and asked, "Where do you want it?"

She motioned to the living room. "How about in there, facing the TV."

Charlie nodded and rolled it into place as Ray and Kendra exchanged greetings.

"How's Sarah doing?" Kendra asked Ray about his daughter, concern evident in her voice.

Ray immediately grinned. "She's doing great. According to her last scans, she's cancer free."

"I'm so glad." She laid a hand on his arm and gave it a friendly squeeze. "She's so darling."

Ray's grin widened. "We think so."

Kendra glanced over at Charlie. "Have you met Ray's family yet?"

Charlie nodded, touched by her obvious concern for Ray's little girl. Before he could answer, Ray spoke for him.

"We had Charlie over for dinner about a month ago, and Sarah announced after he left that we needed to adopt him."

A giggle escaped Kendra. "Adopt him?"

Charlie rolled his eyes, oddly embarrassed. "She just wants me around because I give her piggyback rides."

"You are pretty good at those." Kendra smiled, and Charlie's mind immediately flashed back to the first time he'd met her and insisted on carrying her over the snow. She stared at him for a moment and then nodded at the hall. "I think I'll go change into some workout clothes and put your efforts to good use."

Charlie watched her disappear down the hall and then turned to face Ray. "You said you had an update for me?"

Ray nodded. "Jed Burgess's story checks out as far as we can tell. He did attend award shows repeatedly over the past five years."

"And the award shows correspond with the murders?"

"Five of them, but the O'Riley murder was committed in December, and there weren't any events of significance around that one, at least nothing we could identify," he told Charlie. "I guess it would have been too easy to finally figure out what events were triggering the murders."

"I think we still have to consider that as a possible trigger though," Charlie said. "When were the five murders committed in relation to the award shows?"

"The time of death is a little sketchy on the first two murders because the bodies weren't found right away, but from the coroner reports, all of them looked like they happened within a day or two of the shows. For three of them, the time of death was within twenty-four hours after the award shows ended," Ray said. "Including Joslyn Korden. We were able to verify that she did attend the Grammys."

"That's too big a coincidence to ignore," Charlie insisted, considering. "You know, maybe it isn't the award shows that are the trigger. It could be that they are just a way for our guy to find women who are easy prey, at least for those first four."

"What do you mean?"

"Think about it," Charlie said, his mind whirring. "All the victims were dressed in formal attire. He might be preying on women who attended the award shows because they gave him easy access to the kind of woman he has built his fantasies around."

"Besides Joslyn, there was one other victim who was an attendee of the Grammys right before she disappeared, but nothing like that popped up in the other women's files."

"But the others could have been seat fillers just like Jed Burgess. It's possible that that information was overlooked or wasn't considered important when the local police did the initial investigations," Charlie said, realizing that he was making a stretch, especially when he added, "The one that doesn't fit could be a case of a woman being dressed up for another event but was unlucky enough to catch our killer's attention."

"The timing doesn't work for Kendra either. There aren't any shows coming up anytime soon," Ray told him. "The next one is still a couple of months away."

"I wonder if that explosion backstage at Kendra's concert really was related to all of this," Charlie said. "Could someone else have been the target?"

"The LA office said they're still considering all possibilities, but the MO is the same as the one that occurred before Joslyn Korden's murder."

"What's the status on DeFoe?"

"Nothing yet, but the LA office does have him under surveillance now." Ray thought for a moment. "You know, if your theory is right, we might be looking for a limo or taxi driver. They would have easy access to these women."

"But how would he get into their houses unchallenged?"

"I don't know. Maybe show up claiming that they left something in his limo or cab?"

"It's possible."

Ray glanced down at his watch. "I'd better get going. I have a few things to take care of before I come back tonight."

Charlie nodded. "Thanks again."

"I'll keep you posted."

Charlie walked him out and then locked the door before heading back into the office. He sat down as Kendra's footsteps sounded in the front hall. He could hear her turn on the television, and a few seconds later, he heard the distinctive hum of the treadmill. Satisfied that Kendra was safely occupied, he logged onto the internet and debated where to start researching next.

There were so many possibilities, both for potential victims and possible suspects. Considering the reality that Kendra might be the primary target of the Malibu Stalker, he pulled a notepad out of his briefcase and sectioned off three columns: one with the dates of the murders, one for the dates of the awards shows, and the other for where Kendra was at each of those times.

The first two columns filled in quickly. Charlie then went to Google and typed in Kendra's name. His eyes widened when the results popped up over one hundred seventy million hits. "That's insane," Charlie muttered to himself as he narrowed the search.

He checked out her official website, noting the photos of Kendra at the most recent country music awards. She looked stunning in a streamlined pale blue gown, the scoop neckline and cap sleeves setting her apart from the few other women in the background with their more worldly formal attire.

A sense of unease pricked at him when he noted the date of the photo and realized that it was taken at the awards show just before Joslyn Korden's murder. He then opened up another tab and began searching various magazine and celebrity websites that showed the red carpet photos.

Photos of Kendra were easy to locate since she was always included in the various sites' slideshows. He read one of the captions, smiling to himself when Kendra's blue gown was described as elegant and timeless. At another site, she was called classically modest in her Cinderella-style dress.

"What are you doing?" Kendra asked when she walked into the room an hour later.

"Research," Charlie said as he glanced up. He noted that she must have just gotten out of the shower since her hair was a little damp. She had also changed into a pair of jeans and a long-sleeved T-shirt.

"You're researching me?" she asked flatly, skirting around the desk so she could look over his shoulder at the computer screen.

Charlie nodded absently as he clicked on the next image. "Do you always wear blue?"

"Yeah." Kendra's shoulders lifted. "My mother picked ice blue as my signature color, and I just never cared about that kind of stuff enough to argue with her about it. Personally, I'm about ready for a change."

His blood ran cold, and his eyes lifted to meet hers. The sudden clarity of thought pulsed through him. As much as he didn't want to believe it, Kendra wasn't an image, an illusion of the stalker's obsession. She really *was* the obsession. He also realized that the formal wear could be the key rather than the events the women might have attended.

"What's your favorite kind of flower?"

"My favorite flower?" She looked at him quizzically. "Officially or unofficially?"

"Is there a difference?"

"Actually, yes. According to the public image my parents helped create, I like red roses, but I actually prefer lilies."

Charlie's lips pressed into a hard line, and his mind raced with possibilities. After a moment of silence he asked, "Do you have your dresses custom made?"

"Yeah." She nodded her head. "Henrico Aldaves has been designing dresses for me and my family for as long as I can remember."

"Tell me about him."

She shifted so she was standing beside him instead of looking over his shoulder. Confusion was evident on her face, but she answered him without question. "He's been married a few times, a couple of kids, one from each of his first two marriages." Her shoulders lifted slightly. "My mom was friends with his third wife, Brandi, but when that marriage ended, my mom decided she liked Henrico's designs more than she needed Brandi's friendship, so she kept his phone number on speed dial instead of hers."

"How old is he?"

"Mid to late forties." She shrugged. "Of course, in Hollywood you can never really be sure."

Charlie jotted down the dates of the six murders and then shoved the pad of paper and a pen toward her. "I need you to write down where you were on all of these dates. If you can tell me what you were doing in the few days or even weeks before them, too, that would be great."

"Some of these were years ago."

"I know." Charlie looked up at her, a little ripple of panic finding its way into his voice. "But it's important."

Kendra's eyebrows drew together. "Charlie, what's wrong?"

"I just want to check something," Charlie said, trying to keep his voice casual. "Just give me as much information as you can."

"Okay." Kendra picked up the pen. "But I may need to look on the internet."

Charlie motioned at the chair on the other side of the desk. "Pull up a chair, and we'll work on this." He looked up at her, his eyes dark. "Together."

Chapter 27

He leaned back on the couch and watched the television camera zoom in on Kendra as she started down the red carpet. Even though he had watched this recording dozens of times, his heartbeat always quickened when she moved so gracefully toward where he had been waiting and watching.

Her smile was vibrant as she approached the camera, her sister in step beside her. He hit the pause button when Kendra turned to the crowd and waved. She had waved to him.

The mass of screaming fans had kept him hidden from the cameras, but that was okay with him. He hadn't cared about being seen on television. He only cared about being seen by Kendra.

And she had seen him. After all, why else would she have waved? She knew that she was meant for him. She was just waiting to get to know him, the real him, even if she didn't understand that yet.

He stood up and moved closer to the big-screen TV. He pressed a hand to the image of her cheek and let out a sigh. He was tired of waiting. Her next appearance was only a few hours away, and he would be there. He would be ready to take her away.

* * *

Kendra picked at her dinner, bits of conversations replaying in her head. She forced herself to eat a bite and realized that Charlie hadn't said a word since the blessing was offered on the food. His silence spoke volumes, confirming her deepest fears, a reality beyond anything she could have ever imagined.

"My father was right, wasn't he?"

"What do you mean?"

"My dad has been convinced for years that I've needed protection, that something would happen to me if I had my way and got rid of my bodyguards." Kendra's voice was surprisingly steady. She waited for Charlie to look up at her before continuing. "I'm the one the Malibu Stalker is really after, aren't I?"

"There's no way to be sure," Charlie said unconvincingly.

Kendra nodded, and her lips pressed together as she fought back her emotions. "But it's what you believe."

"Yes, it's what I believe." Charlie let out a sigh. Then he reached across the table and took her hand in his. "The FBI has been trying to find a common link among these murders for years. I think you're it."

"So someone is out there killing women and imagining that he's killing me?" She shook her head, wanting desperately to believe that Charlie's suspicions weren't true. Why would anyone want to kill her? There had to be some other explanation. "This could all be a coincidence. I'm sure there are other blondes at those same events, probably some who were at every one of them."

"You're right. You socialize in a very distinctive crowd, and we'll certainly check that out."

"So you might just be overreacting."

"I hope so," he said, but she could see in his expression that he didn't think so.

She sighed. "Why are you so sure it's me?"

"The explosion backstage at your concert was the first red flag."

She sensed he was holding something back. She couldn't stop herself from asking, "And?"

"The victims are always blonde and are always found wearing a blue evening gown," Charlie said gently. "And there is always a red rose beside each of the bodies."

"What?" Kendra swallowed hard, and her face paled.

"I'm certainly no expert on psychological profiling, but it does make sense. The stalker sees you at the various awards shows or formal events. He fantasizes about you but can't get close—at least the way he wants to. Then he finds a substitute, someone he can pretend is you."

"That's sick."

"Yes, it is." Charlie let go of her hand and pressed his fingers against his forehead to ebb the headache building there. Then he glanced back at her with a look of concern and helplessness. "You have to understand that whoever this guy is, he probably looks and acts normal. You probably even know him, at least peripherally."

Now a new sense of panic skated through her. "You think I *know* the stalker?"

Charlie nodded. "He might be a cameraman or a reporter. He could be someone who works with the company that caters these events or even a limo driver." Charlie hesitated and seemed to gather his thoughts. "Whoever he is, he knows that you have adequate security, and now he's trying to unravel you enough that he can slip past it."

"And if you hadn't found me in Pinewood, he might have."

"Possibly." Charlie shrugged. "Or you might have picked the one place where he didn't know to look for you."

She fell silent for several long minutes as she tried to sort out the jumble of information she had absorbed over the past few hours. Then she drew a deep breath. "One thing I don't understand though. You said there was an explosion at Joslyn's photo shoot shortly before she was killed. Why are we the only two that had that happen?"

"I think Joslyn was the test run." Charlie's voice was gentle, but he couldn't manage to take away the edge of his words. "Joslyn was the only victim who had a bodyguard. She was also the most recent murder."

An ugly sickness started in her stomach and spread quickly. "So she's dead because of me."

"No," Charlie started as Kendra pushed away from the table. Before she could escape to her room, he stood and blocked her path. He grabbed both her arms, waiting for her to look up at him before continuing. "Joslyn and the others are dead because there's a sick man out there who killed them. You didn't do anything to cause this."

"I'm just the woman who wore the blue evening gowns."

"Pretty much." Charlie let out a helpless sigh. Then he pulled her closer, and she let herself be drawn into the warmth of his embrace.

They stood there in silence for several minutes. Then Kendra shifted and looked up at him. "Is this ever going to end? Is the Malibu Stalker going to keep killing people?" She swallowed hard. "And is there any way this can end without me ending up like those other girls?"

"I'm not going to let anything happen to you," Charlie said, his voice barely louder than a whisper.

She stared up at him as a turmoil of emotions bubbled inside her. The fear was still there, the overwhelming terror that the Malibu Stalker would find her and end her life in a horrifying fashion. Humming alongside that fear was the desire to believe Charlie, to let herself trust him to keep her safe.

Warmth spread through her as she remembered the blessing Charlie had given her when they were in Pinewood. She didn't doubt that Charlie was one of the people the Lord had put in her life to help her overcome the challenges she was facing. Now, if she could only figure out how to have faith that everything was going to be okay.

Charlie stepped back, gently easing out of the embrace. "I know you feel stifled when you have a lot of security around, but you have to understand that you can't be alone—ever—until we catch this guy."

"Who's to say the stalker won't be able to get past my security?" Kendra asked, her doubts still lingering. "He got past Joslyn's bodyguard. He even got past Dustin at my concert, and that's not an easy thing to do."

"Dustin?"

"Dustin Brady, my personal bodyguard," Kendra elaborated. "Apparently someone hit him from behind while I was on stage."

"Even the best bodyguards can have an off day."

"Not Dustin. He's a former marine. Special forces. He isn't one to ever get caught off guard." Kendra shook her head. "If he hadn't been one of the best, my father never would have let me go down to only one bodyguard."

"But if the person who knocked him out was allowed to be backstage, Dustin might not have recognized the threat," Charlie pointed out. Something sparked in his eyes, an awareness that hadn't been there moments before. "How tight is security at your concerts?"

"Tight," Kendra said, cluing into his thought process. "Everyone has to have a backstage pass, and those are usually logged as they're given out."

"I'm sure the LAPD is already tracking down those leads then."

"There is one downside. The passes don't have photo IDs on them or anything. They can be handed off from one person to another without the log being altered."

"Yeah, but the police will verify everyone who had a pass and figure out who didn't use theirs and if they gave them away," Charlie stated with certainty.

"Part of me wishes I could just hide out here indefinitely, that I didn't have to show my face again in public." Kendra moved over to the couch and plopped down. "Of course, I'm sure I would go stir crazy within a week. It's only been a couple of days, but I'm already edgy."

Charlie moved to sit beside her. "You know, you can always change your mind about the month deadline you gave us. We can try to arrange protection for longer."

"I can't do that. I'm supposed to be attending a benefit for St. Jude's Research Hospital, and I'm one of the headliners."

"You could cancel."

She shook her head. "I feel bad enough that I won't be at the Red Cross fundraiser tomorrow night. As tempting as it is, I can't stop living my life indefinitely."

Charlie tensed briefly, but then he nodded. "I need to go make a quick phone call, but what do you say we watch a movie together tonight? I saw some DVDs on the shelf by the TV."

"Okay," Kendra said as they both stood up. She surprised herself a bit when she asked, "So is this going to be our first date?"

Charlie rolled his eyes. "I think we passed our first date awhile ago."

"Just checking."

* * *

Elias hung up the phone and then dialed Neal's extension. He wasn't surprised that he answered, even though it was already six o'clock, or that Neal appeared in his doorway fewer than two minutes after being summoned.

"I just got a call from Charlie, and if he's right, we might finally have found the break we've been looking for in this case." Elias motioned to the chair opposite his desk and waited for Neal to lower himself into it before he continued. "Charlie is convinced that Kendra Blake is the person the Malibu Stalker is obsessed with."

"We already suspected that could be the case."

"I know, and he found some more information that seems to be pointing that way. He checked her schedule for the dates of all the murders. Without exception, each woman was killed shortly after Kendra made a public appearance." Elias paused briefly before adding, "And in each case, Kendra wore a pale blue evening gown."

Neal's eyes widened. "Seriously?"

"Not only that. Red roses are publicly known to be her favorite flower." Elias sighed. "If Charlie's right, Joslyn Korden was the practice run for what this guy would see as the grand finale."

"Getting to Kendra."

"Exactly." Elias tapped the notepad on his desk where he had jotted down the information Charlie had given him. "Apparently, Kendra was supposed to attend a charity event this weekend in LA. She bowed out of that one, but she's insistent on going through with a second one next month."

"You want me to cross-check the guest lists for the two events?"

He nodded. "Not only those two events but also the other six events that corresponded with the murders. And not just the guest lists but all employees who worked the events too."

"You got it."

"Have Angie help you out, and make sure you coordinate with the LA office. They might already have some of the information we're looking for. They can do some of the legwork for us."

"I'll get started on it tonight."

"Don't forget to go home and get some sleep at some point," Elias reminded him. "With Kendra hidden away, we've hopefully bought ourselves some time."

Neal nodded and then disappeared into the hallway.

Chapter 28

Charlie walked into the kitchen on Sunday morning dressed in a dark suit. He had strapped on the shoulder holster he normally wore during working hours and was satisfied that his weapon wasn't visible beneath his tailored suit jacket.

Kendra looked up from the table, where she was eating a bowl of cereal, and her eyebrows drew together. "Why are you all dressed up?"

"I wanted to go to church this morning."

Her eyebrows lifted. "You're going to leave me alone to go to church?"

"No, I'm taking you with me," Charlie told her. "I thought we could both stand to get out of this house for a little while."

"I thought I wasn't allowed to leave the house."

"Don't worry," Charlie assured her. "I have a plan."

* * *

He watched her get out of the car and felt the fury simmer inside him. He pushed it back for the moment, forcing himself to be patient. She pushed her hair behind her shoulders, expertly tossing the blonde locks that framed her flawless skin. Then she turned to face the man beside her and flashed him a brilliant smile.

Rage, barely leashed, demanded action. His jaw clenched when the man beside her ran his hand over her bare arm. Seething, he watched as the young couple kissed and then turned toward the door. A surge of jealousy bubbled up inside him and threatened to boil over. How could she let him touch her? Didn't she know what that did to him?

His jaw clenching, he waited until the couple disappeared through the door together. Something snapped inside him, and he shoved his car door open. His tentative hold on sanity still allowed him to plot, to consider his options, but it was time to act. Slowly, steadily, he moved forward, his weapon concealed in the back of his waistband and a single red rose in his hand. Kendra would never cheat on him again.

* * *

"I look ridiculous." Kendra lifted her hand to the wig Charlie had insisted she wear.

"You look normal," Charlie countered.

"This is normal?" Her eyebrows lifted skeptically. Her own blonde hair was tucked beneath the mousy brown wig. With her makeup played down, she definitely looked different, but the changes were anything but flattering.

"Close enough."

"You do realize that we're already late, don't you?" Kendra asked, glancing down at her watch. "And I don't understand why we had to drive across town to go to church if I'm wearing a disguise."

"Just being cautious," Charlie said, pushing open his car door. He circled around to pull her door open for her and lowered his voice. "If we go in after the meeting has started, no one can ask us who we are."

"Good thinking."

"Come on." Charlie took her hand in his and led her through the outer doors and then into the back of the chapel. The opening hymn was just ending when they took their seats in one of the back rows.

Kendra looked down at their hands, at the way Charlie had linked his fingers through hers. She felt an incredible warmth spread through her. She couldn't remember the last time she had gone to church with anyone or even had someone to sit with. When she was on tour, she attended a different ward each week and rarely had time to attend more than sacrament meeting.

Except for her visits with her grandparents and the two or three times a year when she and her sister were together, church was always a solitary pursuit. People often recognized her when she attended, their reactions varying from young girls pointing her out to someone taking the time to welcome her and exchange introductions. Still, those introductions typically took place after sacrament meeting concluded, after she had sat through the meeting alone.

When Charlie released her hand and stretched his arm across the back of her seat, she leaned against him. Her lips curved, and she wondered what it would be like to have someone by her side like this week after week.

* * *

"This is absurd." Sterling Blake glared at Detective Dan Eadelton. "You come here asking me ridiculous questions about my social calendar when my daughter is in danger?"

"I wouldn't ask these questions if they weren't important," Dan said with, what he considered, admirable patience. "And I need the backstage passes you had to your daughter's last concert."

"I already told you, we didn't use them."

"Yes, sir. I understand that, but I need to verify that they are still in your possession," he insisted. "Whoever planted the explosives at your daughter's concert gained access somehow. We are tracking down everyone who had a backstage pass to narrow down where security could have been breached."

"I'll go get them," Monica Blake said as she turned and left the room. She returned a moment later holding two bright blue laminated passes the size of large index cards. "Here you go."

"How much longer will it be before Kendra can come back home?"

"I'm sorry, sir, but I'm not privy to that information. All I know is that the FBI wants to keep her in protective custody as long as she is agreeable. Our evidence continues to suggest that she is the next intended target."

Sterling shook his head, clearly annoyed. "For all I know, she was forced into protective custody."

Dan's jaw clenched. "I find that highly unlikely. The FBI doesn't force anyone into protective custody."

Monica Blake crossed the room and put a comforting hand on her husband's arm. "Detective Eadelton, I'm sure you can understand that my husband and I are concerned. Other than one phone call right after the incident at Kendra's concert, we haven't had any assurances of her well-being, other than what we have been told by others."

"I do understand your concern."

Frustration vibrated off of Sterling. "Have you made any progress with your investigation?"

"Yes, we have." He nodded and held up the two passes. "In addition to these, we are pursuing several other promising leads. I assure you, we are doing absolutely everything within our power to identify and stop the man after your daughter, but we need your cooperation and your patience."

"I'm afraid patience is something I don't have a large supply of, especially when my daughter is in danger."

"I understand that, sir," Dan said. He took a step toward the door. "I will certainly contact you as soon as we know anything further."

Sterling gave him a curt nod, and Dan turned and left the room.

* * *

"Thanks for taking me to church," Kendra said as soon as they walked in the front door. "It was so nice getting out for a change."

"You're welcome." Charlie fought back a grin as Kendra immediately started fiddling with the wig so she could pull it off. "You didn't want to stay a brunette?"

She turned and glared at him, but humor was in her eyes. "No."

"Well, take good care of that wig. You'll need it for church next week." Charlie led the way into the living room. He picked up a Styrofoam wig stand from off the coffee table and held it out to Kendra.

Kendra settled the wig on the stand and then combed her hair with her fingers so it fell in soft waves around her face. "Don't you think people will get suspicious if we slip into church every week during the opening hymn and then leave during the closing hymn?"

"We'll go to a different building next week." Charlie shrugged out of his suit jacket and laid it over the back of a chair. "We don't want to fall into any specific pattern, or we might get noticed."

"I guess that makes sense." Kendra sat down on the couch and picked up her guitar that was leaning against it. She pulled the guitar into her lap and rested her arm on it, her eyes landing on Charlie's holster. "Do you always have to wear that?"

"I'm supposed to have my weapon with me at all times," he said as he unhooked the harness and set it on the table. "I only wear the shoulder holster when I'm wearing a suit though. I prefer using a waistband holster."

"Can I ask you a personal question?"

"Depends on the question."

"What made you want to join the FBI?"

Charlie considered the different events that had influenced his decision, one in particular coming to mind. "A few years ago, my sister was taken hostage overseas. She had been working in the U.S. embassy in Abolstan."

Kendra's eyes widened. "I remember when that happened. I had no idea your sister was one of the hostages."

"She wasn't just one of the hostages. She was the only hostage who didn't make it out with everyone else," Charlie told her, remembering all too well the days of waiting for news and finally flying overseas with his father to help find her. "She and one of her rescuers were left behind enemy lines for two days before they made it out."

"So how did that help you decide to work for the FBI?"

"I remember staying at my parents' house when we were waiting for news and hating it. I wanted to be the one who was doing something about bringing her home." Charlie sat on the couch beside her. "One of my brother's friends was in the FBI and helped out during that time. It got me thinking about choosing this as a career."

"Have you ever had any regrets?" Kendra shifted to face him more fully.

"Only once."

"When you and your old girlfriend broke up?"

"No, I wasn't thinking about that." Charlie shook his head as he fought against the guilt he felt whenever he thought about his former partner.

Kendra waited for a moment. Sensing that he didn't want to talk about it, she glanced back at the chair where his weapon was hanging. "I guess knowing that you're armed should make me feel safe, huh?"

"Just about anything you can put your hands on can be used as a weapon. A gun is just a tool of last resort," Charlie told her, relieved that she'd changed the subject. "Being here where no one can find you is what should make you feel safe."

"And having you here with me," Kendra said as she shifted and started fiddling with chords on her guitar.

Charlie's eyes met hers, and he nodded. "And having me here with you."

* * *

FBI Agent Rick Michaels looked down at the two bodies, and his stomach rolled. He knew he should be used to crime scenes by now, but he doubted he would ever get past the shock factor that came with each useless death. The man sprawled lifelessly just inside the door appeared to have been shot twice at close range.

The woman's body was on the pool deck, dressed in a blue gown, a red rose by her side. Like the other victims of the Malibu Stalker, she had been killed by a single gunshot through the heart.

Rick moved closer to the woman, noticing the bruises on her arms. His eyes narrowed when he looked closer and saw that her wrist appeared to have been broken.

"This is unusual," Rick commented to the coroner, who had worked all the previous stalker crime scenes. "Do you think she fought back?"

The coroner lifted one of the woman's hands and examined her manicured fingernails. "It doesn't look like it. If I had to guess, I'd say our guy was in quite a rage. This looks to me like he was losing control." He shook his head. "The other victims didn't have a mark on them except for the bullet wounds."

"We've never had a second victim either."

"Something has definitely changed."

"Or we could have a copycat."

"We should be able to figure that out once we get the ballistics report back," the coroner commented.

"I'll see if I can get the lab to put a rush on this one. We need to know if we're really dealing with the same killer."

The coroner looked up at him with grave eyes. "I don't know whether to hope that it's the same guy or a different one."

"I know what you mean."

Chapter 29

"Hey, Ray." Charlie pulled the door open and waved him inside. "I didn't expect to see you here so early."

"We've got a problem."

"What's wrong?"

"We've had another victim. Two, actually."

"Two?" Charlie's eyebrows lifted.

"A man and a woman this time." He held out the file in his hand. "The ballistics report just came in. It matches the others."

Charlie led the way into his office as he opened the file and started reading the summary page. He scanned through the details, flipped through the crime scene photos, and then read the autopsy reports. "What do you make of this?"

"He's getting sloppy."

"Or frustrated." Charlie rubbed a finger over his chin. "If Kendra really is the primary target, this could be the first time the killer had to choose a substitute without having the time to plan it out first."

Ray nodded in agreement. "He figured Kendra would be at the event on Saturday night. When she wasn't, he found someone else that looked enough like her to give him someone to take out his frustrations on."

"That would explain the woman's broken wrist and other bruises—and why he didn't take the time to get her alone."

"Was the LA office still tracking DeFoe and Zack Prescott?"

"Yeah, and get this. Both of them were at the fundraiser."

"You're kidding."

Ray shook his head. "Since Kendra was supposed to perform, Prescott and all her other band members had tickets."

"What about Steve DeFoe?"

"Apparently, he works for the caterer," Ray told him. "He also worked backstage at the Grammys before the third murder."

"Did we have a tail on him?"

"We did, but DeFoe gave him the slip. He must have realized he was being followed because he drove there and then left in a different vehicle. He still hasn't shown up to pick up his car."

"I assume someone is waiting to bring him in as soon as he does show up."

"Yeah." Ray nodded. "I'm heading into the office for a little while. I'll let you know if I hear anything."

"Thanks."

* * *

Kendra clasped her hands together as Charlie rolled the dice. They had been coexisting in relative harmony at the safe house for nearly two weeks now and had fallen into a similar routine to when they had arrived in Pinewood. They both kept to their separate corners of the house when they were working during the day, and then they spent most of their evenings together.

At times, Kendra wondered if this was what it would be like to be married, but she tried to chase those thoughts away as quickly as they appeared. For one thing, a married couple certainly wouldn't have a chaperone show up by ten o'clock every night. And even though she felt like she knew Charlie pretty well after being practically inseparable for the past several weeks, she could hardly start thinking of a future with him when the main reason he was with her was his job. Except for kissing her that first night, Charlie seemed determined to keep things platonic between them.

She watched him make his move and tried to decide how to broach the subject of the upcoming charity dinner she had committed to and the preparations that she still needed to make.

"It's your turn," Charlie said after moving one of his backgammon pieces into the home position.

"Oh, sorry." She rolled the dice and moved her pieces, not realizing until a few seconds too late that she had missed an opportunity to bump him.

Charlie jiggled the dice in the cup but didn't roll them. "Are you going to tell me what's bothering you?"

She looked up at him. "What?"

"Kendra, something is obviously bothering you." He motioned to the board. "I never get this far ahead of you, even when I have a phenomenal game. So tell me what's on your mind."

She let out a sigh. "You're going to think it's silly."

"Maybe," Charlie agreed. "But tell me anyway."

"I need a dress."

His eyebrows lifted. "A dress?"

"Yeah, for the benefit concert coming up." Kendra took a deep breath and let it out. "I know it probably seems silly, but there are always so many reporters and photographers at these events. I will be expected to show up wearing something suitable."

"Something suitable," Charlie repeated, looking as though he were torn between concern and laughter. "So what are you asking me to do?"

"I need to talk to my designer to have a new dress made," Kendra told him. "He's probably already started on one, but it would be the same blue that I always wear. After everything that's happened, I want something different."

"That sounds reasonable." Charlie nodded.

"It does?"

"Sure." He rolled the dice, considered his options briefly, and then made his move. "Give me his number, and I'll have someone contact him. I assume he already knows your size."

She nodded. "I'd need at least one fitting before the benefit, but that can wait until a couple of days beforehand."

Charlie nodded again, but humor danced in his eyes.

"What?"

"You know, you're really cute when you're nervous."

Kendra rolled her eyes and let her dice fall. "You're just trying to distract me."

"You already distracted yourself." Charlie motioned to the board as Kendra made her move. He was within two rolls of winning the game, and Kendra didn't have a single piece home yet.

"Maybe I was just softening you up so you'd help me order my dress."

"Oh, is that it?" Charlie rolled again. He gave her a smug look when double sixes fell to win him the game.

She smirked at him and nodded. "I can be sneaky when I have to be."

"That's good to know." Charlie motioned toward the kitchen. "But loser gets to fix dinner."

She couldn't help but laugh. "How come when I win, the winner gets to clean up or fix dinner or do dishes, but when you win, it's the loser that gets extra chores?"

He wiggled his eyebrows. "Because I can be sneaky too."

* * *

"You must understand Mr. Blake's concerns," Alan Parsons said from the seat across the desk from Rick Michaels in the FBI's Los Angeles office.

"Exactly what is it you're asking of me?"

"My father's company has been providing security for the Blake family for nearly a decade. We need to know if you are any closer to apprehending the man you believe is after Kendra or if we need to be prepared to alter our security plans for her when she leaves your protection."

"We do have a person of interest at this time, but we need time to investigate further before we bring him in for questioning."

"Can I ask who?"

"I'm afraid I can't divulge that information."

"I see." Alan pulled a business card from his pocket and offered it to Rick as he stood up. "Please let me know if there is anything I can do to help. Obviously, we want this situation resolved as quickly as possible. Kendra belongs at home."

Rick stood as well. "I appreciate your concern."

* * *

Elias picked up his phone, his attention still on the computer screen in front of him. "Washington."

"Elias, it's Rick Michaels. I need a favor."

"What can I do for you?"

"We've been trying to locate Steve DeFoe."

"Yeah, I read the report. Any luck?"

"Actually, we think he's heading your way. He used his credit card to rent a car this morning. The GPS on the vehicle shows him heading east on Interstate 10."

"If you know where he is, why aren't you having the local LEOs pick him up?"

"Our case is still pretty circumstantial. Without the murder weapon, all we have is a couple instances of him being in the right place at the wrong time," Rick said. "The search warrant just came through, so I'm going to head over to his apartment right now, but odds are that if he has the weapon, he has it on him."

"Great," Elias muttered. "So I assume that you want us to stake out Kendra's condo to see if he shows up."

"Exactly."

"Any hits on hotel reservations for him?"

"No, but I did e-mail you his photo and the rental car info so you can track him. If we're right, he should be arriving in about five hours."

"All right. We'll keep an eye on him, and if he shows up here in Phoenix, I'll send someone over there to keep an eye out."

"Thanks."

"No problem. Let's just hope that he shows up. I'm ready to close the book on this one."

"That makes two of us."

* * *

"Is all of this really necessary?" Kendra looked at the travel plans spread out on Charlie's desk. "The fitting is only going to take an hour at the most."

"It's going to take a lot longer than that to get there." He tapped his finger on the winding route they would take through the valley to get to the hotel room where they would meet her designer.

Even her designer would be picked up by an agent tomorrow at the airport and escorted by similar fashion to the private villa that had been reserved for him at the Arizona Biltmore. Charlie had arranged for a decoy vehicle to bring Henrico to see Kendra.

"I still don't understand why you didn't push this back another week." Kendra thought of the dreaded wig. "Henrico must have rearranged his whole schedule to have made my dress in only three days."

"He was very accommodating," Charlie said cryptically.

Kendra caught his look, and suspicion bloomed along with a surge of annoyance. "Did you question him?"

"Me?" Charlie shook his head. "No."

Her voice took on an edge. "Not you personally. The FBI. Did they question him?"

"That's what we do." Charlie's shrugged, but his concentration was on the map in front of him. He made a note on his master plan and then glanced up at her, apparently oblivious to her shifting emotions. "We couldn't bring him out here unless we were certain he wasn't involved with any of the killings."

"That's why you were asking about him," Kendra realized, a sense of invasion crowding her for the first time since agreeing to protection. Resentment hummed through her voice. "Is everything I say just more data for you to analyze for your case files?"

Charlie looked up at her and let out a sigh. "I told you before, my primary goal is to keep you safe, but I also want to see the man after you behind bars."

"Am I just a case to you?" Kendra asked.

"What?" Charlie's eyes narrowed. "Where did that come from?"

"It comes from realizing that every conversation we've had was really an interrogation," Kendra said as temper replaced annoyance. "When I talk to you, it's because I want to know you better. You talk to me so you can solve a case."

"That's not the only reason, and that case has everything to do with your safety."

"Well, I'm safe for now." Kendra turned to leave the room, but she only made it two steps before Charlie reached out and grabbed her arm.

He waited for her to turn and look at him before he spoke. "Kendra, I may be here on protection duty, but you're not just a case to me. I thought you knew that."

"I don't know what to think." Her words vibrated with anger.

His eyebrows lifted, and he cocked his head to one side in a way that made him look confused and unexpectedly vulnerable. "I don't know what you want me to say."

"Tell me how you feel," Kendra insisted. "Tell me if I'll ever see you again after you catch this man, if you even want to see me once this is all over."

"Of course I want to see you, but I'm also trying to be realistic. I live in Phoenix. You live just about everywhere else."

"That's just geography, Charlie." Kendra's stomach went to war with a thousand butterflies, but she forced herself to push on. "Except for my family, I've never felt as close to anyone as I feel to you."

"Kendra, I don't know what you expect from me. Do you really think that we could make a long-distance relationship work? What are we supposed to do, steal snatches of time between your concerts and my stakeouts?"

"It doesn't have to be that complicated. But that's not the point. If this is for real, I have to think that the Lord would help us figure things out. The question is whether or not you want to try." She took a steadying breath. "I could fall in love with you, Charlie, and I'm afraid you'll break my heart if I do."

Charlie blinked rapidly three times before he managed to look at her. Then his shoulders relaxed marginally. "I think I started falling for you when you tried walking in the snow with sandals on." He reached up and tucked a lock of hair behind her ear. "You matter a lot to me—enough that it scares me. But I'm afraid that if I let myself get distracted, I won't be able to do my job, that something will happen to you because my focus isn't where it's supposed to be."

"And when your job is over?"

"I would really like it if you could stay in Phoenix for a while. I'd love to take you out and get to know you without worrying about who might be hiding in the shadows."

Kendra managed to smile as a sense of satisfaction spread through her. "I'd like that too."

CHAPTER 30

Rick pulled on a pair of gloves as the apartment manager unlocked the door to Steve DeFoe's unit. As soon as the door was unlocked, he thanked the manager and then walked inside, followed by fellow FBI agent Anthony Martinez. The moment the door was closed behind them, they began their search, both of them feeling a sense of urgency. In fewer than four hours, their prime suspect would be arriving in Phoenix, a short distance from where Kendra Blake was currently being hidden. Protective custody or not, no one wanted to let him get too close.

They started in the living room, quickly dispensing with the few possible hiding places due to the simplicity of the furnishings. They then worked their way back to the bedroom. Like the living room, the furniture was streamlined and modern. Other than a newspaper on the nightstand and a pair of shoes on the floor, everything in the room was exceptionally tidy.

"What do you think?" Anthony asked. "Is this guy a neat freak, or does he have a maid?"

"Maid," Rick answered. "Neat freaks don't leave their shoes in the middle of the floor."

"I'll check out the closet."

Rick nodded and pulled open a nightstand drawer. He looked through the drawers in both nightstands and then moved to the dresser. The haphazardly folded clothes suggested that he was right about the maid, a maid who clearly didn't do the man's laundry. Meticulously, he searched through the clothes until he reached the left bottom drawer. Nestled in the corner, beneath a stack of swimsuits, was a handgun.

"Got something," Rick called out. He pulled the weapon free and held it up to show Anthony. "It's the right caliber."

Anthony glanced down at his watch. "If we hurry, we should be able to get the gun to the lab and get the ballistics report before DeFoe gets to Phoenix."

Rick nodded as he bagged the weapon. "Let's go."

* * *

Charlie was still reeling from his talk with Kendra when Ray arrived that night. He looked up from his desk in the study, surprised to see Neal Coramavich walk in with Ray. Before Charlie could ask why Neal was there, Ray asked, "How's it going?"

Charlie tapped a printout on his desk. "I've got those travel plans finalized for tomorrow."

"We may have to put that on hold," Ray told him.

"What?"

Neal spoke now. "Steve DeFoe is on his way to Phoenix. We've been tracking the GPS on his rental car since early this afternoon, and he's definitely heading this way."

"We might be able to use that to our advantage," Charlie considered. "Maybe we can time Kendra's fitting to be while he's being questioned."

"We aren't just picking him up for questioning. We have enough to charge him," Neal told him.

"I thought everything we had was circumstantial."

"It was, until a couple of LA agents found the murder weapon in his apartment. We just got the call a little while ago."

"Are you serious?" Excitement rippled through Charlie. "That's huge!"

Neal nodded. Then he glanced down at his watch and looked knowingly at Charlie. "It's too bad he'll probably get picked up after hours."

Charlie couldn't help but grin. Everyone knew that spending time in the federal prison system was preferable to the local jail, but if it was after five, the local police would be called in to take him into custody instead of the U.S. Marshals. "Yeah, that is a real shame. Too bad it isn't Friday."

"Well, we can't have everything," Neal said. "Anyway, I need a key to Kendra's condo. I thought it might be more effective if I can wait for DeFoe inside. He might be able to spot a stakeout on the street."

"Good thinking." Charlie nodded and led the way into the living room, where Kendra was sitting on the couch cross-legged, her guitar resting beside her as she scribbled in her notebook. "Hey, Ken. I need the key to your condo."

She didn't look up but waved a hand in the direction of the kitchen. "It's in my purse. Outside pocket."

Charlie walked into the kitchen and picked up her purse from off the island, oblivious to the speculative look that crossed Neal's face. He opened the outside pocket, fished out her key ring, and flipped through the half dozen keys, all labeled with what they went to. He slid the correct key off the ring and handed it to Neal. "Here you go."

"Thanks." Neal pocketed the key as Kendra shifted her guitar onto her lap and began playing an unfamiliar song. Her voice joined the music, and all three men stopped and stared.

Charlie smiled when he recognized a few of the lines he had heard Kendra working on the night before. Realizing that she had completely tuned them out, he turned his attention back to Neal. "Watch your back tonight, and give us a call when you know anything."

"Huh?" Neal stared at Kendra for a moment longer before facing Charlie. "Oh, yeah."

Charlie left Ray in the living room with Kendra and walked Neal to the door. Neal shook his head, and envy filled his voice. "Boy, did you luck out on this assignment."

"More than you know," Charlie muttered. "I'll talk to you later. Good luck."

"Thanks."

* * *

Neal Coramavich was ready. Images of the crime photos, of the victims, were imprinted on his memory. Nothing could bring those people back or reverse their individual tragedies, but at least he knew he could give them justice and stop the Malibu Stalker from claiming any more lives.

He might have envied Charlie his assignment and the easy friendship he obviously now shared with Kendra Blake, but right now he couldn't think of anywhere else he wanted to be. The surveillance team outside had already alerted him to Steve DeFoe's arrival, and only a moment ago, he'd received word that DeFoe had started up the stairs leading to Kendra's front door.

Footsteps sounded on the landing, and Neal flexed his hand on the grip of his gun. The doorknob rattled, the lock turned, and the door swung open.

"FBI. Freeze!" Neal demanded before DeFoe could even pull the key free of the lock. Neal's finger itched as he thought of the victims once more. He found himself sorely disappointed when Steve DeFoe stared at him wide-eyed and simply raised his hands over his head.

* * *

Charlie hung up his phone, an immeasurable sense of relief flowing through him. Finally, Kendra was truly safe. Finally, her nightmare was over.

"Kendra!" he called for her as he hurried into the kitchen, where she was putting away the leftovers from dinner. His face was alive with excitement when he grabbed both of her arms and her eyes lifted to meet his. "They caught him."

"Who?" Confusion crossed her face. "The Malibu Stalker?"

He nodded, and his hands slid down her arms, his fingers linking with hers. "Neal just caught him red-handed entering your condo."

Her jaw dropped open at that news, but then the reality that she was finally safe caught up with her. "It's really over?"

"It looks that way." Charlie pulled his hands free of hers and slid them around her waist. His gaze lowered to her mouth, lingering there for a moment before his eyes met hers once more. The beginnings of a smile lit his face. "Which means I'm finally free to do this."

His expression was full of fun when he leaned down and touched his lips to hers. She lifted her hands to grip his shoulders, and the subtle scent of her shampoo tickled his senses. What had begun as a playful kiss slowly changed and deepened. Warmth sparked inside him and spread as he gathered her close, a sense of freedom rushing through him.

He was going to miss her, he realized suddenly. He had been spoiled, being able to see her all day, every day. More than anything, he wanted to keep Kendra right here with him, and he didn't know if he should be comforted that his heart was open once again or if he should be terrified.

Memories stirred within him, images of her singing late at night, of her walking out of her room with her eyes still heavy with sleep. Relief and regret melded together as he reveled in her safety but knew he was no longer needed in quite the same way.

He pulled back and looked down at her, his eyes dark. "I don't know how I'm going to get to sleep now that I won't have you singing to me."

She shrugged and reached up to kiss him once more. "I guess you'll just have to download all my music."

His eyes sparked with humor. "What makes you think I haven't?"

"So what happens now?" Kendra asked. "Can I just leave? Or do I need to stay here awhile longer?"

"My boss wants to keep you here for another day or two just to be safe. We've already got everything set up for you to meet your designer tomorrow, so we might as well stick to the plan."

"Do we still need to use all that security now that the FBI caught the guy?"

Charlie nodded and glanced at his watch. "I don't think my boss is going to want to take you out of protective custody until after they question DeFoe."

Kendra stepped back and looked up at him, completely stunned. "*Steve* is the Malibu Stalker?"

"Yeah. It looks that way," Charlie told her. "In fact, you gave us a lot of the information that helped us figure it out."

"It can't be Steve." Kendra shook her head. "He was a jerk sometimes, but other than the fight with Alan, he never acted like he would hurt anyone. He couldn't even stand the sight of his own blood." She looked up at him and shook her head again. "There has to be some mistake. I'm sure there's some logical reason why he was at my condo."

Charlie took her hand, realizing that Kendra was still working through her shock. "Kendra, the murder weapon was found in his apartment."

"But if he was at my place to hurt me, why didn't he bring his gun?" Kendra asked now. "That doesn't make any sense."

"I don't know why he left it behind." Charlie shrugged. "Maybe he wasn't planning on hurting you. He might have hoped to win you back, especially since we believe you are the person he's been obsessed with all this time." He hesitated for a moment as he considered the oddity of Steve not bringing his weapon with him. "Regardless, the weapon that was used to kill eight people was in his apartment. He also managed to shake the agent we had tailing him on the night the last murder was committed."

She stared up at him, a deflated expression on her face. "I can't believe it's him. I never would have even thought it could be him."

"Serial killers aren't easy to identify," Charlie said gently.

"More like impossible."

"I know it's a lot to take in." He gave her hand a squeeze. "I do have some good news, though."

"What's that?"

"My boss said that since they've made an arrest, you can call your family if you want."

Her face lit with excitement. "Really?"

"Yeah." Charlie grinned at her. "You can use my phone."

"That would be great. Thanks, Charlie."

"No problem." Charlie pulled his phone out of his pocket and handed it to her. "Just do me a favor and don't tell anyone where you're staying."

Kendra's eyebrows lifted. "You don't want me to tell my dad that we've been living together for the past month?"

Charlie winced. "Definitely don't tell him that. He might not be active in the Church, but I don't think that's the kind of news any father would want to hear."

Kendra laughed. "Yeah, I guess you're right. I'm afraid he's already suffered enough while I've been gone."

Chapter 31

"Honey, I can't tell you how glad I am to hear your voice," Sterling Blake said as he sank into his favorite chair and let the stress of the past month melt away. His baby girl was safe, and she was coming home.

"I'm sorry I couldn't call you, Dad. Everything has been so crazy since my last concert."

"I know, but at least you'll be home soon."

"Kind of," Kendra said, and he could hear the hesitation in her voice.

"What do you mean 'kind of'?"

"I'm coming home for the St. Jude's benefit, but then I'm going to come back and stay at my condo in Phoenix for a while."

"Why would you do that?"

"Because I want to take some more time to write," she told him. "Even though this month has been incredibly stressful, I've gotten so much work done."

"You can write here in California."

"It's not the same, Dad. I'm never really alone when I'm in Malibu."

He caught it then, something in her voice that told him she wasn't telling him everything. "Is your music the only reason you want to stay in Arizona?"

"It's the main reason," Kendra said. "And there's someone I started dating here. I'd like the chance to spend more time with him."

"You're staying there because of a boy? How did you start dating someone while you've been in protective custody?" Sterling demanded. "Who is he?"

"If all goes well, you'll meet him when I come home for the benefit. I'm hoping he can come with me."

"At least come home and spend the week here with us."

"Dad, I'll be home next week," Kendra told him. "Henrico is flying over tomorrow morning to do a fitting for my gown, and my sound check for the benefit isn't until the day before the concert."

"I'll still feel better when you're home and I can see for myself that you're okay."

"I know," Kendra said. "I love you."

"I love you too." Sterling hung up the phone and looked up at Bruce and Alan Parsons, who were both standing beside him. "You were right. She's fine."

"What was that about her dating someone?" Bruce asked.

"She didn't say who, but she's planning on bringing him with her to the benefit." Sterling let out a sigh.

Alan spoke now. "When is she coming home?"

"A week from Friday." Sterling shook his head. "She made arrangements for Henrico to fly out tomorrow to do her fitting. I have half a mind to fly over there myself and camp out at her condo until she's ready to come back to Malibu."

"I don't think that's necessary," Bruce said. "I'm sure she'll be home soon enough."

Sterling rubbed a hand wearily over his face. "I'm sure you're right, but boy am I glad all of this is finally over."

* * *

"I'm sorry I won't be able to come with you today, but Angie is a good agent. She'll make sure you stay safe," Charlie told Kendra as he knotted his tie.

"I'm sure I'll be fine," Kendra assured him. She gave him a wry grin. "Of course, Angie and the agent driving Henrico to the resort will get to see my new dress before you do."

"Maybe I'll just have to convince you to try it on for me tonight."

Her eyebrows went up. "Do we have plans tonight?"

"Do you want to?"

"I think I do."

"Good." Charlie slid his tie into place and straightened his collar. "This protection detail should be called off by tonight, and I think it's about time I take you out to a nice dinner."

"That sounds great." She smiled at him, but a trace of nerves danced in her eyes. "I was also hoping you could work out your schedule to come to that benefit with me."

"In California?"

She nodded. "I'll understand if you can't make it, but I'd really love for you to take me. It gets pretty old always being the only person there without an escort."

"I'll see what I can do." He leaned forward and kissed her. "I'll call you as soon as I finish at the office."

"Okay. Be safe."

His grin flashed. "Always."

* * *

"Hey, Charlie. Welcome back," Sam Pressman called out to Charlie as he stepped off the elevator. Sam was only a year older than Charlie, and they occasionally got together to shoot some basketball after hours. "How does it feel to be back among the normal people?"

"You consider yourself normal?" Charlie asked jokingly.

"Close enough." Sam fell into step with him as Charlie headed toward Elias's office. "Seriously though, how was it living with Kendra Blake? You were with her for what? A month?"

"More or less." Charlie answered the easier of the two questions and then quickly changed the subject. "Has DeFoe been questioned yet?"

"He's down in interrogation with Elias right now."

"I'd better get down there," Charlie said, changing directions. He walked into the viewing room and saw Elias sitting across the table from a slender, dark-haired man in his mid-twenties. Charlie turned to Neal, who was watching through the one-way glass. "Has he confessed?"

"Not yet. He hasn't asked for a lawyer either. Says he didn't do it."

"Don't they all?" Charlie muttered.

"Elias said to send you in as soon as you got here. He thought you might want to take a shot at this guy."

Charlie's mouth pressed into a hard line. "I think I would like that."

He walked out of the viewing room and then moved down the hall a few yards to the door of the interrogation room. Charlie pushed the door open just as Steve insisted once more that he didn't kill anyone. Rather than interrupt, Charlie simply closed the door behind him and leaned back against it.

Elias glanced up at Charlie briefly before firing another question at DeFoe. "Where did you go last week after the charity dinner?"

"One of the guys I work with was catering a private party in Beverly Hills. Afterward, a bunch of us drove up to Mammoth Mountain to do some skiing."

"Why didn't you take your car?"

"My car wouldn't start."

"What about the gun we found in your apartment?"

"I don't even own a gun."

"Really? Then how do you explain that the gun used to kill eight people was tucked away in your swimsuit drawer?"

"I didn't kill anyone," Steve insisted again. "I don't even know any of these people, except for Joslyn, but everyone knows her."

Elias glanced up at Charlie, sending a silent signal for Charlie to take over.

Charlie pushed away from the door and took a step toward the table. "How did you get the key to Kendra Blake's condo here in Phoenix?"

"She gave it to me."

"She gave it to you?" Charlie asked doubtfully.

"Yeah." Pride and ego filled his eyes when he added smugly, "We were close once."

Charlie ignored the way his stomach twisted at Steve's words and pressed on. "Why were you at her condo today? I understand that the two of you broke up more than three years ago."

"Yeah, we broke up. That bodyguard of hers wouldn't give us two seconds of privacy."

"So you knocked him out and planted a bomb backstage at her concert."

"I didn't do the bomb, and it's not like Alan didn't have it coming."

Charlie and Elias exchanged looks.

"Alan?"

"Yeah, Alan Parsons." Steve blew out a breath. "He must really have it in for me to set me up like this."

"What do you mean?"

"He's the one who told me that Kendra wanted to see me," Steve told them. "That's how I knew about her condo here in town."

Charlie looked at him, confused. "But you just said Kendra gave you a key."

Steve's ego deflated a little. "Well, Alan's the one who gave it to me, but he said she wanted me to have it."

"When was this?" Elias asked now.

"Yesterday."

Elias's eyebrows drew together. "And Alan suggested that you go see Kendra?"

"Yeah." He nodded. "He made it sound like it was pretty important. I thought maybe she'd come to her senses and wanted me back."

Snippets of conversations flashed through Charlie's mind. *The Parsons have been with us since I was a teenager. The threat against me when I was a teenager.*

"It's Alan." Charlie's jaw clenched. "He set up DeFoe so we would back off."

"Where's Kendra now?"

Charlie's face paled. "She's supposed to have a gown fitting today."

Urgency filled Elias's voice. "Who's the agent with her?"

"Angie Boyter."

Elias pulled his phone out and called Angie's number. He looked over at Charlie and shook his head. "Angie's not answering. Try Kendra."

Charlie pulled his phone free of his pocket and hit speed dial. The phone went straight to voice mail. "Her phone isn't on."

A sense of urgency seized him, and a single command flashed through his mind. *Go now!* Charlie didn't hesitate. He sprinted from the room and out to the parking lot. Fewer than two minutes later, he peeled onto the road as he offered up a constant litany of prayers.

Chapter 32

"It's perfect, Henrico," Kendra said, running her hand down the silky gold fabric. "Thank you for going to so much trouble for me."

"For you, it is no trouble at all," Henrico said with his thick Italian accent. He looked down at his watch, "But now I have to catch my flight."

"Thanks again." Kendra took a step toward the door to walk him out of the bungalow that was nearly as large as her condo.

"I can see myself out. You go change out of that dress. It needs to be perfect for the benefit."

"I know." She smiled at him. "I'll go change right now."

Kendra turned toward the bedroom, knowing she didn't have long before Angie would come inside to take her back to the safe house. She had insisted on taking up position outside the bungalow, and Kendra could only imagine that after an hour of waiting, she would be ready to leave.

A set of French doors on the side of the room led to a patio and the swimming pool beyond it. From the bits and pieces of information she had picked up, the FBI had arranged with the Biltmore to keep the bungalows near hers unoccupied during her fitting. She thought the effort was overkill, especially now that an arrest had been made, but she could admit that the solitude was comforting.

Turning away from the picturesque view, she stepped in front of the full-length mirror on the far wall. She studied her reflection, wondering what Charlie would think. She scooped her hair up with her hands, imagining she would wear it up for the benefit—and for the cameras, because if she had her way, it would be her first public appearance with Charlie Whitmore.

She wondered if he had thought of that, of the fact that the paparazzi would be out in force at the benefit and that his name would undoubtedly be linked with hers long before the weekend was over. Of course, the press could make a story out of so many things. Besides the possibility of her name being linked with the capture of the Malibu Stalker, she imagined some fashion magazine would notice her deviation from her signature color.

"Your dress isn't blue."

Kendra whirled around, her hand lifting to her pounding heart. She relaxed marginally when she saw Alan behind her. She supposed she should have known her father would send her a bodyguard even though she insisted she was fine. Briefly, she wondered how Alan had found her then quickly realized that he'd probably used his contacts with the FBI. Either that or he'd followed Henrico.

Knowing that Charlie would be taking her out tonight chased away her typical annoyance that such a ploy would have evoked, and she managed to smile at Alan. "No. I thought it was time for a change."

She turned now to face him fully, and her eyebrows drew together. "How did you get in here?"

"I always imagined you would be wearing blue," he said as though he hadn't heard her question.

She took a step back as she wondered why Angie had let him come inside the bungalow alone. "What are you doing here, Alan?"

"I came for you," he said, his voice eerily calm as he held up a single red rose.

The alarms in her head nearly exploded, and Kendra took another step back. She'd known Alan as her protector for years, but this wasn't right. When he took another step forward, a horrifying thought flashed into her mind. *Imagined me wearing blue? Could Alan be the person responsible for killing all those women?* Her blood ran cold at the possibility. The odd expression on his face only amplified the panic skittering through her.

"Does my father know you're here?" She glanced at the French doors on the opposite side of the bed. She took another step back and toward the phone by the bed. Alan was standing a few feet inside the doorway, effectively blocking her path to the front door and to where her cell phone was tucked away in her purse in the living area.

He laughed softly. "Your father is the one who brought us together."

"What do you mean?" Kendra asked.

He edged forward, and Kendra took the last few steps to the phone. She picked it up, sickened to find there wasn't a dial tone.

"I've known since you were sixteen years old that we were meant to be together. A few letters, a few suggestions to my father, and then, there you were." He waved a hand absently toward the telephone as though her efforts didn't bother him in the least. "The phone doesn't work anymore."

Kendra's heart pounded, terror and panic shooting through her. Silent prayers ran through her mind as she begged her Heavenly Father to help her find a way out. She swallowed hard and tried to keep her voice steady. "My father trusted you to protect me."

"And I have," Alan insisted, moving another step into the room. "I've been close by, even when you didn't know it." He shook his head as though suddenly confused. "Why couldn't you see me? Why didn't you know that I was there watching out for you?"

Think! Kendra demanded of herself. Had he really been following her around all these years? She thought of the women he'd killed—the women he'd pretended were her. But they weren't her.

"What about the other women?"

"The others?"

"You weren't watching out for me when you were with them."

He shook his head quickly as though suddenly agitated. Then his placid expression returned. "There's never been anyone else. It's always been you." His voice turned wistful. "I tried to talk to you at the party your parents threw for you to celebrate your first Grammy."

Confusion filled her.

"You were standing by the pool." His eyes stayed on her, even as he was captured by the memory. "You had gone outside to get away from the crowd. I tried to tell you then."

Images of that night flashed into her mind, along with a vague recollection of seeing Alan in her father's backyard. He had handed her a red rose that he'd picked from the garden and had said he wanted to tell her something. Then her father had come out and insisted she rejoin the party.

"You remember."

"I remember," Kendra managed to say as prayers continued to rush through her mind.

"And you remember that you never came back to talk to me. You never cared to know what it was I needed to tell you, that I just wanted to love you and that I wanted you to love me. You never gave me that chance."

Kendra stared at him in disbelief. Could it really be that a single careless moment had brought her to this? Her life was finally becoming what she wanted it to be, and now it might end before she had the chance to explore a future with Charlie. If only he had come with her today. Charlie would have stayed inside the bungalow. He would have insisted on being close to her. He would have been prepared to use his weapon to protect her. Then she remembered Charlie's words. *Anything you can reach can be used as a weapon.*

Alan took a step forward, and his eyes glazed over. "Each girl, each time, it was as though I was asking you again, giving you a chance to fix what you had done. But they weren't you. And I hated them for that." Alan motioned toward the French doors, to the swimming pool beyond them. "We should take a walk."

Kendra shook her head. "Alan, you need to leave," she said, desperation humming through her voice. Grasping for words, she motioned to her dress. "I need to change."

Alan ignored her words and kept moving forward. Kendra edged back until the night table was directly behind her. Without looking, she reached back, searching for something, anything she could use. Her fingers brushed against a thick decorative lamp and a heavy ceramic vase. She chose the vase.

Her teeth clenched together as her fingers curled around the base of it. He was only a few feet away now, and she knew she couldn't let him get any closer. She picked up the vase with one hand, gripping it tightly as she swung it toward him. He jerked back instinctively, enough that the vase barely grazed his jaw.

His hand came up to his face and pressed against where her impromptu weapon had connected. Then his mouth drew into a hard line, and he shook his head slowly as he stared down at the vase still clutched in her hand. "That was not very wise." His voice was distant as he added, "I only wanted you to love me."

Fear spiraled inside her, panic clawing at her throat. Kendra lifted the vase again, this time holding it out in an effort to maintain the distance between them. Alan simply shook his head and stuck out his hand, knocking the vase to the floor.

Trapped, Kendra reached back again, groping for something, anything, but it was too late. He closed the distance between them and grabbed her arms.

Her scream pierced the air. "No!"

Then his hands were at her throat, squeezing so that no more sound would come. She gasped, her windpipe burning as she fought for air. She was vaguely aware of her surroundings, but all she could think of was that she couldn't breathe.

Suddenly, Alan's grip loosened, and something seemed to snap inside of him. In one fluid motion, he reached back, and his hand disappeared beneath his shirt. Understanding flashed through her—the realization that he was reaching for a gun. She remembered what Charlie had told her, that each of his victims had been shot through the heart. Panic, desperation, and courage melded together as she struggled against him, using both the force of her body and her flailing hands to somehow knock the gun free of his grasp.

She heard the gun drop, but before she could scramble for it, Alan grabbed her from behind and whirled her around so they were both facing the door. She caught sight of Charlie standing in the doorway and desperately wondered if her prayers had been answered or if Charlie was too late.

Chapter 33

"Let her go, Alan." Charlie kept his voice steady, though terror dominated. His weapon was in his hand, but he already knew he couldn't shoot. He couldn't get a shot off safely while Alan was holding Kendra in front of him.

He took a brief moment to glance at Kendra's face. She was pale, but she looked determined. She had already managed to knock Alan's gun to the floor, and it was a few inches from her feet. Now Charlie had to find some way to help her get free of his grasp. With his weapon basically useless, he decided to try reason. "Come on. You don't want to hurt her."

Alan stared at him with pale blue eyes, his breath coming rapidly. Charlie could hear sirens in the distance and hoped that the backup Elias had sent wouldn't spook Alan further. He considered the psychological profile, remembering the various memories of Alan that Kendra had shared during their time together.

"I know how much you love her," Charlie began, a bead of sweat running down his back. "You've loved her for years. That's why you sent those letters to her dad when she was a teenager."

"She needed someone to watch out for her, to make sure no one took advantage of her," Alan said.

"And when Steve started hanging around, you were furious."

Alan shifted his grip, and his eyes darted down to the floor where the gun lay. "He was never good enough for her."

"Of course not, but you protected her. You made sure he couldn't hurt her."

He nodded, his whole face tensing with a sudden fury. "I saved her from him, and what did she do? She pushed me aside."

"I didn't know," Kendra managed weakly, her voice hoarse, her eyes on Charlie.

Alan seemed to forget that Charlie was there, instead focusing solely on Kendra. He loosened his grip slightly so he could look down at her face. "You picked Dustin over me. You let that old man watch over you when I should have been the one by your side."

"It wasn't her fault," Charlie said now. "She didn't have a choice."

"It was always her choice."

"No, Alan. It was her father's. He didn't trust anyone with his little girl."

He shook his head vehemently, and his eyes went wild.

"Alan, look at me," Charlie said. He could feel Alan's fragile control slipping. "Let Kendra go. You're supposed to protect her. You aren't supposed to hurt her."

"If I can't have her, no one can." Alan's face was riddled with derision. "No one."

Charlie saw his intent, and a silent prayer raced through his mind. Movement blurred as Alan leaned down to reach for the gun, pulling Kendra down with him so she was still shielding his body. Alan's fingers gripped the weapon, and Kendra gasped as she practically fell to her knees before being jerked back up again.

Then Alan swung the weapon toward Charlie, and Charlie automatically shifted to the left. A dozen thoughts ran through his mind in that split second when he had to decide whether to retreat or shoot. His training told him to think of his own safety first, but his heart wasn't listening. His gun was still raised, still aimed at the part of Alan's head that was visible behind Kendra.

He knew he needed to take the shot, but the fear of missing, the possibility of ending Kendra's life, terrified him. Then he let himself look into Kendra's eyes, and the answers were all there. He saw the fear and a steely determination, but besides that, he saw her trust.

Kendra's arm reached back toward the end table, just as another clear and sudden realization illuminated his mind. *You can't help her if you're dead.* The thought startled Charlie into action. He darted into the hall so he could use the wall as cover just as Alan fired his weapon. The bullet impacted in the hallway wall right behind where he had been standing.

He heard a muffled thud and quickly shifted back into the doorway, leading with his weapon. Alan was sprawled out on the floor, and Kendra was standing over him, a thick lamp in her hand. Alan shook his head, his left hand lifting to where Kendra had presumably struck him.

Kendra took a hurried step back, but Alan managed to grip the bottom edge of her gown. The material ripped as Kendra tried to pull free, her breath coming in gasps.

Alan looked up at her, evil insanity filling his eyes. He lifted his weapon. Kendra screamed, and Charlie pulled the trigger on his gun.

* * *

Kendra sat in the padded chair in the hospital waiting room, her hands clasped together, her head bowed as she uttered yet another silent prayer. The elderly man beside her flipped the page of his hunting magazine, a teenage girl across from her stared openly at Kendra, and a thirty-something woman fiddled with her wedding ring while she kept her eyes fixed on the door.

The door opened, and the woman's eyes brightened expectantly. Then she sighed and continued her steady stare. Kendra didn't notice any of it. All she could think was that another woman might die because of her.

Angie Boyter had tried to stop Alan when he'd approached Kendra's bungalow earlier that day. Her efforts had resulted in two stab wounds. One had been relatively minor: a slash across one of her arms. The other was the real concern: a knife straight to the abdomen.

Kendra started when a hand came down on her shoulder, and her eyes whipped up to see Charlie standing beside her.

"Any news?" Kendra asked, her hand instantly reaching up to cover his.

"Not yet." Charlie glanced around the waiting room and then motioned to the door. "The nurse said she's going to be in surgery for a while yet. Why don't we go for a walk? You need some fresh air, and I bet you haven't eaten since breakfast this morning."

"I'm fine."

"Kendra, please." Charlie's voice was low. "Come walk with me."

She wavered briefly. Then Charlie linked his fingers with hers and helped her stand up.

"We won't be gone long," he promised as he led her to the door and out into the sterile hallway.

* * *

Charlie escorted Kendra out of the main entrance and walked down a path lined with benches. They passed by a couple talking quietly by the door, and Charlie could feel the waves of guilt rolling off Kendra. He understood the guilt. He shared it. If he hadn't gone into the office that morning, it would have been him at the hotel room instead of Angie. He would have recognized Alan and might have been able to stop him before anyone had gotten hurt.

They continued on to the end of the path, and Charlie motioned to a bench where they could talk without the risk of being overheard. He waited for Kendra to sit before taking his place beside her. With his hand still holding hers, Charlie shifted to face her. "None of this is your fault."

"I don't know what I'm going to do if someone else dies because of me."

"You aren't listening." He reached out with his free hand and tilted her chin up so their eyes met. "This isn't your fault."

"Charlie, we both know that isn't true. Angie is upstairs in surgery right now because she was trying to protect me."

He recognized the truthfulness of her words and realized that the only way he was going to be able to help Kendra was to help himself first. "I never told you why I moved to Phoenix."

Kendra's eyes narrowed. "I thought FBI agents just went where they were assigned."

"Usually, we do, but my transfer was deliberate." He took a deep breath. "My first assignment out of the Academy was at FBI headquarters. FBI agents are usually sent somewhere new, where no one knows them, but somehow that rule was broken with me."

"Why?"

"I'm still not exactly sure, but I've always suspected that someone pulled strings because of my father. Either someone thought having me around would help the FBI get what they needed from Capital Hill or someone figured they were doing Senator Whitmore a favor by keeping his son at headquarters where he would be safe."

His shoulders lifted restlessly, and he forced himself to continue. "After almost a year of working a desk, I was finally partnered up with a guy named Brian Mueller. He was a field agent—a good one—and he took on the job of being my trainer." The guilt sliced through him as though it had been yesterday, but he forced himself to go on. "A few months ago, we were following up on a lead. It was routine. Knock on some doors, flash our badges, and ask some questions."

"What happened?"

Charlie let the images form and fought to keep his emotions in check. "We went into a warehouse where we suspected some contraband was being stored. Something wasn't right from the moment we got there, and Brian called for backup. Then we heard shots fired.

"We drew our weapons, went in together, and total chaos broke loose." A fresh wave of guilt crashed over him. "I fired a couple times, but the shooters were well covered. Then one of them worked their way up on some crates. He had me lined up in his sights, but right before he fired, Brian pushed me out of the way. He took the bullet meant for me."

"Did he . . ." Kendra's voice trailed off.

"No, he didn't die." Charlie shook his head. "But we're still not sure if he'll ever walk again."

"And you feel like it's your fault."

"He went into the line of fire to protect the son of a senator, so yeah." Charlie nodded. "I feel like it was my fault."

"Maybe he was just protecting his partner," Kendra ventured.

"Maybe, but either way, he might not walk again because he saved my life." Charlie shrugged.

"Just like Angie was trying to save mine."

"Exactly."

"Does the guilt ever go away?"

"I don't know. I hope it will." Charlie squeezed her hand. "I pray that it will."

"Me too."

* * *

They had barely made it through the waiting room door when Ray approached them with a dopey grin. "Angie's out of surgery. She did great."

Kendra reached for Ray and gave him a hug, tears of relief in her eyes. "I'm so glad."

"Any news about her prognosis?" Charlie asked.

"She's going to be out of the action for a few months, but the doctor didn't seem to think there would be any permanent damage."

"I sure hope not," Charlie said.

"Come on." Ray motioned for the door. "The doctor said she's going to be out for at least a few hours. Let's go get something to eat, and we'll celebrate the end of Kendra's nightmare."

Kendra looked from Ray to Charlie and nodded in agreement. "Sounds like a great idea."

Chapter 34

"Kendra!" Sterling Blake rushed out his front door and scooped his daughter into his arms. "Thank God you're safe."

"I'm fine, Daddy." Kendra's arms encircled her father's waist as she indulged in a long hug. For the first time in recent memory, she actually seemed glad to be home. She clung to him as he breathed in the familiar scent of her favorite perfume mixing with a hint of his own cologne, the same one that had been named after him. When she finally eased back, she motioned to the man who stood silently behind her. "Dad, this is Charlie Whitmore. He's the one I told you about."

Sterling had barely looked at the man until he noticed the easy smile his daughter sent him. In a smooth move, Sterling shifted Kendra to his side with one hand and reached out to shake Charlie's hand with the other. "Good to meet you, Charlie."

"You too, sir."

"Come on inside." Sterling started up the front steps. The moment they were through the front door, Monica came rushing toward Kendra.

"Oh, you're home!"

Kendra was passed from father to mother, and everyone exchanged introductions once more.

Sterling led the way into the living room but didn't bother waiting for everyone to sit down before he opened the dialogue. "Now tell me what happened in Phoenix. All I know is that someone from the FBI called and said you were safe and on your way home."

"I'm the one who called," Charlie said. He wisely chose the chair beside the couch instead of taking the spot next to Kendra. "There was an incident in Phoenix where we apprehended the man we believed to be the Malibu Stalker."

Sterling's eyes whipped over to look at Kendra again. She looked calm, composed, but all he could think about was that someone had tried to hurt her. Someone had gotten too close. "What happened?"

"Your daughter can share those details with you if she wants. What you really need to know now is who the stalker was." He glanced over at Kendra, a silent signal passing between them.

Sterling lowered himself onto the loveseat beside his wife. Then Kendra reached forward and took his hand. "Daddy, it was Alan Parsons."

"What?" Sterling and Monica said in unison.

Sterling shook his head and pulled his hand away. "That's ridiculous! You must be mistaken."

Charlie's voice remained calm. "No, sir. We're not."

"How can you possibly think that the man who has been protecting my daughter all these years is the one who was trying to hunt her down? That's absurd."

"He manipulated you," Charlie said bluntly. "He's the one who wrote the letters, threatening Kendra when she was a teenager. He gave you a reason to need extra security, and he used the reputation of his father's business to gain access. At first, being around her must have been enough for him, but when he was taken off her protection detail, something must have snapped."

"I'm sorry." Sterling pressed his fingers to his temples, and he looked at this man who had brought his daughter home, a man he had barely met. "I just don't understand how Alan Parsons could be a serial killer."

"He used his position in his father's company to meet women who resembled Kendra in order to gain their trust. He had the skills necessary to bypass security systems and elude the authorities, and he also had the knowledge necessary to plant the bomb backstage at Kendra's concert."

"Wait a minute. He didn't even have a backstage pass to that concert."

"No, but he did have access to this house. We believe he used one of your passes while you were out of town, and then he returned it before anyone even realized it was missing."

"That's crazy." Sterling shook his head in denial, but Charlie continued laying out the facts he didn't want to hear.

"The LA office also confirmed that he has been in contact with them as your representative on this case."

"What?" Sterling felt his reality crumbling. "I never asked him to do that. I was personally dealing with the detective on the case."

"We know that now, but as I said, Alan Parsons was very adept at using his position as a bodyguard to cover up what he really was."

"Where is he now?"

"He's in the hospital." For the first time, Charlie's voice wasn't completely steady, but his eyes remained direct. "He has already been charged with attempted murder, but I expect that several murder charges will be added as soon as we can connect him to the victims."

A sick feeling spread through Sterling. "You're telling me that I hired a man who tried to kill my daughter?"

"Dad, there wasn't any way you could have known." Again, Kendra reached for his hand, and Sterling looked down at her narrow fingers resting in his. He had been so careful. He had taken so many precautions, and still, someone had pushed through all his defenses.

For a moment, he was speechless. Then he considered the security challenges they would face for the upcoming benefit. He certainly couldn't let Bruce Parsons keep working for him under the circumstances. "Maybe we should cancel your appearance at the benefit."

"No. I'm done hiding." Kendra's eyes met his. "Whether you admit it or not, no amount of security is going to keep me one hundred percent safe."

"Maybe not, but you have to at least give me time to find a new bodyguard for you."

"Dad, it's time you let me run my own life," Kendra insisted. "Charlie is going to escort me to the benefit. I'll say my prayers every night, asking to make it through each day safely, and I'm going to trust that everything is going to work out."

Sterling stared at Kendra. He wasn't sure prayers alone could keep her safe, but he was willing to entertain the possibility that they might help. He had certainly had a few prayers regarding his daughter's safety rattling around in his brain over the past few weeks. But his protective instincts were strong. "Are you sure you're ready to go out in public after this?"

"I'm sure." Kendra smiled. "Although I do need to call Henrico to see if he can make me another dress. The one he just fitted was damaged after he left."

"I still can't believe all of this. It's my worst nightmare come true." Sterling squeezed Kendra's hand. "I don't know how you are able to sit there and look so relaxed."

"Maybe I inherited your acting talent." She gave him a wry grin. "If it's okay with you, I thought maybe Charlie and I could stay here this week."

"We would love that," Monica spoke before Sterling could wrap his mind around Kendra's words. All he could think was that his little girl was finally home. Then he remembered his last conversation with Kendra, the one when she'd mentioned she was planning on living in Phoenix for the foreseeable future.

"Are you the reason my daughter has decided to stay in Phoenix?"

Charlie nodded, and his eyes stayed focused on Sterling when he answered, "I am the one benefiting from that decision."

"I see." Sterling studied the man across from him. He wasn't sure how he felt about this boy who clearly had strong feelings for his daughter, but one thing was certain: even though Kendra and Charlie hadn't spoken the words, he had little doubt that Charlie was the man responsible for saving his little girl. "Kendra can show you where the guest room is."

"Thank you." Charlie stood up and motioned to the door. "I'll go get our bags."

"And Charlie?" Sterling spoke before Charlie could leave the room. "I shouldn't have to tell you that I expect you to stay out of Kendra's bedroom and vice versa."

Charlie's eyes met his, and he nodded. "No, sir. I respect your feelings completely."

* * *

"Explain to me again how I let you talk me into this." Charlie looked at Kendra's reflection in the mirror as he tugged on his tuxedo jacket to make sure his shoulder holster wasn't visible.

"I asked you to come." Kendra leaned against the doorjamb of the guest room, and humor danced in her eyes. "And you said yes."

"Must have been a moment of temporary insanity," Charlie muttered. He adjusted his shoulder harness and tugged on his jacket once more. The weight of his gun served as a constant reminder of the day at the hotel when he had nearly been too late.

He still had some bad moments when he thought of how everything had played out, not so much because he had pulled the trigger but because he had come so close to losing Kendra. He didn't think he had ever prayed as hard for anything as he had on that drive from his office to the Biltmore that day. He had almost been too late, probably would have been too late had it not been for that flash of inspiration during the DeFoe interrogation.

Charlie knew that it had been inspiration that had helped him arrive in time, just as he knew that the Lord had watched over both him and Kendra to allow them to survive that day. Perhaps it was that knowledge that had kept him from dwelling on the fact that he'd been forced to pull the trigger again. As a result of his actions, Alan would spend the rest of his life in a wheelchair. Whether that life would be spent in a mental institution or on death row still remained to be seen. Regardless, he wouldn't be able to hurt anyone ever again.

Charlie pushed those thoughts aside and turned to face Kendra. His breath caught as he took in the stunning effect of Kendra in full makeup, her hair artfully piled on top of her head, and her saffron-colored gown shimmering in the lamplight. "You look beautiful."

"Thank you." She smiled fully and took a step inside the room. Casually, she brushed at a speck of lint on his jacket.

As though his parental radar were tuned perfectly, Sterling Blake's voice boomed through the hall. "Kendra?"

"In here, Daddy." Kendra called out and turned toward the door.

Sterling looked into the guest room. He gave Charlie a stern look and then spoke to Kendra. "I thought we agreed that you were going to stay out of the guest room while Charlie is here."

"Yes, Daddy." Kendra fought back a grin but obediently stepped back out into the hall and pulled Charlie with her. Then she asked her father, "Is it time to go?"

"Yes." Sterling nodded. "The car is waiting downstairs."

"We're ready," Kendra told him. When Charlie tugged on his jacket again, she ran a hand down the front of his tuxedo. "It looks fine. You can't even tell it's there."

Sterling's eyes narrowed. "What's there?"

"My weapon." Charlie straightened his shoulders, not sure how Sterling would feel about him going to the benefit armed.

"You have your gun with you?"

"Yes, sir. I'm supposed to keep my weapon with me at all times."

Sterling stared at him for a moment but nodded. Then he looked over at Kendra. "I think I might like this guy after all."

"I thought you might." Kendra laughed. "I need to go get my purse. Dad, we'll meet you outside."

"Don't dawdle," Sterling called out as he headed down the stairs and Kendra started down the hall.

She returned a moment later, purse in hand. When she reached Charlie, she glanced downstairs and then looked up at him with a mischievous smile on her face. "You know, this may be the last time we're alone for hours and hours."

"In that case . . ." Charlie's hand wrapped around her waist and he lowered his lips to hers. That familiar sense of rightness and belonging spread through him, and he could feel his future snap into place.

When they parted, Kendra rubbed her thumb over his lower lip. "Sorry. I got lipstick on you."

"I gather it isn't my color."

"Well, we might not want to leave it there, even if it is." She wiped the last smudges off and laughed. "What would everyone think?"

Charlie took her hand in his and brought it to his lips in a sweet, old-fashioned gesture. "They won't think—they'll *know* that I'm the luckiest man alive."

About the Author

Originally from Arizona, Traci Hunter Abramson spent much of her childhood exploring the little town of Pinewood. She is a graduate of Brigham Young University and a former employee of the Central Intelligence Agency. Since leaving the CIA, Traci has written multiple novels, including the *Undercurrents* trilogy, *Royal Target,* and the Saint Squad series.

When she's not writing, Traci enjoys spending time with her husband and their four children. She also enjoys cooking, although she prefers an electric stove to the wood-burning variety.